AJ Grayson drinks extraordinary amounts of coffee and likes to write on an old Corona Standard typewriter, though is enough of a technical enthusiast to buy whatever Apple dangles from its latest stick. Time not spent writing books is time spent reading them, walking (perhaps unsurprisingly, in parks), working with youths and adults in various counselling settings and teaching.

Please be in touch with AJ Grayson on Twitter, Facebook and Instagram @GraysonForReal

Also by AJ Grayson

The Boy in the Park

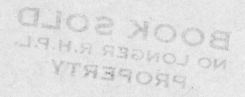

THE GIRL IN THE WATER

AJ GRAYSON

KILLER
READS

Killer Reads
An imprint of HarperCollins*Publishers* Ltd
The News Building
1 London Bridge Street
London SE1 9GF

www.harpercollins.co.uk

A paperback original 2019

2
Copyright © Harper 2019

A J Grayson asserts the moral right to
be identified as the author of this work

A catalogue record for this book
is available from the British Library

ISBN: 978-0-00-832102-4

Set in Sabon 10.75/15 pt by
Palimpsest Book Production Limited, Falkirk, Stirlingshire

Printed and bound in Great Britain by CPI Group (UK) Ltd, Croydon CR0 4YY

To those who have suffered:
A tribute.

For David who didn't make it: the fondest
of memories.
And for Rachael, once again.
Don't give up.

He's hiding something from me. I know he is. He's hiding something, and it's going to change everything.

There's nothing I can pinpoint; no concrete, indisputable fact that makes this a certainty, but I'm certain all the same.

He's lying. And he's never done that before.

I'm not sure what to make of it. It could be nothing. Could even be good. Men hide things, usually because they're cowards, but sometimes because they think we want them to. They consider it wit. Maybe he's hiding a necklace. Or earrings. Or tickets for a surprise holiday, maybe back to the coast again. He knows I always like the coast, especially in the springtime.

But I don't really think it's any of those, not if I'm honest. My skin is a pepper of fire and suspicion.

His briefcase is in the walk-in closet of our little

1

bedroom. I know it's always locked, off limits, but he never holes it away or tries to conceal it. Yet today I found it, unprompted – a pair of synthetically shiny gym shorts slung over the top, as if this would somehow mask its shape. As if I wouldn't be able to see.

He's lying. He's lying.

My beautiful man is lying . . .

Prologue

The first body in the water was a woman's. She was a beautiful creature, despite her unfortunate condition. Her black hair was cropped short. Her cheeks were soft. She had rose-painted lips. Above her body, stranded forever in place, the clouds floated smoothly across the sky.

The river, by all accounts, received her body with reverence. It seemed, through some wordless comprehension of nature, to know this was the arrangement and would, for a time, continue to be. 'Everything in its appointed place,' it seemed to affirm, and that, perhaps, made things a little more right in the world. Or wrong.

It's sometimes hard to know the difference.

The last body in the water would be mine.

That's a hard thing to admit, and harder to accept, but it's the way things go. The vision, crystal and clear.

My golden hair, swaying in the motion that water always has near the shore. My clothes untorn. An altogether different appearance in death than that girl. A stripe in my flesh, bleeding crimson into the water around me. My fingertips, as always, with their nails nibbled down to the skin. My blue eyes open.

It's an odd thing, to play the observer at one's own death. Part of me is ashamed, certain I should feel more emotion. There should be anger. Grief. But then, how can I feel those things, really? Of course the shore must be the end. Of course there is water and silence. My story was probably always going to end like this. Like most, the final page was presumably written long before the first, the conclusion the one sturdy fixture towards which everything before it was always going to lead. However they begin, there's no story that doesn't finish with the end.

So I see it. Real. Certain. I float in the water, my light blouse transparent against my body, suggestive in ways that, in life, would be provocative but which in death evokes only pity. I'm dead, and I'm quiet, and I'm screaming. My lips are stalled a lifeless pale, but I'm screaming. Screaming with all the breath that is no longer there.

PART ONE

BEGINNINGS

1

Amber

Every morning, as I stand in the bathroom and gaze into the mirror, my eyes look back and taunt me. The fact that their colour doesn't match my name has always disappointed me, and it's like they know this, and are so prominent on my slightly freckled face purely as a way to rub it in.

They should be amber, and they should be magnificent. Instead I possess the name, feminine and graceful, forever without the matching gaze. Amber on the tongue, but in the eyes, cursed with blue.

This is overstatement, of course. Something I'm prone to. I don't genuinely consider my blue eyes a curse, and others have sometimes even found them beautiful. *'They're gorgeous, Amber, like twin pools of the sea'* – a splendid compliment, though more than they deserve. They're not the deep blue of royal porcelain or a navy blazer, but something softer. Just light enough, just bright enough to mark themselves out.

David loves them, too, and for that alone I suppose I shouldn't complain. Maybe if my face had been punctuated by some other colour the first time we met, he wouldn't have noticed me, wouldn't have collided into 'hello' and that catchy smile, and all the romance that followed. Maybe, if I had the amber eyes I've always craved, I'd have ended up all alone.

I shrug, seeing them in the mirror now, and go about my familiar routine. Morning is morning, and every step is practised. The mascara shade is a light brown, harder to find than a person might think, and it complements a soft brush of Clinique's cleverly named 'Almost Powder' in Neutral Fair. Understated, but just enough polish to let me feel like a well-cared-for piece of art, pleasing without being showy, which is what my mother taught me always to aim for. And mothers, as no one but mothers ever suggest, always know best.

But there's a headache forming behind my eyes – and I can almost see it in the mirror, too, with the rest that's visible there. A strange pulsing at the sides of my face, as if the pain has shape and can be caught in the reflection in the glass.

I blink twice, the blue orbs of my eyes disappearing and then reappearing before me. I can't dwell on the pain in my head. It has long since become a customary feature of my days, and work starts in forty-five minutes. There's no use dwelling on what can't be changed.

Just keep going. And I do.

The routine concludes a few minutes later. My face is done, my hair brushed, and my teeth are the glistening off-white of Rembrandt Extra's best efforts for a heavy coffee and tea drinker.

My feet, seemingly registering all this even ahead of my brain, are already moving me out of our teal-tiled bathroom towards the kitchen.

Like they've lives of their own.

By disposition, I'm not a morning eater. A cup of tea, I've always thought, is a perfectly complete meal before midday. Add milk and it's two courses, and entirely satisfying. Recently, though, David has been trying to change my habits of a lifetime.

Because it's good for you, Amber. It's healthier. Trust me, you'll grow to like it.

Sweetest of men, David, though on this front, at least, disastrously wrong.

A tall glass of the monstrosity he calls a 'smoothie' has been left on our kitchen's Formica countertop. It's his latest effort, fitted nicely into the current trends of our health-conscious West-Coast culture. Its shade is something close to the purple of a badly overripe plum, and he's probably got plum in there, the ass, along with banana, and berries, and spinach and Christ in heaven knows what else. *'The flavours mix together so well, you don't even know what you're drinking.'* The fact that this is a lie has never stopped him from saying it. The drinks taste exactly like what they are. Reality can't be masked, not that well. What's in the mix always makes itself known.

I take a single sip. It's enough. I know David wants me to take at least two, to give it the honest college try, but I can't bring myself to do it. Won't. It's simply beyond my strength to stomach the stuff, so the rest of the smoothie is down the drain in a colourful swirl, and I'm comforted by the fact that blended breakfasts flow out of existence so cleanly. If David were to cook me, say, eggs (something I loathe with an almost equal fervour to smoothies), the uneaten remains would be harder to conceal. We don't have a disposal in the sink – the landlord suggests installing one would raise our rent $75 per month, which is simply shit – and the trash can would be obvious. Maybe I'd have to dig a hole out in the garden in which to conceal the evidence, but it seems like 365 days of uneaten eggs would get noticed some time before day 366.

I rinse out the glass and set it in the rack. There's a note on the counter, next to a ring of condensation. *'Morning, hon. Enjoy, and have a good one. Love you, -D.'* The blue ink of the ballpoint pen has met the moisture where the glass had stood, the lower curve of the 'D' blurring like a watercolour.

The note warms me. I've never particularly cared for 'hon' as a term of endearment, but from David's lips, or his pen, the word is a little embrace. I'm smiling without really noticing the change in my face that produces it, and I'm thankful, too, because I have someone who can have this effect on me – who can make my cheeks bend and turn as if he were physically connected to the muscles beneath my skin, provoking my body to move in its most intimate of gestures.

Even if he does make smoothies.

There's coffee left in the carafe – David makes a fresh pot every morning and always leaves me some – and I pour out half a cup to gulp down before I head for the door. Not tea, but it'll do. Sadie's already been walked and fed and is lolling with typical canine disinterest in the corner near the fridge.

'Bye, Sades,' I say, my first vocalised words of the morning. I'm nibbling a nail as I say them and the words come out misformed, but my girl knows her name. No children in our little family, though we've been casually trying for the past year at least, and Sadie does her best to fill that void. We're no longer spring chickens, David and I – though I won't hit forty for another two years, so I refuse yet to be labelled middle aged – but it's starting to feel like our efforts in this area just aren't going to lead anywhere. I suspect, sometimes, that Sadie may be as close to a child as I'm ever going to get, though in dog years she could easily be my mother.

She acknowledges my presence with a slightly lifted head and a huff, then lets her nose flop back to the ground. Her pink tongue is askew in her teeth. Her morning walk with David is enough to last her until I get home, and I'm certain she plans to nap for the bulk of the interim. The laziest dog in creation, and I love her.

A few moments later, I'm outside. The front door to our apartment building closes with a click, and I take in a deep breath of the morning air. The sun is already well over the hills, and the flowers that line the sidewalk are glowing. Gardenias fill my nostrils – a heavy, tactile scent, perfume and honey colliding at the back of my throat. A water feature chortles gently in the corner of the lot.

The day is beautiful. The sort of day we sometimes wonder if we'll ever see, and usually don't appreciate when we do. I try to soak it all in. Absorb it.

It's almost enough to make me forget the throbbing that pulses at the side of my face, and the fire that threatens to burn away the edges of my vision.

2

Amber

I'm at the bookshop by 8.25 a.m., a full five minutes ahead of schedule. There was little traffic between Windsor, the quirkily British-sounding, northern California suburb town where David and I have set down our roots, and Santa Rosa, and I've got a heavy foot when there's not a mass of stop-and-go cars before me. It's an all too frequent occurrence on this tenmile stretch of Highway 101. My little 'put-put', as David calls it, might only have 104 horsepower beneath its hood, but I like to put every last one of them to work. Nothing says Modern Woman of Determination like a floored car maxing out its power at 77 miles per hour and getting passed by delivery vans and teens on mopeds.

The shop is already starting to bustle with the customary movements of the morning. A few customers are perusing the racks of new arrivals. The espresso counter has a line of eager attendees. The morning delivery of periodicals and papers has just been brought inside, the boxes waiting to be opened and sorted onto their shelves.

I love the place. I know that book sales are declining and paper going the way of the digital dodo, that Kindle reigns supreme and that there is a whole generation of people who've never held a physical book in their hands, but there is a romanticism to the bookshop that I can't believe will ever truly disappear. The scent of the fresh pages mingled with the thick aroma of coffee, the beautiful hush punctuated by the subtle tones of friendly chatter. It's a paradise. A little refuge from the noise of the world outside, with a thousand stories to tell and mental universes to expand.

Of course, it's traditionally more of a young person's milieu, or at least it was until young meant digital and books meant old-fashioned. There are more grey-haired heads in here these days than brown or blonde, though I haven't yet spotted the first white streak on my own. Can't be long until I do, though. I don't feel a day over thirty – hell, I don't really feel different to how I did when I was in my twenties – but there are going to be forty candles on my cake soon enough, and I can't play the child forever. Forty. One of those round numbers nobody appreciates: no longer young, not yet venerable. And you have to live with it for a few years, since 'the forties' are much the same as forty itself, until you hit the edge of fifty and suddenly you're catapulted from 'in her prime' to 'middle aged'. Damn, if the categories aren't a bitch.

But whatever age may be or mean, work in the bookshop is a joy. Enough in the way of responsibilities and activities to keep me busy, without becoming crushing. Stress isn't something I crave, nor the 'fast-paced action' of a more pressing grind. Leave the mad rush to others. I crave the quiet. The solitude. The rhythm of a nicely patterned life.

The solitude, of course, is relative. One is never alone, even in the dim lighting of a small bookshop. I talk with the customers now and then, though the conversations are usually brief and rarely terribly personal. And I have colleagues, some of whom have become friends – an extension of the little family that David and I constitute at home.

'Double-caf, half-fat, cooled down, no foam latté, as the lady ordered.' As I approach my corner of the shop, I'm greeted by Mitch Tuttle, one of those collegiate family members and, in fact, the owner of the little shop. He says the words in his usual sing-song style. He's sporting a tired pair of trousers, untended wrinkles long since transformed into permanent creases that spider out from his crotch and knees. A belt holds them in place, hidden somewhere beneath the paunch of a stomach wrapped in a badly patterned shirt. The stress of managing such a bustling hive of worldly activity, he regularly joked, had ravaged his otherwise classical good looks. A boss with a sense of humour is not the worst thing in the world.

But his timing is off. Mitch is jovial, now, at 8.25 am – a time of day when this is more or less inexcusable.

He's carrying a paper cup in his enormous hands. There's a smirk, two bushy, unkempt eyebrows coming almost together as a smile wrinkles the whole of his face. Too many wrinkles for a man who hasn't yet seen fifty.

Of course, the drink he's announced is all wrong.

'Shit, Mitch, I take tea. Just black, plain, tea. A miracle this shop makes a profit at all, with you at the helm. You've got a memory for details like a sieve.'

I take the cup, wrapping both hands around its warmth and shaking my head. *Tut tut, Mr Tuttle*. But it's a ritual, not frustration. We both know the familiar script and all the gestures that go along with it. 'Not like it hasn't been the same order every day since we met,' I say.

'Thought I'd be spontaneous, force you to try something new.' He grins, his teeth uneven but spectacularly, unnaturally white. The peroxide blonde of the dental world.

My eyebrows aren't as pronounced as his, but they'll still mount a good rise when the moment calls for it, and I prop them up in mock disapproval. Then a sip of my drink – tea, despite Mitch's pronouncement, strong and hot and exactly as I like it. Of course. And in a cup from Peet's, which we've collectively decided has Starbucks outgunned on all counts. We've all long since grown tired of the coffee we brew in-house. That's for the patrons. We ourselves will take something a little more refined, thank you.

'Susan still keeping you to the new diet?' I ask him. The script had run its course, and I'd noticed Mitch had opted out of his usual coffee and sported a cup with a teabag – orange-coloured, probably indicating something herbal and revolting – dangling out of its lid.

'The fascist,' he mutters, looking defeated. 'If it hasn't been brewed from a weed or a berry, I'm not allowed anywhere near it.'

'Commiserations.' I'm laughing as I answer. 'I'm still getting smoothies.' There's no need to elaborate. Mitch knows the story and shakes his head empathetically. If there were more hair there, it would flop with the exaggerated motion.

He's carrying two additional paper cups in a holder, filled with whatever contents are bound for their recipients on the far end of the shop, sighing for good measure but still smiling as he walks away. Big steps, lumbering but confident – a great, heaving land mass on the move. Mitch, needless to say, doesn't cut the slimmest of figures, and I can see why Susan wants him on a diet. Still, poor thing. I probably shouldn't refer to him as a land mass.

I'm momentarily captivated by the motion of this boisterous, generous man, hunting down the prey to serve as the targets of his daily good deeds. I catch the look of satisfaction that covers his creased face when he spots the smiles they offer in response, and for a moment feel the melancholy that comes from wondering why there aren't more selfless souls like Mitch Tuttle's in the world. And definitely more bosses. But I also catch the sly sleight of hand that flicks a donut from the counter into his grasp as he saunters back, and my devious smile is instantly back. I feel exonerated from the guilt of the heaving-land-mass reflection.

'I know I said I wouldn't nag you.' I let my words stretch out as he approaches. My eyes point to the deep-fried treat poorly concealed in his grip.

'A promise I'm glad you consider as inviolate as the oath that put that ring on your finger,' he answers, motioning towards my hand, before I can go further. He steps into his small office at the side of the shop, divided from the floor by a glass wall, and plops his overweight frame into his seat. I can hear the donut drop onto the desk next to his herbal tea.

A second later, I'm quite certain, it's gone.

Libra Rosa is hardly the largest bookshop in our part of the world. Even in a society where they're fast disappearing, the Bay Area still has its share of some of the greats. Green Apple in San Francisco has branches scattered around the city, some covering multiple storeys and bringing in authors and speakers while cultivating book-sharing and the lovely art of the second-hand. Johnson's in Berkeley caters to the hip. Iconoclasm in Marin fosters the new age, as do a half-dozen others like it. There's a little bit of something for everyone. The only thing the shops share in common is the Californian-liberal ideal that they should be nothing at all like the high-octane bookstores of New York and 'the big cities'. They're quiet little holes-in-the-wall with small-town vibes and a pace deliberately laid-back to suit the pot-happy lethargy of the NorCal literary culture.

Libra Rosa is, among the mix, pretty standard. A tribute to its location in Santa Rosa – an oversized town just fifty-five miles north of San Francisco and the last opportunity for residence that San Fran careerists can reasonably consider for a daily commute – the shop has been shaped by Mitch into his vision of a perfect, if miniature, out-of-town literary tribute to the old Haight-Ashbury days. Rows of new books, stacks of classics, and a small section for the second-hand, with beanbags in corners, vinyl LPs on the wall and an overall atmosphere of being committed to life in 1965. Most of what we sell can be bought on Amazon, but Mitch has ingratiated himself with enough of the local community that the shop has a decent following who come in dribs and drabs throughout the day, never more than a handful at a time, though the addition of the coffee bar and seating area two years ago upped the daily visits a little.

In one corner of the shop, on the far left as one enters and barely visible from the glass frontage onto the street, is the periodicals section. My terrain. I have a small desk surrounded by rotating racks for the newspapers and fixed shelving for the magazines.

Periodicals are even less viable these days than books, given that almost every smartphone in existence carries their content in full colour and with instant access, but keeping up the periodicals corner is something of a hobby horse for Mitch. *'It's called* print *media, and print requires paper and ink.'* God love the man for more than just his kindness. I'm not a technophobe, and I browse the Net with the best of them. But the *San Francisco Chronicle* and the *New York Times* are just never the same on the screen. You need to be able to hold them, get the ink on your fingers. It's a life experience not to be dismissed.

So I arrive each morning. I unbundle the packs and boxes, which feels almost like working in a proper, big shop in the city – except that I know the mailman who delivers them is called Bruce, a wooly-haired gentleman who's been on the downtown route for twenty-six years and who delivers our items 'promptly at the exact time I get here', and follows the delivery with a twenty-minute linger over a double black coffee, which doesn't quite seem full octane to me. Nevertheless, I set the papers into their assigned racks, glancing through the magazines as I place them on the old shelves. It's a job with a slow pace, deliberately as much as a simple function of location, but with an upside: it allows me to read as I go and catch glimpses of the world's reporting on life outside.

It usually takes me an hour or two, and then I settle into the routines of maintenance, selling, curating. And simply being present, as a shop without attendants is nothing more than a warehouse. Though a shop without customers is, too, and some days we barely pass that test. So I sit at my small desk, smile as guests enter the shop, answer questions when they have them – which on rare occasion are about books or papers, but more often about their children's recent sporting success or a vague complaint about the state of politics, or another pothole on Main Street – and spend the many quiet moments between browsing the Internet that still has stories to tell even once I've read all the day's papers through.

I have my own computer for that task, and I have to admit that as much as I cherish paper and ink, I do love this thing. The latest model, thinner than my calculator and an elegantly understated shade of what Apple optimistically calls gold. I can't say that my previous model, whatever it was, had been all that bad; but I do love a shiny new thing, and the shinier the thing that's new, the darker the memory of what it's replaced. God bless Apple for keeping the shiny things coming. If I weren't happily married and Tim Cook, CEO of Apple, hadn't announced himself as being the other way inclined, I could see myself having an extraordinarily torrid affair with that man.

Pinned to the wall beside my desk is a photo of David and me, taken a year and a half ago near Lake Berryessa, and another of David and Sadie both lying on their backs, bellies up, out in the backyard. Two frozen moments of happiness I keep right at eye level. Tacked around them are notes and posters and all the usual fare of a bookseller's trade; but right in the centre, right at the core: two manifestations of bliss, and both with furry bellies.

I wrap my hands around my tea. One of the boxes from this morning's delivery has already been cut open by someone else, and I reach over and grab out a copy of the Chronicle. I have a few minutes before I need to get to my chores. Right now, tea and a paper – a morning crafted for happiness.

And I'm at work.

Life is sometimes truly good.

A sip, and the tea is warm on my tongue. With a jostle of the newsprint page the day's headlines leer up at me in bold black. Single-phrase proclamations, shouting their way into my attention. Speaking of the weather, the traffic, the political climate. Some of it interesting, most of it routine.

Ordinary.

Normal.

That's usually how it is, just before the world changes.

3

David

Looking back, staring into the past from all that my present has become, I can honestly say that the world we inhabit is a mystery. I've never in all my life had to come more to grips with that fact than now. A mystery, and a puzzle.

I met her on Tuesday morning at 8.25 a.m.; I remember the timing exactly. The contours of my watch's face, the position of its hands, I remember them in the same way poets remember the flowers on hillsides or the scents in the breeze on the days they experience love. Impossible to forget.

I'd been told a little about her. I was familiar with the kinds of details shared about individuals on a printed page, cutting a lifetime of reality down to basic facts: the length and colour of her hair, her height. Weight, at least approximately. As if these things mattered. Yet they were there to be had, and I had them in hand as I first walked in to meet her. Everything a man could possess to go on.

Except her. The experience of her simply couldn't be compared to what I'd imagined. Or anything I'd ever experienced before. She was altogether more.

The first thing I noticed were her eyes. I'd never encountered eyes like those. I'll never forget how they first moved me.

I think she knew, even then, that I saw something in them. That the sight of her captivated me. But, despite their potency, their vivid hue, it wasn't their colour that captivated me. There are only so many colours eyes can take, and I've never found the variations to be all that engaging – whatever she or others might think.

It was their intensity. God, staring into them was like beholding a cry that had been given physical form. Her eyes were her plea, and they seemed to hold, just behind the shine of their lenses, an entire world that was screaming to be set free.

And then we spoke, and reality began to fall apart.

4

Amber

The change today came in an instant. My headache had been getting worse, despite the tea. It was still early, but the throbbing at my temples was becoming more than a mere distraction. It's like this too often, though, and I'd already swallowed two pills to combat the customary. I'd be a Tylenol addict if they didn't tell me it would melt my liver into goo, so I'm an ibuprofen addict instead, popping two or three at a time throughout the day, for the little good they do me.

I'd downed them in a single swallow, then set about my morning tasks. They hadn't taken long, and the papers – which I'd already skimmed through – were now racked and the latest editions of the magazines placed prominently on their shelves. The boxes they'd come in were flattened and out back with the recycling, and I'd managed a handful of sales to the business types who

27

wanted a paper to go with their croissant as they headed off to the office.

And then I was alone. The bliss of the job. I'd opened my laptop at a moment when the ebb and flow of the shop had been mostly flow, and called up a familiar selection of news feeds. Maybe it's the fact that I'm in this little shop in this little city that makes me so keen on keeping up with the news. It hardly matters to me, most of it, but I read it with diligence.

My headache notwithstanding, I refocused my eyes on the computer screen. Minutes, maybe fifteen or twenty, had passed since I'd started my usual scanning, and thus far the online media wasn't proving itself much more enticing than the day's print versions I'd already perused.

The headlines were hardly works of art. I know a lot of effort goes into them by the poor saps whose job it is to dream up one-liners that make the boredom-inducing sound enticing. But effort isn't always enough to breed interest.

*STOCKS TRADE DOWN – BROKERS
KEEP HOPES UP.*

That, in the journalistic world, is apparently what passes for catchy. The down and the up; directional contrapposto. Whoever wrote that got full marks in Journalism 101.

*BART TRAIN DELAYS THROW PASSENGER
PATIENCE OFF THE RAILS.*

This attempt to convey poignantly uninteresting content about the Bay Area Rapid Transit system under the guise of a catchy tagline – it's an art. Like a record producer fronting an album with one catchy tune and filling the remaining eleven tracks with artless crap. By the time anyone hears them, the've already bought the record. (Though I can hear Tim Cook yelling at me now: *'No one "buys a record" any more, Amber. It's all about streaming, about personalized subscription!'* then smiling seductively and somehow charging me another $9.99 a month.)

CRACKS IN BRIDGE DIVIDE COUNTY OFFICIALS.

I'd paused at that one, tapping to see the paragraph-length summary. The concrete of a sixty-year-old bridge outside Napa, in our neighbouring county to the east, was suddenly the cause of 'grave concern' amongst the county administration (note the adjective 'grave' in a story that might involve tragedy: I read enough to know that's strong copy), despite the fissure in the concrete having been visible for more than three decades.

I tapped my keyboard again, my waning interest spent.

Then, without any deliberate intention, my glance wandered upwards. A few headlines above the one I'd clicked, less than an inch away from scrolling off the top of the screen, a different caption grabbed me.

I can't identify precisely how it did it – how it affected

me. It was a spark, and it launched a fire in my spine that shot through me like badly wired electrics. Before I'd even taken full account of the words, I could feel the voltage in my head change.

I shoved my tea aside with a jolt, slammed the palm of my hand against the spacebar to stop the feed scrolling off the screen, and glued my eyes to the headline. I was barely aware that I had all but stopped breathing. My eyes didn't want to focus.

The words were simple and unadorned.

WOMAN'S BODY FOUND ON SHORELINE.
FOUL PLAY SUSPECTED.

And there it was, that buzzing at the surface of my scalp again. Electrics. An immediate tension in my chest.

There was nothing in the headline that should have caused such a reaction. It presented none of the witty word play of the other titles (wit, I have often observed, is generally disapproved of in writing about death, since almost nobody successfully navigates the line between banter and respectability). It was unfussy. A simple statement of fact.

WOMAN'S BODY FOUND ON SHORELINE.
FOUL PLAY SUSPECTED.

I read it again, and again, and gradually became aware that my spine had gone rigid. I'm sure there was a thin film of sweat between my fingertips and the etched glass of the trackpad.

The noise of the bookshop seemed to have vanished, and if there was anyone left in the store, they had become invisible to my attention. My mind, drawn in by this headline for reasons I couldn't explain, raced through the limited details that could be inferred from such a minuscule amount of text. 'Foul play' means possible homicide. Fine. I mean, horrible, of course; but comprehensible.

But my reaction, it was not comprehensible at all. I blinked, and my eyelids left trails as they rose back into their folds.

WOMAN'S BODY FOUND ON —

The words grabbed hold of me. Assaulted me. Inexplicably, at that instant, I wanted to scream out from the very depths of my belly.

Isn't that the very strangest thing?

Then, with the shift of no more than a second, the agony fled. The headline was just a headline, clear and crisp on my screen with a stark lack of factual detail, and I was disinterested and dismissive and —

And it was back, as quickly as it had gone. My breath outpaced my pulse, my eyes clamped closed, and in an explosion of the unexplained, I couldn't even make out the conclusion of my own thoughts. Though for a moment, just for a moment, I thought I heard them telling me that my world was coming to its end.

5

David

I was perched across from her, the day I met the woman that changed my life. I don't know for how long. It doesn't matter. I was in my government-issued moulded plastic chair, clipboard in hand, diagonally opposite her position in the little room.

I didn't know who she really was then when we first began. I only knew what was in the official reports and my stack of references.

'I've read your file, Miss.' I listened to the doctor's voice as he spoke directly to her, facing squarely across the metal table between them. 'What the records say about you is pretty clear.'

He spoke in cold, formal phrases. He was a medical professional, of course, and of many years' standing. But he was also an officer of the state, and she was not here under circumstances any would consider friendly.

Her expression didn't change. Her eyes remained motionless. From my position in the shadows at the side of the room, I felt unnerved by her solidity.

'We both know what's brought you here,' my superior added. Dr Marcello was an old hand at this, and I'd heard him make similar beginnings before. I craned my neck, trying to observe some emotion on the woman's face.

'Do you realize why you're in this room, at this moment?'

A common formula of approach. Begin with a querying of the context; find out how much the person in front of you is willing to admit of their position, and proceed from there. With an assistant at the side, from the pharmaceutical wing, taking notes in silence in order to help with the medicinal diagnoses.

Thus far, Dr Marcello was keeping things by the book.

The woman said nothing. She was alone in the room, for all her expression would have suggested. She just stared through the walls into a space I couldn't see.

'You're not here because you asked to be,' Dr Marcello added, stating the obvious. No one came into that room by choice. Still, the comment might jog her.

Her eyes had begun to drift upwards, as if something on the ceiling was attracting her attention. My superior almost spoke again, but then a sound – nearly imperceptible – emerged from the woman's lips.

'Not . . . by . . . choice.'

It was the first time I heard her speak.

She was mimicking Dr Marcello's speech, or so I thought, but still – her voice. Almost. She whispered the words, as if holding back a more personal moment.

I leaned forward in my chair, frustrated by the odd angle that kept me from gazing at her face-on. I tried to make out everything I could. She had short black hair, cropped and fine. Visible softness in her cheeks. Rose gloss on her lips that glistened in the fluorescent light as she whispered.

She was beautiful. It might have been wrong for me to think that way. Inappropriate to institutional objectivity. Too subjective and personal. But she was, and I noticed. Even from an angle, even out of reach. She was beautiful.

Dr Marcello remained impassive.

'Call you tell me your name?' he asked, hoping to elicit more words from her with a question that hardly required analysis.

The woman's eyes fell back from the ceiling, straight into his. And then, to my shock, she swivelled her head and stared straight into mine.

Our first gaze. The moment my life changed.

'My name,' she said softly, 'is Emma Fairfax.'

6

Amber

Somehow, the day has disappeared. I'm not sure how it's happened. I've been in the bookshop since it began, going about my usual routine, and it doesn't seem it's lasted that long. Not long enough for end-of-the-workday noises to be emerging from the street outside, or for quick drinks at Trader Tom's around the corner to be the subject of conversations by colleagues, not quite out of earshot, as the metal blinds are lowered inside the windows. Yet I hear them, just like that, and the clock on my monitor agrees with the voices.

Time, I suppose, gets away from us all, now and then. Einstein may have theorized that time changes relative to speed, but I'm pretty certain it also changes relative to concentration. Focus on something hard enough – as I'd apparently been doing with the news on my screen and the other work of the day – and the clocks slow down. Then you blink a few times, smear away the haze of all that intensity from your eyes, and you find you're back in the present, situated awkwardly in the skin of the person you'd forgot you'd been a few moments before.

So I refuse to be too surprised by the noises around me, now, of a workday at its end. Nor am I overly disappointed. I love this little den of respite, yes, but I'm not a lonely woman, wedded only to my work to give my day its meaning. I have my corner of the shop, my papers, my computer, my employment that feels half like a retreat. But I also have home.

I have David.

I'm out the door by 5.07 p.m.

Mitch walks behind me. With all that mass, it's rare he walks in front.

'You going straight home, or you up for a drink?'

His questions are always pure, though he says them with the kind of raunchily exaggerated tone of voice that suggests we might follow up that drink with a steamy escapade, entwined in each other's naked skin in a hotel that charges by the hour. But it's all smoke and sarcasm with Mitch. In reality, he is devoted to Susan, the most doting wife in the world, and he knows I'm well and truly hitched and not looking to break that bond. He's just a kind man, and one who's fairly certain alcohol won't be on the menu when he gets home. Nor, for that matter, any particular act that could be described as an 'escapade'.

'Not today, Mitch.' I smile, pausing to allow him to

catch up and lowering a hand onto his wide shoulder. There's the uncomfortable sensation of moisture rising through the fabric of his shirt. I force myself not to lift my hand away. 'Thanks for the offer, though.'

'You sure? Wouldn't take more than an—'

I switch my grip to a pat. The motion accentuates my headache, which has grown worse throughout the foggy day. 'I'm sure.' A bigger smile. 'Stuff on the mind. But go have one yourself. Susan's not bound to have a glass of Jack on the counter, is she?'

He heaves a resigned but happy sigh, muttering something indiscernible about pigs and flight, then chortles. 'Till tomorrow, Amber.' And he turns, and I blink, and he's already halfway to his car.

The drive home is, as always, twice as long as the commute in. The roads are packed, the commuter congestion I'd avoided in the morning now at its predictable height. To emphasize the plight, the woman's voice on the National Public Radio affiliate for the Bay Area suggests there's no hope for improvement ahead. I settle passively into the time set out before me.

I have a water bottle in the cup holder at my left, its flimsy plastic only slightly sturdier than the interior of the car itself. The myth that water eases headaches is a lie, but it does make popping the ibuprofen easier. Another two are down before I'm fifteen minutes into the drive, leaving their lingering, slightly sweet taste on the back buds of my tongue. It's too familiar. Advil's parent company should offer me some sort of loyalty card.

The details of what I'd read during the day peck at my attention as I play tap-dance between the accelerator and the brake.

My spine tingles again with the memory of the head-line that had captured my attention. An ice cube projects itself up my back.

This woman in the river.

It had been on the computer, not in print, which meant it was fresh. Probably only became known after the papers had gone to press for the day. I'd looked through them again, just to be sure, but found nothing there.

I'd gone back to the Internet, oddly enthralled, and chased up what few details were available. *Age, 40.* The woman who'd been found was just a year my elder. Her body had been discovered at approximately 9.45 p.m. by an advocate of late-evening walks who reported his find to the local authorities. It was situated on the Russian River – the 110-mile-long gentle beast that stretches out from near Lake Mendocino, twisting and turning south and west until it joins the Pacific Ocean in Jenner, two hours north of San Francisco. I know the river as well as anyone does who lives in the area, more by simple proximity than first-hand experience. I've driven along stretches of its length that run near the highways, that's about all I can say. At places it appears mighty, at others barely more than a stream.

As I drive, now, I recall the process of searching for

these facts on various police websites. It had taken over an hour. Maybe several. The day, as I say, had kind of slipped away from me.

The details, though, continue to cycle through my mind.

A hiker coming upon the body, still floating in a gentle bend in the water.

It wasn't an overly bloody find, or particularly terrifying or grotesque. This wasn't a dismemberment or chainsaw attack. What was disturbing was, in fact, the simplicity of the whole situation. The fact that it was almost . . . scenic. The river water, flowing. The mention of someone out for a casual stroll. 'Rambling', as the English would say, which seems appropriate as I drive towards a Californian town called Windsor.

A foolish song I knew as a child tussles at my memory, its tune playful and ridiculously out of concert with the topic of my thoughts.

> *Rambler, brambler, with rushes at my knees,*
> *Walking, talking, to bushes and to bees . . .*

I shake my head in protest. It seems inappropriate that my mind should wander to such things at this moment. I try to push the tune out of my thoughts.

Beyond the victim's age, none of her private details – name, residence, so on – have been released to the media, except to indicate that she was a Caucasian female and apparently in good physical condition.

I fidget. But it's not a fidget, it's a squirm. I'm uncomfortable. *The air in my car is too hot*, I realize all at once. I switch on the A/C and turn the knob as far as it will go towards the little snowflake symbol. It lights up with a reassuringly blue glow – blue having at some stage become a colour we all associate with being refreshed and cool. For a moment, this meaningless fact distracts me.

The tune, though, won't leave my head. *Rambler, brambler, with rushes at my knees . . .*

I stomp my foot beside the accelerator to shake the melody from my mind. *Enough!*

The cause of death I'd found was listed only as that ambiguous 'suspected foul play'. Any further detail is apparently under embargo. Hardly surprising, as the case is so new, but it doesn't close the door to informed speculation. As a woman who reads the news religiously, I know that 'suspected foul play' usually means there's some physical evidence of additional trauma – maybe a gunshot wound, maybe stabbing. Something more than simple drowning, which would be the more obvious cause of death in a river. Drowning could indeed be murder, of course, but it could also be just a fall. Or suicide. 'Suspected foul play' hints there's something more.

My temples are starting to throb. *Stinking, ineffectual pills.* And the air con is doing shit, blue snowflake or not. I can feel my blouse clinging to the sweat on my back.

I recite the details over and over, making them almost a chant.

A *thirty-nine-year-old woman's body.*
Found at the river's edge.
White.
Cause of death – unannounced.
Foul play.
Sinister.

I'm sure there were other things I looked at in the news today, other happenings that will have attracted me at the bookshop. But my mind is stuck on just this. On this, and . . .

Rambler, brambler, with rushes at my knees . . .

The song won't leave my head. My breathing has become heavier, and for some reason my right leg is starting to ache. I can't think of any reason for that. I try to reposition myself on the seat.

The lane to my left suddenly shifts to life. I click on the indicator and push myself into the moving traffic at the first opening. Distraction from the odd sensations. Triumph. We clock a stellar seven miles per hour before the motion slows again, and within a few seconds we're back at a standstill. The lane I left is moving. I clench my fists tight on the wheel. The urge to unleash a satisfying barrage of profanities is almost overwhelming, but I try not to recite the curse words David describes, with mock old-world flare, as 'so awfully unwomanly'.

Though, to be honest, he always says it with a very un-old-worldly grin, which makes me think he half-likes those moments when I lose verbal control.

I blink heavily two or three times. There are trails there, again, following my eyelids as they move.

The traffic starts to flow once more, and I attempt to distract myself, shifting my attention to the hillsides and vineyards alongside the road. All the locals along this particular stretch of Highway 101 refer to it as the Redwood Road, though I've yet to spot a Redwood tree anywhere near it. An enormous growers estate, entirely modern but designed to look ancient and historical, sits off in the sweeping green hills to the left of the highway. It's a winery, of course, as most things are around here, but I can never remember the name of it. It's built like a castle, complete with turrets and triangular flags. An odd way to sell wine. But the visual effect is dramatic, and the delivery trucks pulling in with supplies could as easily be wagons with mounted drivers, their diesel horsepower replaced with the actual thing. It wouldn't look the slightest bit out of place.

But then there's a Beyoncé cutaway on the radio and a new update on the refugee crisis in Eastern Europe, and the world again seems so very, recognizably, modern. Even the vineyard castle suddenly looks pallid and uninspired. Just another hoaxy specialty shop along the roadside, different only in size from the shed a few miles back and the Safeway warehouse at the next intersection.

That's how quickly the world changes. A soundtrack,

a flash of circumstance, and it's a different land. A familiar one, where David is waiting at home and the universe is as it should be. God, how I want that, in this moment. My normal world. My comfy home. My wonderful man.

But suddenly I'm sweating fiercely. My breathing has become tight and rapid. The northern California landscape around me is as it was a moment before, nothing at all has changed – and yet it has, all the same and all at once. The woman's situation has thrust itself back into my mind, powerfully, her circumstances flashing like lights in my vision.

I think I might hyperventilate – maybe I already am. My pulse, I'm sure of it, is out of control. This isn't a headache any more. I don't understand what is happening to me. The edges of the highway are glowing white, a phosphorous light that is too bright for me to look at directly, bleeding into every inch of my vision.

And I can see a girl, like a picture from a perfectly told story. She's right there, in the glow of white that has overtaken the world. I am an observer at the solemn portrait of something ethereal and other-worldly.

And . . . wrong.

I can no longer see the traffic around me. I'm not sure if I'm still in my lane, or even in my car. Life itself has gone out of focus.

I only see the girl. Her. The girl from the headline – of whom no photos have yet been released. The girl whose face I have no reason to know from Eve's. There's something peculiar to her eyes. Something wrong with her neck. Yet it's her, I'm sure of it, and she's there, her face bathed in white, staring at mine. Her life ebbing away. And for some reason I want to call her Emma.

7

David

The way things went, after I first gazed into her eyes, first heard her voice – it's not the way I necessarily would have wanted it to go. I would have liked there to have been less trauma. I would have liked to have avoided the pain. The pain I bore, and the pain I had to inflict.

But this is what happens. This is where you end up.

I hadn't expected that any woman would change my life. My experience with women had never been good. When one you love dies, so early in your life, you're not exactly left with the most optimistic hopes for the future. And if another, who ought to love you, doesn't, that doesn't help mend the wound. I'd been through both scenarios, with a sister in the grave before her time, and a mother who, together with my father, hadn't left for the next life soon enough. Childhood was a mass of misery in my head, and in my youth I'd hoped one day

I'd flee from it. Get far enough away to at last be free. But time was a vicious teacher, and eventually I had to learn to be satisfied with an unhappiness as deeply set as my bones and my blood. And eventually I did: I simply got used to it. Give a man enough pain, and for long enough, and he'll stop hoping for anything else.

But that encounter, that first moment with her – it changed things. I'd long since given up on escaping my pain; hell, I'd made a career of wallowing in it. Surrounding myself with more of the same. I had become a man condemned to live in the never-ending cycle of sorrow I'd carried as long as I could remember.

And then, in a single instant, something new. A doorway into a new life.

Not that the pain would leave, even then. Not for me. That was, in the end, simply too much to hope for. In the days that would come I would smile, and hope, and sing, and even find the means to rejoice. But never to sing the pain entirely away.

Some pain, we learn too late, exceeds the songs that are sung of it.

8

Amber

I don't burst through doors, it's just not my way. Never has been. But today, just now, as I tentatively push ours open enough to catch the sight beyond, I wish I was the kind of person who bursts through doors. The day's been too strange, and I want the surety, the comfort that I know waits on the other side – and I want it now, instantaneously, all at once.

But I don't burst through. I push gently. Wood parts from wood and scrapes across our much-abused carpeting. And though the opening is tentative, the reveal is what I long for. The open door gives way to the reality of genuine happiness. This is home. Within . . .

My heart always rejoices when I see David, and today I need that rush more than most. I rush forward, grab him by his fleshy, muscular shoulders, and pull his lips towards mine. They're parted even as we meet and I lock us into a long, warm embrace. It extends into a span of time I really couldn't measure, and wouldn't want to try. I am a woman who knows true love; and when you know that love, you don't try to understand it.

Finally, our lip-lock breaks. 'Well, hell, good to see you too.' David's face is a wide grin. Stubble, firm cheekbones, that slightly olive skin with its twinkle of shine – *'It isn't oily, babe, that's Mediterranean sexy!'* Everything is familiar and welcoming. A touch of my pink lipstick has clung to his chin. 'I take it life in the shop wasn't all that bad today?'

I'm shaking my head, kicking off my favourite retro flats with an overly girlish motion, like Dorothy flipping her slippers to an unheard musical beat. It's a playful gesture that made him laugh once, and which I've repeated a hundred times since. My shoes wind up somewhere in the corner, lopsided, near Sadie's plastic water dish.

A flash of white light at the edges of my vision – to be ignored. It's nothing. The remnants of a migraine. I do so often get those.

'Work was fine, David. I'm just happy to be home.'

The flipping of shoes has roused Sadie to life. She's already at David's feet, looking pleased to have the household back in proper assembly. Her orange fur droops against the tiles beneath her as she saunters over and shoves her snout against my ankles. I tap at her head and give the usual 'That's a lovely puppy' utterance in baby-talk tones, which sends her tail wagging.

Wagging. A breeze. Wind . . .

I'm sure I'm not the only one who's always been amazed how quickly our thoughts can take us to another place. The present moment is a spectacular case in point. The day, the house, the dog – they all coalesce, and suddenly they're all gone. All I see in this instant is a seaside walkway in the Marin Headlands, a vividly blue sky, and the sound of seagulls squawking over steep hillsides that abruptly end in cliffs sheering down to the Pacific.

A good memory, this one. I permit it to sweep through me without resistance.

I was hiking north, that's how I remember it, and at a good clip. Years ago. The shoreline on my left lay at the bottom of cliff faces that lifted up in brilliant severity from sea level, with the hills on my right dressed in spring wildflowers that almost concealed the cement remains of the naval turrets and bunkers that had been active in these hills until the end of the Second World War. In the distance, only grey-blue seas and low clouds over the minuscule Farallon Islands. Beyond them, nothing at all until Hawaii.

I was alone, as I always was, and lost in grey thoughts that clashed with the bright skies. I was walking with sticks, those retractable kinds that look like ski poles but cost twice as much. He was at the front of a group of two or three, walking in the opposite direction. I don't think I noticed him first. It was the other way around.

'Excuse us,' he said, politely. The wind was blowing

(a given; it was the Pacific coast in early spring – the wind is always blowing). He was covered in a puffy red coat that looked as if it had been injected with a little more stuffing than required, giving his torso the appearance of a badly packaged tomato.

It could have ended right there, our first encounter. It could have been our only. But in a moment out of a children's cartoon I sidestepped left when it should have been right, my eyes downcast, on my feet rather than on the strange tomato person in front of me. He did the same, and a second later our bodies collided – heads first, with the requisite crack, and then chests and arms and hands to keep each other from falling.

The way things begin.

'Oh, Hell, I'm so sorry,' he said, reaching out to stabilize me. 'That was entirely my fault.'

'No, it was mine,' I freed a hand to rub my forehead. And I looked up, wincing in the slanted light that suddenly felt too bright.

That's when our eyes connected for the first time. That magical, painful, wonderful moment.

David's eyes were, and are, a stranger hazel than most I've seen before. Blue and green in equal mixture, but they have brown centres, just around the iris. Something unique. I must have stared into them longer than social norms would allow because the next words were his, awkward and accompanied by a glance that broke mine and tried to find some other landmark on the barren horizon at which he could stare.

50

'At least we're both still upright.' His words were cheesy and superfluous, but I didn't care.

'I should pay more attention to where I'm going,' I offered. Sheepish grin. Foolish girl. I wished I had stronger words to say, but I had't been feeling myself, and those words didn't come.

'It happens,' he answered. The profundity of our conversation was truly epic. 'These surroundings, they can . . . they can take you in.'

And there was his smile. The first time I'd seen it. The one I've grown to know so well over the years. One too many teeth in an otherwise nicely balanced mouth. That cute, very cute, face, bordered with slightly disorderly locks of black hair and a refreshingly masculine touch of stubble on his chin. I've never understood women who don't go for stubbled chins and hairy chests. They're an incomprehensible demographic, too influenced by the wax mannequins that pass for men in magazines. I've always gone for the Chia Pets of the race.

The skin around his eyes bunched as he smiled, full of warmth and sincerity. 'I'm David,' he'd finally offered, reaching out a hand with its glove considerately removed. 'And these guys over here' – he gestured towards the men a short distance behind him, who didn't seem to notice – 'are my work colleagues.' One of the men might have nodded, but seemed too chilled to consider approaching and reaching out a hand himself. He was huddled with a third member of their party, stood a few steps away, engrossed in a gathering of sea birds diving for fish over the edges of the cliffs. I might have been on Mars for all they appeared to notice me.

I raised my hand to David's and felt a powerful grip.

'I'm Amber,' I answered. 'It's . . . it's lovely to meet you.' The words were almost flirtatious, like nothing I'd ever uttered before.

It made him smile again.

Then, the strangest thing of all. I spoke not only flirtatiously, but with an openness completely uncharacteristic of everything inside me.

'I'm staying just up the way, by Muir Beach. At the Pelican Inn. If you . . . you know, ever wanted to bump into each other again.'

In the midst of my confusion, wit. Spectacular.

Or maybe not quite spectacular, but definitely more than was normal for me.

I cringe at the memory, but it's that wonderful cringe of something so horrible, something that could have gone so terrifically, spectacularly wrong, that ended up going just the opposite. It wasn't two nights later, or three, that David crouched his big frame through the short, barrel-wood door of the Pelican Inn, 'just stopping by' with the hope to say hello. It was the same evening. The very same.

There was something magical on the coast that day. That's the only explanation. Something magical that brought me out of my shell. That brought us together.

And now we're here, in our kitchen in the little town of Windsor, California, standing in front of the refrigerator on which an orange paper cutout of the word 'Bump!' remains the perpetual reminder of our first meeting. We're still locked together, bodies close, though the kiss has ended. There's beer on David's breath – the scent of more than one. Usually means a long day in the shop, and the need to get out from behind the pharmacy counter for one or two before heading home. I have a fleeting desire to ask him about the mundane details of his day, but it passes quickly. Work is work. For today, his is behind him, mine's behind me.

But I'm not wholly in control, and that conviction bends. The thoughts that come are an invasion, not an invitation. Into the swirl of memory floats a river with a bend I don't recognize. The woman I'd read about on the computer and thought about so vividly on the drive home. The unexplained.

In this intimate moment I can feel goosebumps rise on my arms.

It almost happens. I almost touch that buzz of electricity that pulls my world out of order and into the mêlée of impulse and memory. I can tell I'm right at the edge of it. There are so many draws.

But I'm anchored in an emotion that's more powerful than them all. I have my means of resistance. My solidity and my rock, firm and stable in my arms, with his big, beautiful smile.

I pull David's face towards mine again. I can taste the beer on his lips, and I push him towards the door.

9

Amber

It happened in the night, somewhere in the darkness of the drawn curtains and the muffled lampshades, beneath the cotton sheets and in the midst of the heady scent of all that goes on in the dark room of a husband and wife who've found their way there by stumbling up their staircase, falling into bed as clothes are thrown at walls and ceilings.

Somewhere in the midst of all that, the strangeness closed in.

Our bodies were as tightly wound together as two bodies can be. My chin was pressed into his neck, my lips somewhere near his ear, his whole body slippery with anticipation. His breathing was heavy, rhythmic. Mine was keeping pace.

Then came the flash of light. An image, bursting into my mind. A stranger's face, loving and peaceful and kind and wicked and cruel, all at once. One of Cinderella's sinister stepsisters, only far more beautiful.

I suddenly remembered the bookshop. The headline, my hours on the Internet, and something beyond all the details I'd read. Someone else's games and mysteries and . . . *wrongs*. My whole body suddenly felt the immense, overwhelming wrongness of the world. And I remembered the highway, the flashes of my thoughts and fears on the drive instantly back before my eyes. The image. *The face.*

And I can hear whimpering, and crying; the utterances of a creature, crying out and asking me to know its pain. A judgement, cascading into my present.

And in my embrace with my solidity and my rock, my arms wrapped around David's fiery chest, I said it. The single word that echoed out to me from that strange, white darkness.

A name. Her name.

'Emma.'

I don't know where it came from, why it made my lips move. But her name was suddenly there, and I couldn't keep it to myself.

'Emma.'

I could feel David's body go rigid beneath me. There was ice. The cessation of everything. And then the world stopped, and started to fade away.

10

David

It pains me to think that Amber might start to understand. There are so many things a husband and a wife share, but there are also things we can't. She and I can never share the truth. Not this truth. It would destroy her. It's only the lies that keep us alive, and keep us together.

I've struggled with this fact countless times. Since childhood it's been engrained in all of us that truth is what liberates, and it alone. It will set you free – such a pithy saying, and probably as a general rule it holds true. But not always. No, not always. Sometimes truth is the greatest form of slavery.

At one point in my life I would have rejected that premise with all my energy – I'd have spat out that lies have absolutely no place in life, that they lead only to darkness and torment. That ought to be argued as a matter of principle. But I simply can't. I won't. Experience sometimes proves right what social norms insist are wrong.

Everything I've built with Amber is a lie. I admit that. It's all facade. That's what makes it work – for me, for her. A beautiful, artistic, warm facade of manufactured reality. It isn't true, perhaps. That depends on your definition. But it's real.

It's been real since that day in the Marin Headlands when – for all Amber knows, or ever will – we met for the first time. That happy little headbutt above the sea, the little sidestepping dance that forced the moment not to pass but linger. Some might say the staging of it, the weeks of thoughtful planning, of following her movements and learning her itineraries, of making sure I'd be on just the same path at just the same time, were manipulative or false. But no one accuses a man who plots out a typical first date of being sinister for doing so – deliberating what flowers to buy, what restaurant to go to, what music to 'accidentally' have playing on the car stereo during the drive. It's normal, all of it.

Is what I've done really so different? Only the circumstances are out of the norm, and for damned good reasons.

And I still have means of rescuing the situation. Tools. Resources. Not everything is lost.

This is a world I'm not willing to let fall apart.

11

Not *every den of torture looks like what we're given to
expect. Like what the storybooks tell us we should see
there. It is possible that there are those which fit the
stereotype: dark, damp stone walls with old chains
hanging from hooks on the ceiling, the devices of abuse
crusted with dirt and gore.*

It's possible.

*But reality can be more hellish than those props. Strip
away the myth, and what's left behind – what's left to
be real – is something different. Something worse.*

*It's a basement, though not because there is any
particular power to darkness or to being underground.
It's a basement because basements bar sound better than
ground-level living rooms, and though there isn't usually
that much noise involved in the way torture really*

works, one does want to guard against even the remotest possibilities.

It is furnished nicely, if simply. The carpeting is higher grade than discount, the walls are a muted tan. There are bookshelves with nondescript volumes – the kind that bespeak a degree of education but not an excess of wealth – and a small desk in one corner, with an old tube-style television on a table in another. The chequered fabric sofa with pull-out bed is the centrepiece of the wall to the right, as one enters, and the door itself is wood-panelled with a knockoff brass knob. The prefab sort with a lightly marked up, push-button lock.

The only sign of the room's real purpose is the sturdy chrome bolt lock that's been added above the knob. An ordinary basement den, with no windows or external exits, doesn't have a deadbolt fitted towards the interior hallway. Especially not the kind that is key operated only, from both sides.

The kind that, once locked, keeps you in as well as out.

12

Amber

As all days do, the new one that began when the daylight crept over the hills has rolled through its usual routines. It's brought the sun and home and work, but I haven't been seeing them in a bright light. This day was inaugurated differently, and as it began, so it carried on.

Differently.

I arrived at work at 8.50 a.m. It should have been 8.30 a.m., and I should have been in better cheer, but there's only so much control one can exercise over the ebbs and flows of life. I was late, grumpy, and had been praying solely for a lack of conversation and an empty path between the front door and my desk.

That I made it through Classical Fiction and New Releases en route to my periodicals corner, past the coffee kiosk, arriving at my desk without interruption, felt like the first bit of unmitigated good news of the day. My unusual tardiness meant the bookshop was already bustling with customers, and someone else had already gone through the day's delivery packs, at least enough to get a few copies of the morning papers on the racks in time for the day's first push. I'd probably end up being scolded for thrusting that role onto someone else by my absence, but I would simply have to face that.

Mitch had left a cup of tea on my desk, though his office at this moment was empty. I sighed, marginally disappointed with myself for being relieved, but I simply wasn't in the right frame of mind to have interacted well if he'd been there in his usual cheer. When you're in a pissy mood the cheerfulness of others is doubly revolting.

I popped the plastic lid off the Peet's tea and drew in a long sip, taking advantage of the distraction to avoid the disorder of the boxes around me. The tea was tepid, but it still satisfied. It washed the latent coffee taste from my tongue, and with it a bit of the tension of the morning.

Then it was onto automatic pilot. Sorting. Shelving. Cutting boxes and recycling. Bringing order to the most changeable corner of the shop. Then, when it was all done, settling into the quiet that invariably followed. Reading the papers. Scanning the glossy magazines. Gold computer, open – the surest sign I was fully caught up despite my late arrival and could settle into the calm of the day. Eventually, a little chime announced that all was well with the technological innards of my laptop and the screen shifted to display the desktop. I called up my usual starting pages: AP, Reuters, *The Times*. All auto-refreshing to the day's latest.

The rhythm of ordinary life in a low-intensity job is a decent tonic for anxiety, and it's cheaper than Xanax. A comforting montage. *This is my morning*, I reflected, *my every morning. It's today's, and it will be tomorrow's.*

It was yesterday's.

I'd stiffened a little at that. The word didn't feel right in my head. *Yesterday.* As if it weren't an actual day.

Next to my computer, opposite the memos, was a little notepad. I've been repeatedly reminded I can take notes on the computer itself, but I suppose I feel the same way about paper and pen as I do about novels with covers and words on actual pages. On the cover of the notepad is a garishly pink Hello Kitty logo, augmented with purples and reds that only a colour-blind teenage girl could admire. I'd grabbed it out of a stationery shop's discount bin a few weeks back without closely examining what I was buying, and every time I look at it now, it makes me feel ten years old and ridiculous.

I flipped open the cover.

Yesterday.

I tried to cast the word out of mind as I scanned over the few notes I'd written. They were all various jottings about that headline. *Yesterday's headline.* The story that had so enrapt me.

Woman.

The shiver, again.

Thirty-nine.
  White.
    Suspicious circumstances.

The words, penned in my own hand, made me increasingly uneasy.

  Cause of death unknown.
    No match to any known missing persons.

Yesterday.
I shoved the notebook aside and stared at the newsfeed on the computer. Those jottings had been what *yesterday* was all about, and they'd started from a banner on this screen. The new day's headlines were scrolling by now, though, at their usual rate, and I wasn't spotting anything more about the body. I'd have thought there would be more stories by now. More information. I used the trackpad to move backwards through the listing by time, but it seemed to have disappeared from the day's radar.

Then, disrupting the intensity that had been building up to this moment, comes Chloe – right now, as I'm focused on all this and the beginnings of the workday blend into the present.

Chloe: my closest friend at the bookshop. She's one of the few under-thirties here, as eccentric in her own right as the rest of us combined. I halfway suspect she chose to work here because she is simply too weird to be hired anywhere else.

Her head pops into my personal space with her typical intensity. She, who is always brimming with exuberance and wit, and whom I absolutely do not want to see at the moment.

'Hey girl!' she announces, taking no notice of my condition. Her head is not quite bobbing, but almost. The pitch of her voice is entirely too high, and she stretches out the two words to a span of time that could easily have accommodated an entire sentence.

'I thought I heard you sneakin' on in here!' Her affected accent is as shocking as always. Chloe's most conspicuous failure of self-awareness is her apparent belief that she can simply will herself to become a busty black woman with a drawl that makes ordinary phrases sound charming and profound. The phenomenon emerged precisely at the time she went on an Idris Elba fan binge on Netflix, re-emerging from that two-week stint more Southern and succulent than any character he's ever played. I've tried, on numerous occasions, to remind her that she's more than a decade younger than me, from Oakland, B-cup at the most optimistic, and on her very best day a pasty white that most bleach brands would set as a target for the 'after' of their comparison washing ads. But that's just how she is. Chloe's quirkiness is inflexible, and her friendship comes at you like an out-of-control freight train, or it doesn't come at all.

At the moment, I'd give anything for the latter option.

The tension in my neck is fierce, and with an as-yet unexplained urgency, I desperately want to get back to reading about . . . whatever this story of the woman in the water is.

'What's wrong, hon?' Chloe flaps her lashes with the question, broadcasting the mildest irritation that I've not yet acknowledged her presence.

'It's nothing, Clo.' A horrible abbreviation for her name, but I've never thought up anything better. 'Just distracted with my own stuff. Can we talk later?'

Her look is unreadable. For a moment there are hints of disappointment, then pouty annoyance and the threat of an even poutier resentment. It eventually morphs into a tight smile, though she speaks through barely moving teeth. 'Sure, if that's what you need. If, you know, your stuff is *so important*.'

She stresses the words with mock disdain, but disappears behind a bookshelf and pretends to be busy with re-organising the stock there before I face the delicate task of replying.

The headlines on my screen have kept scrolling. There's still nothing about the girl in the river.

In the river.

Last night bursts back into my head. And this morning. The way things weren't supposed to be.

This morning, from the moment I awoke, David was different. His movements were different. He lingered longer than usual before he left for work, petering about upstairs, in his third-storey 'home office', with whatever it is he works on in there. Usually it's only a few minutes – *'Just grabbing my things, then out the door . . .'* – but not today. Today he changed his routine. And David is not a man who changes his routine.

I would swear he was trying to avoid me, hiding himself away in a spot he knew I didn't go. Trying to move through our apartment unseen so he didn't have to lay eyes on . . .

But I stop myself, because that's such a very silly thing to think. Even if the thought has been with me since the day first began and the face in the mirror did its usual thing.

Every morning, as I stand in the bathroom and gaze into the mirror, my eyes look back and taunt me. The fact that their colour doesn't match my name has always disappointed me, and it's a bit like they know this and are so prominent on my face purely as a way to rub it in.

They teased from the mirror in their customary way, today, but I merely shrugged. I'm used to this, and I went about my ritual as usual. Mornings are a well-honed routine. The actions of each minute are tuned to fit into their allotted space just as they ought, and so I went through the steps in their customary order. My face was done, my hair was brushed, and my teeth were as clean as is ever the case for a heavy tea drinker. I was suitably polished up for the day. My feet, seemingly registering all this even ahead of my brain, were already moving me out of our teal-tiled bathroom towards the kitchen.

Like they'd lives of their own.

They pointed me down the stairs, the same as they might on any average day. Toe into the not-so-plush carpeting of each step, then heel, bend of a stiff knee above – not creaking yet, I'm not so old as that – and repeat. I let my body guide me. *Like normal, like any other norma—*

But I didn't feel quite myself, it has to be said. And it's an odd thing, to start the day feeling not quite one's self.

The quarter-inch synthetic rag of the staircase drove its way between my toes in exactly the way it always does, and yet it . . . well, it didn't. I'm not sure I can say it any better than that. And it wasn't just the floor. Moments earlier, when my face stared back at me from the mirror, it was there, too. Something in my features I couldn't pinpoint, something that in another context I might describe as pain. And a buzz in my ears. And a stronger edge to my eyes.

I felt, deeply, that I ought to know what brought me into this day in this state; that it's strange, and somehow incomprehensible, not to know why one feels the way one does. But I woke without that knowledge, and like so many other things in life, I simply had to accept it.

One foot in front of the other, toes in the carpet, head on fire.

At the bottom of the staircase I'd rounded the corner into the kitchen, brushed my straw-coloured hair from my exposed neck and tried to rub away a bit of the firmness there, but I was pressing fingers into rocks. I'd gone to bed a woman. I'd woken up made of stone.

The lights had flickered when I switched them on – then a sudden burst of white. *White*. The memories came on strong, in the confused flurry that generally shapes morning thoughts.

The murder along Russian River. Not a dream. Work. Engaging, yet peaceful work. Long hours in front of my computer. Real.

The drive home. *White lights in my vision, a face . . .* The dreams pressed for their own.

But then – home. Passion. *David*. Tight embraces.

And then coldness and rejection. That wasn't a dream, either. That was real, and horrible, and I was quite certain I wasn't imagining it.

The evening had begun with passion. I may be hazy-eyed but I remember that clearly enough. All the signs of the red-blooded night every couple dreams of, and we were bringing that desire to life. But then it stopped, so abruptly. A single word, and everything ground to a halt.

There may have been more involved than that, but I just don't remember. I didn't remember this morning in the kitchen, and I don't remember now at my desk.

I only remember . . . *oh, God*. In the kitchen my shoulders clenched further as the memories returned. The flash of a face on the motorway. A name somehow appearing in my mind.

Emma.

And then my whispering that name into David's ear. The truly inexplicable. Even now, my skin tingles to think of it.

Who the hell is Emma?

And why for the love of God would I whisper another woman's name into my husband's ear while our bodies were entwined together and heat filled our room?

But I did. I said it, and the night was over. David froze as the final, whispered syllable crawled its way out of my lips, then rolled out from beneath me with a motion that wasn't meant to be graceful. When I'd adjusted myself to face him his shoulders were to me, his head pressed into his pillow.

'What is it?' My question was innocent enough. 'What did I do?'

'It's nothing,' he answered, in a way that made it clear that it was certainly not nothing. I could tell he was controlling his breathing. The melting bumps of goose-flesh wilted on the sides of his back.

I briefly felt badly, wondering whether I'd stirred up some old pain. David isn't a fragile man, but he's not exactly the most open with his feelings, either, which makes it hard to know when I might accidentally knock the scab off some emotional wound he's never fully shared. That's the rub in holding things back from people you love: you open yourself to being tortured by them, since they can never know what territory of your heart is whole and what is tender.

'David, if I said something to upset you, I'm—'

'I said it's nothing!' No concealing the clap to his voice, like thunder when you haven't seen the lightning; but then a long, controlling sigh. A softer tone emerged from the thunder a few seconds later, though the words were still stiff and forced. 'Don't worry about it. I'm just tired.' Hesitation. 'We're both tired.'

I wasn't tired. My body was still on fire, tingling and energized. I reached out to his shoulder and tugged on it provocatively. It was still hot, his body disagreeing with his words.

'I'm sure we can get a little energy back if we try.'

David pulled the shoulder away in a strong, singular motion.

'Enough, Amber. Enough.' Then a sustained lacuna, as if he were pondering what to say next.

'Let's just go to sleep. I have a busy day ahead of me in the morning. We probably shouldn't have started this anyway. Drink some water, you need to hydrate. Get some rest.'

He pulled the sheet up over his shoulders and curled himself yet further away from me. And there I was, naked and uncovered on my half of the bed, utterly confused as to what had just happened.

I don't know when I fell asleep. I had my long draw of water as David had recommended. He always encourages me to keep a bottle by the bedside; saves having to traipse downstairs if I get a midnight thirst – and it's just like him to think of my welfare, even at a moment he's obviously upset. It soothed a little, but neither my body nor my mind were in the mood for rest. I remember staring at our bedroom ceiling for what felt like fifteen or twenty years. I got to know every feature of its poorly textured surface, probably once billed as 'eggshell white' but now suspiciously more the colour of dilute urine. We really, desperately need to repaint.

When I turned to David again he was soundly asleep. Somehow I got a handful of the sheets back and covered myself up. I don't remember much after that, except for frustrated jostling and annoyance at the fact that counting sheep just never works. They're revolting, shaggy creatures anyway, fluffy-white only in comic strips. In reality they're dirty and matted and pooping on absolutely everything, and they always just bleat and jump and carry on coming, and . . .

Morning eventually came, with David's adjusted routine and the noises from the den. Finally, he left for work. I got a peck on the cheek before I rose from my pillow. That much, at least. All wasn't lost.

The memories overlap in my mind. The sounds, the kiss, the usual routine in the bathroom. The stairs. The kitchen.

Beneath my feet the linoleum was cold, and the lights had finally flickered wholly to life. The revolting colours of the inbuilt décor glowed under them and the vision assaulted one of my senses, while the scent of coffee, gradually overpowering the lingering remnants of David's cologne, assaulted another.

71

Coffee. There was half of a pot still in the carafe, dutifully prepared before David had left, and an empty cup beside it. An invitation, a gesture of reconciliation.

And a smoothie, some repellant shade of green, in a tall glass near the fruit basket, sitting atop an appointment reminder from the dentist's office in lieu of a coaster.

But there was no note. And I can't remember the last time David didn't leave me a note.

13

David

There is no other choice. Not now. With what Amber said as we went to sleep, the way forward has become painfully, but perfectly, clear.

It might be politically correct to wish there were another way, but there isn't, and I've learned not to waste my time with those kinds of emotions. We're perilously close to falling off the only path that keeps us alive. Course correction is required, and a man shouldn't lament what is simply necessary.

The solution – the only solution – doesn't lie in anything new. The path we're on is the right one. What needs to be adjusted isn't the act, it's the art of the dosage. I'd thought it had been high enough. Obviously I was wrong.

The particular concoction I've settled on acts deeply, almost at the core of the psyche, but that doesn't mean more won't sometimes be required.

One of its perks is that its interior impact lasts, even while its more physical effects – the grogginess, the confusion, the loss of control – wear off swiftly. An ideal pairing.

So this morning I did what I always do, adding it to what I know she'll drink, this time with a few additional drops. It's always been the easiest way to get it into her system. Some here, some there. Prep everything just right, make it a kind of invitation. She never resists.

I mixed the smoothie, trusting that the sound of the blender was so familiar now that it wouldn't rouse her. There are other ways to get the job done – when we're on a trip, or camping, or otherwise out and about. But when we're home, when it's the routine, this has become the standard.

The drink's contents just filled a glass, and I left it on the counter.

Then the coffee. Always, always the coffee. An essential part of it.

A drop here, a drop there.

It will all have its effect. It will just take a day, maybe two – and everything will be made right.

14

Amber

My thoughts have been wandering too long. The book-shop is moving around me now, quietly but with gentle activity. I think I've tended to a few customers who've ventured to my corner and didn't already know what they were after, but I can't say I'm entirely sure. My memories, permitted freely between activities, have never-theless seemed to invade the whole.

But it's impossible to be oblivious to Chloe as she re-emerges from behind a bookshelf covered in paperback detective fiction and thrillers. A favourite genre of hers. As she appears, I impulsively fold down my laptop's screen, which I'd been once again perusing from behind the stacks of magazines on my desk. I'm not sure I want her to know what I'm looking at.

I recognize that the motion might appear rude, so I glance up at Chloe with a try for a smile. Immediately

I realize my error, and try desperately to halt the change in my expression. I'm still not in the mood to talk, and smiling generally encourages Chloe to speak. Even here, in my quiet corner where I'm so often left in peace.

'Noticed I didn't hear none of your usual flirting with Mitch today,' she says, proving my point. There is egging in her voice, together with that stupid drawl. She fancies herself a detective, with all the time she spends nose-deep in the books, but with Chloe it's mostly guesses and innuendos. She wags her head towards our boss's office door in an appropriation of subtle suggestion. Little stints of investigative splendour like this would be flaunted in my direction more often if Chloe's normal post wasn't on the till near the front door, too far away to pass sly comments with any degree of subterfuge.

'Haven't seen him since I got in,' I answer. 'I assume he's down in the warehouse.' Curt. Short. 'And I never flirt.'

'Come on now, we all flirt! You don't have to hide nothin' from—'

I can't stand it. I just can't stand another syllable of it. I'm upset with David, with myself. I'm confused about the odd emotions I seem to harbour about the story of the woman in the river, frustrated that I can't find more details on it, and I'm not prepared for such an exchange. Not today, and not with this throbbing in my ears.

'Noth-*ing*,' I answer, cutting her off and staring straight up at her. 'I don't have to hide noth-*ing*.' I catch myself. Shit. '*Any*-thing. Christ sakes, quit pretending you're

76

Agatha Christie meets queen of the bayou. You work in a bookshop!'

That's a good snap, for me. I usually don't react like this.

Chloe is silent for longer than I've ever known her to manage the feat. The miracle spans a solid ten seconds.

'Bitch,' she finally says, flatly. Her accent is now wholly Californian. 'Just trying to be friendly. And I can talk however I want. It's my life.' Then a pause, and then for what I assume to be the good measure of ensuring it sunk in: 'Bitch'.

I feel bad. Chloe may not yet be thirty, but she's already a single, twice-divorced mother of a seven-year-old boy whose stated goal in life is to grow up to be 'a more bad-ass fucker than dem shits from Oakie' and whose usual terms of endearment for his own mother alternate between 'wench' and 'yo, lady' She deserves a break, and certainly more than my attitude.

'I'm sorry,' I offer. 'I didn't mean to—'

'No, to hell with you,' she cuts me off. 'I don't want to hear about your long morning or your tired body or your worn-out temper, or your great throbbing bastard of a headache.' Chloe is almost prescient in her huff. 'You just sit there and tend to your pile of newspapers and dross, I'll mind my till, and we'll both pretend you're not the pompous self-centred cow we both know you are.'

She's disappeared among the rows of shelves again. Despite the impressive array of insults having just been flung my way, I'm not willing to become too apocalyptic about the exchange. I re-open my computer. Chloe and I have tragic, earth-ending disintegrations of our friendship on more or less a weekly cycle, so I know this will pass.

Though not, perhaps, quite as quickly as it actually does.

'You'd think you'd be grateful for a little help with your snooping, since the art of the search clearly isn't your forte.' I hear her voice, soft and back-in-black, from somewhere behind a row of rarely visited classics. A strange comment. My ears are suddenly a degree more alert. My face comes up from my monitor and Sadie's fuzzy underbelly is facing me from the photo on the wall.

I'm entirely uncertain what sort of 'help' Chloe could be in a position to offer me – there's a solid 50/50 shot it's advice on hairstyles or improving my sex life, or just an all-out ploy to get me to do some menial activity she doesn't want to do herself – but her reference to snooping jostles my attention. She hasn't said it with the tones that normally go with jokes, and the word itself sounds foreign in my ears.

'My snooping?' I finally ask. I don't get up.

And I can't explain it, but there's that tingling in my spine again.

'Yeah, help, woman,' Chloe answers. Power is coming back into her voice, and after a strong intake of breath, she launches into a long collection of words she's clearly been storing up since she first said hello.

But I only hear the first three.
'It's about Emma.'
And she keeps talking, but I suddenly can't breathe.

15

Amber

I am positively, spectacularly certain that I've never spoken with Chloe about my private, quiet little obsession with learning all I can about the murder of the woman in the river. It's been entirely my own, tucked away in my corner and in the secret folds of my thoughts. Besides, a conversation like that would have been torturous, and while many of my emotions over the past twenty-four hours have been unusual, I'm not that out of it.

But Chloe didn't just mention the subject of my sudden interest. She mentioned a name. *The* name.

'What do you mean, "It's about Emma"?'

I can barely form the last word. The name that came to me on the road, the one that stopped David mid-thrust and sent yesterday spiralling out of normalcy into disarray. The name I'm all but positive I didn't even know before I left the shop yesterday.

Yesterday. That word, again.

'What do you mean, what do I mean?' Chloe's been talking non-stop for several seconds, her voice a background murmur behind my thoughts, but she halts at my interruption, genuinely puzzled. 'Haven't you been listening to I word I just said?'

I shake my head, too anxious to be embarrassed. 'Start again.'

'I *said*,' she draws out the word, emphasizing the condescension implied in her willingness to repeat herself, 'that you being so interested in random bits of the week's news seems to have paid off, in terms of curiosity value. The murder you're so bent up on, up in the Russian River. Story's got more involved overnight.'

It's solid now. She knows concrete details. Like she's been in my head.

'What the hell are you talking about?' I demand, fire in my voice. I'm not normally this assertive, and the strength in my breath is doubly out of place in the quiet of the shop.

Chloe's left eyebrow rises so high it looks like it might go into orbit. 'The hell am I? What . . . Calm down, girl. I'm *trying* to share the juicy details I dug up for you.' She looks like she might spit at me if I don't change my tone, but I can't seem to stop myself.

I didn't ask Chloe to do anything for me, dig up anything. I'm mishearing. My palms are growing sweaty, sticking to the newsprint of the paper on which I've laid them.

'That woman you've gone all Hercule Poirot over.' Chloe's voice stomps through my thoughts, instantly proving me wrong. 'You're not the only one who can play detective, you know. Come on, you're talking to the queen. Try to name a detective novel published in the last five years that I haven't read. Come on. I dare you.'

I don't. She rolls her eyes.

'Anyway, I scoped out everything I could find on that woman last night,' Chloe continues. 'Web's a fantastic place for the curious. Turns out she's single, never married and no children. One site said she was gainfully employed, but didn't say where. No ongoing relationships. No history of major drugs. No criminal background.' Chloe lists off the facts in a way that stresses, again, that she'd just said this a moment ago, when my brain wouldn't allow me to listen. 'I did manage a little more this morning,' she finally adds. 'Since I knew you were interested. Looks like they've got a cause of death now, and some other stuff. Saved it on my phone. You want it as an email or a text?'

I abruptly stand up. The newspaper clings to my wet palms and I frustratedly shake it free.

'What's going on, Chloe? Why are you nosing around into these things?' I'm affronted by what feels like her invasion into my inner world. Has she been watching me? How could anyone know I was so taken by this? How could she?

'Who asked for your help?' I blurt out.

Chloe's face drops out of banter mode. It's not a facade she often abandons.

'You sure you're feeling okay, Amber?' Her voice is once again more Oakland than fake Floridian, and she looks genuinely confused. When I nod my head but say nothing, her eyes go a little wider. 'Because, I mean, what kind of question is that? You asked me, obviously. Who else would have?'

I suddenly feel dizzy on my feet. I want to snap back at her, but I can't find any words.

Liar. Cow. I haven't talked to you about this. I haven't talked to . . . But the reactions stay firmly in my head. If I could see my face, I'm certain I would see it going white.

'We, we talked about this? You and me?' I try to make the question sound calm, rational, but inwardly I'm imploring her to say no, to announce some joking Chloe-esque detail that puts an end to this spontaneous charade. Maybe she caught a glance at my computer screen yesterday, or my notepad. Damn that oddly enticing Hello Kitty logo. She's just goofing around, playing the clairvoyant.

'I wouldn't say so much that we talked,' she answers. *I knew it! Cow!* But Chloe doesn't stop there. 'It was a weird conversation. A few scattered words. But I caught your drift in the end, hon.'

My eyes are back into hers. They must ask the question for themselves.

'You were just sitting there at the periodicals service

desk, muttering,' she continues, nodding at my cluttered workspace. 'About three o'clock. Shop was in the afternoon lull, and you'd been lost in your little world a while. Come on, you're honestly saying you don't remember?'

I don't want to admit that, even to myself. 'Remind me,' I say instead.

'Your eyes were glued on your laptop, Amber. Your whole body was rigid, like you'd really been captivated by something. Weren't saying much, but you were obviously enrapt.'

'And?'

'And, well, it isn't every day you start out a conversation asking for help. So I paid attention.' She pauses – long, expectant – but I don't have anything to say.

Asking for help? *This makes no sense.*

'After that,' she continues, 'you just said a few words, pointing at the screen.' She indicates my laptop. '"My story. The dead woman in the river, her name is Emma. Help me." You obviously wanted to explore the story, and heck, I'm always up for diving into a bit of snooping around.'

It's suddenly gone very cold in my corner of the shop. Chloe's words are not nearly as disturbing as the fact that I have absolutely no memory of saying them.

I finally peer back at her. She's eyeing me with what feels like too much curiosity. Then, joltingly, the intensity breaks and a devious wink flickers across her eyes.

'You want my opinion, hon?' she asks, her voice toying.

'No.' But that answer's never worked with Chloe before, and it doesn't now.

'I think you need to get yourself laid.' She leans forward, her small chest heaving as rapaciously as she can manage. 'Nothing better for clearing a foggy mind and that pasty looks like a good—'

'Was I right?' I suddenly find myself asking, eager in equal measure for an answer and to keep Chloe from finishing that particular sentence. Her face is instantly a question.

'Right?'

'When I said . . . you said I said the girl was called Emma . . . All those other details, but you haven't said whether what I said was . . .' The sentence is convoluted. I'm not sure how to frame my question in any other way. 'Was I right?'

Chloe's eyes are now as wide as I've ever seen them. She doesn't answer immediately, and her silence feels foreign and uncomfortable. Finally she replies, with a tone bridging tenderness and concern, 'Yeah, hon, you were right. Course you were. Doesn't take a mystery fan to figure that out. Name's public record.'

'She really is called Emma?'

'Emma Fairfax.' I can see Chloe trying to normalize her expression, hoping to re-rail a conversation that hadn't gone at all the way she'd anticipated. But when I keep silent, it becomes clear that Chloe doesn't know how to continue. She begins the slow departure back towards the front of the shop.

'Whatever, girl. I'll shoot you off an email with a few more notes later, see if I can help you make all the nice plot points fit together.' Her voice retreats to a whisper before it fades away all together. 'Not like I don't have my own things to be doin'.'

I wish I could say that I'm able to move on and accept Chloe's strange words as just her being her. I wish I could just get about my day, but I can't. I only manage to get myself back into a seated posture by the most extraordinary exertion of will.

Chloe's words mingle with those already in my head.

Single, never married, no children.
        Emma.
Gainfully employed.
        Emma.
No relationships. No domestic problems.
        Emma.
Foul play. Murdered.
        Emma.
           Emma.
              Emma.

As I whisper the name now, I remember whispering it yesterday. Uncomprehendingly. Innocently.

And again I remember David's body, rigid beneath my own.

16

David

'Not . . . by . . . choice.'

When those words emerged from Emma Fairfax's lips, as I first met her two and a half years ago, a little more, they opened a door. A door I'd been waiting for my whole life, without even knowing it. She became a revelation, and a revelation only for me.

She'd been admitted to the ward nine days before her first interview with Dr Marcello, and she'd already gone through the usual battery of psych evaluations that accompany every arrival. Even when one is committed by law, rather than choice – when there's at least the legal assertion that the individual has substantial psychological problems – there's a routine that has to be gone through in order to arrive at a formal diagnosis. Intake interviews, broad-level diagnostics, then assignment to an appropriate ward for specialist interviews prior to the prescription of treatment. She'd come to Dr Marcello only after the first few rounds of those had already been accomplished, ready for the diagnostic comb to be finer and the focus of treatment more precise. And I sat at his side, as I always did in those days, watching, learning, taking notes, offering thoughts. The pharmacy wing always had a representative at consults like this, to counsel the doctor on options to form part of any treatment, and to receive instructions in turn on the precise drugs a patient's regime would require.

So there we were. The system, in its glory.

All this had fallen upon Emma Fairfax because of the day she got into a car. A blue Chevy Malibu with a custom JBL ten-speaker sound system, still blaring Coldplay, of all things, at full volume when the emergency services unwrapped its wrinkled metal frame from a tree trunk in Santa Cruz. There would probably have been an arrest following her hospitalization in any case, given the nature of the crash, but a stomach filled with a nearly lethal combination of Valium and Xanax, stirred together with most of a bottle of cheap tequila, changed things. Attempted suicide always gets a psych eval.

Attempted suicide. With pills. At first, an innocuous case. Later, that feeble attempt at taking her own life would make so much more sense.

The tree Emma had hit stood in a front yard in a residential neighbourhood inhabited by twelve children under the age of fifteen (the prosecutor had been insistent to identify the exact number and ages, even though none had been injured in the crash), and that meant Emma had been labelled 'psychologically disturbed with criminal liability', which in turn meant she'd ended up in DHS-Metropolitan, the Department of State Hospitals facility in LA County, rather than in a cell in the women's prison in Chowchilla or Valley State.

Which meant she came within the scope of my vision.

It took days for her conversations with Dr Marcello to open up beyond the blank stares and occasional mutterings that had characterized the first encounter. Part of that was due to the sedatives forcibly delivered to her in a little paper cup each morning, but part went beyond the medications. Something was haunting this young woman. I could see it, even from the side of the room. And my interest grew, because there was something there that was familiar. Something that stirred at memories. Something that made me want to . . . help her.

'You know, you can talk to me.' Dr Marcello said this almost every morning, usually towards the beginning of the prescribed thirty-minute sessions. It was a truth that needed to be gradually absorbed by the patient, softening up the clay that had hardened into her rock-solid defences. She'd eyed him each time he said it, sometimes glancing over in my direction as well, but usually little more than that. Only in the fifth session did she finally begin to open up.

'It'll help if you talk, eventually,' he added that day. 'You've been here two weeks now, a little more. Time's got to come to speak, Miss Fairfax.'

She grunted. We weren't to be believed. Her look was momentarily all revulsion, peering up and down at Marcello, then at me. Then the emotion evaporated. The doctor jotted a note down on his pad, just visible to me on his knee. *Resistant to authority. Maybe to men.*

'Though I suppose, from another perspective,' Dr Marcello added, 'we could say you don't have to speak at all.' He laid down his pen over his notes. 'You can stay silent, if that's what you want, and we can just sit like this. You're going to be in here for a while, in any case. You know that.'

'Not long enough.'

I barely caught the words. She barely said them. But the whisper made it to my ears, and my shoulders rose, encouraged by the first sign of a real communication.

'What does that mean, Emma?' Dr Marcello asked. 'Is it okay if I call you Emma?'

She shrugged, dismissive and annoyed. It was 'I don't care' and 'fuck off' in a single, well-practised thrust of the shoulders. But it was also a solid sign of comprehension, and a concrete response.

'You can call me whatever you want,' she finally answered. 'It doesn't matter any more.'

I was startled at the strong accent with which she spoke. With her first full sentences it came out noticeably, and the elongated vowels and reassigned consonants of country bumpkin drawl clashed with her simple beauty. Her 'whatever' came out 'wat-evuh' and her 'doesn't matter' was a punctuated 'don't mattuh'. I couldn't immediately tell whether it was authenticity or affectation, but Emma had the motions to go with the sassy tones. There was a tedious roll of the eyes and a dismissive flick of the head. *Ain't much for ya, fukkuh. Piss off.*

'Why is that?' Dr Marcello asked, keeping his attention focused. If he was as surprised by her voice as I, he didn't show it. 'Why doesn't it matter what I call you?'

'Nothing matters now I'm here. It's all done.' She rolled her eyes again. Her arms remained folded across her chest.

'Your life isn't over,' he said. 'You were fortunate – you didn't harm anyone but yourself. The car's totalled and you probably offed the tree, but it didn't go further than that.'

When she laughed, the sound was pitiful. Mournful. I remember I was amazed that someone who seemed so determined to be brash could exhibit such a contrary emotion.

'Didn't harm no one!' she jabbed back, her eyes suddenly going glassy. 'That's the whole problem. I've harmed plenty, and no one knows.' She swung her head my way, stared into my eyes, as if I might understand what she felt the doctor didn't.

I lowered my head, unsure how to meet that stare. I had a clipboard across my lap, intended for clinical notes on prescriptions the doctor might require, but I found myself scratching illegible lines across it with my pen. Muscle memory was moving my hands.

'Is that why you were taking the drugs?' Dr Marcello asked. Suddenly my own throat caught slightly. The mention of the pills – it wasn't the first. But the attempt at suicide, it suddenly hit me. Not as simply a clinical fact, but as a memory. One I'd worked so hard to push away.

The pills . . .

I swallowed hard.

'Was it guilt?' Dr Marcello continued. 'Guilt over the people you feel you've hurt in your life? The Xanax, the Valium – you had a lot in your system.'

God, Evelyn. I shoved the memory away. Back into its box. This wasn't the time. The past was the past. This woman wasn't my sister.

Emma Fairfax glared at Dr Marcello, her eyes pitying and condemning at the same time.

'I don't *feel* nothing,' she answered. Her eyes rolled and her arms crossed tighter at her chest, defiant. I escaped the clenched feeling in my chest enough to see Dr Marcello underline the phrase as he transcribed it onto his notepad. A sentence fairly well drenched with possible interpretations.

'So you feel you don't sufficiently register emot—'

'I'm not speaking psycho-shit, Doctor,' she snapped. But she wasn't angry. 'I don't *feel* I've hurt others. I know it. It's a fact.'

There was a sob in her eyes and it shook her tongue. She stopped talking, tossing her hair aside in a show of dismissiveness. *I don't care. Nothing can make me care.* The forced denial of someone who cares deeply – more than they wish or want.

'Can you tell me about that?' Marcello asked. He'd

drawn a firm line across his paper. This was a new area, one that hadn't come up in our brief encounters to date.

My heart was racing. The conversation was taking me in new directions, too. The memories were hitting like a flood.

The pills.

The death.

My sister's absence.

I could barely stay in the moment.

'It weren't supposed to turn out the way it did!' Emma cried out. There were tears then, streaming down her cheeks and pooling at the curve of her chin before falling onto her lap.

'What wasn't, Emma?' Dr Marcello kept his voice soft.

'It were bad. We all knew it were bad. But it got out of hand.'

She wasn't registering his questions, so he stopped asking them.

The sob was back, this time long, vocal and heart-wrenching. A few words fumbled out from between Emma's lips, but none of them had anything to do with the car accident.

'Emma,', Dr Marcello leaned in towards her in a carefully practised, unthreatening way, 'I'm not sure what we're talking about. Fill me in. Why don't you start with where, with when?' Concrete facts, sometimes easier for traumatized patients to deal with than emotions.

She gazed more through him than at him.

'You don't want to know,' she said. 'These nice looks

you give me, the "it ain't so fuckin' bad, you're a good girl" sentiments, you're not gonna have 'em for long if I tell you what . . . what . . .'

Her throat seized up. She wanted to be defiant, but a sob stopped her.

Marcello leaned forward. Despite the torrent of my memories, my emotions, I leaned forward too.

'Emma, there's nothing you can tell us that will cause me to change my desire to care for you.'

It's a lie he'd been trained to tell. All of us, actually, even if we're just pharmacists in a prison ward – and we're taught to believe it, too. Our goal is to help the patient. Nothing can change that. There's nothing they can say that ought to cause us to look at them differently. No deed a person has done that devalues his worth or affects our duty to care.

But it's a lie. A terrible, dreadful, hideous lie. Maybe I was never meant to become a man of Dr Marcello's moral objectivity, maybe my own experiences meant I couldn't maintain that ruse of unflappable dispassion, but reality's reality. There *are* things a person can say – things a young woman can say, in a little room beneath fluorescent lights before an analyst and a pharmacist at a metal table – that should make any human person change their mind radically about them. Things a person can say that show they're not people at all, but monsters. Monsters whose existence makes the world itself groan, repulsed by more than their actions.

Repulsed by their very existence.

17

Amber

I have to get home. I have to get to my husband.

I've managed, somehow, to go through the remaining motions of the day. No customers want newspapers after 3.00 p.m., and if you haven't caught your glossy copy of *Esquire* by lunch, chance is you're not going after it until tomorrow – so the second half of my days tend to be even quieter than the first. There is always a bit of restocking to be done, some tidying up of the reading areas. An attempt at making the periodicals service desk, which I like to think of as my own, slightly more present- able beneath its stacks of papers and magazines.

As customary as the flow of the day is, however, I near its end with anxious relief. Anxious for reasons that are still difficult to understand. The day has been a haze, and every time I exhale I'm propelled through its fog, back into a maze of very different thoughts.

A maze that keeps drawing me towards my husband.

I don't know precisely what it is I want to tell David, in light of what I've learned today. Something happened – last night, this morning, somewhere inbetween. The bridge from yesterday to today involves him.

In my immediate surroundings, Chloe has kept to herself throughout the afternoon. Demonstratively. She hasn't spoken a word to me since our exchange in the morning, and I linger now with her promise of an email with a few more details before the day's end. I'm sure it will come, and equally sure that she's delaying sending it simply to rub in her displeasure with the bizarre nature of my reaction earlier. I'm going to have to apologize to her eventually. Chloe may be a nut when it comes to social skills, but she's not a liar, and if she says I talked to her about all this, then I have little choice but to believe her. The evidence is there. At least my outburst was minor, more odd than offensive. She'll get over it soon enough. If she doesn't, a gift will certainly do it. There are few crises in Chloe's life that a Mars bar or a pack of Marlboro Reds can't remedy.

But I'm a different story. My interior state is neither as manic nor as mutable as Chloe's. My ups stay ups and my downs downs, with a long haul required to change them. It's always been that way. From childhood. My mother yells at the ten-year-old version of me in a burst of anger – a skill she'd expertly cultivated – and the next two months are sulky, all the weather grey and dismal. My father lashes out and strikes (*'It's just a goddamn slap, Amby'* – such a deplorable nickname, though linked to one of the few vivid memories I retain of him – *'Used to hand them out in schools, back when children knew their place'*) and I'm down for weeks. I remember those emotional pits. They were always deeper than I'd thought they'd be, their walls made muddier by the betrayal of people who shouldn't have pushed me into them in the first place. Still, you crawl out eventually. Chloe would probably have coiled up some internal spring and bounced out in an instant, smiling by the time she arced back down to earth. I had to climb, fingers in the mud, dirtied and darkened by it all, carrying the grime with me. But there's always an upper rim, even to the deepest pit.

Then there are the highs, too, with me just as long in life as the lows and stirred up in their own, unique ways. The kind words from a friend. The gold star on a childhood art assignment. Bumping into just the right man on just the right walk. They catapult me onto mesas, those things. From their heights a person can see the whole world, and on that world the only thing that shines is bright, golden sunlight. It's all a matter of the right prompt.

The details Chloe brought me, and the bits and pieces I already knew – they aren't the stuff of mesas or mountaintops. You'd think I might be interested simply by the fact of something out-of-the-ordinary happening in our area, even if it does involve a death. A curiosity. There's something exciting in that. Instead, the details drag my emotions down, against my will and beyond my control. I can smell the mud of a pit I can't yet see. It smells of moss and roots and decay, and something about it terrifies and depresses me. I've been in pits before, and I remember how dark the world can be.

I'm about to experience it all anew. I can feel it. And once again, I can't explain why.

18

The second body was a man's. He was middle aged, slightly overweight but overall in decent form: lean, not too thin, not too fat. His silver hair matched a grey buttondown shirt that wasn't off the rack. Attention to fashion was visible everywhere. Upturned, contrasting-colour cuffs. Alligator-print belt. Perfectly polished shoes. What looked to have been a good hairdo, before the struggle changed that.

He lay prone on the unyielding tile floor. His skin was already bluing, and his eyes, like hers, were wide open, though they didn't sparkle with light. They were hollow, sucking in the grey ceiling rather than reflecting the light of the sun or moon.

There was no serenity surrounding him. His end had been violent, and the signs of the violence were every-where. Rips marred the silver shirt. Bruises that looked like they might have come from fists speckled the skin of his arms. A wild look of recognition was frozen on his face. He'd seen what was coming. He couldn't escape it.

And a knife-wound flowered at his side, bleeding now only a few remaining drops into the crimson pool that had emerged beneath him.

This was reality.

But it wasn't the way the story was supposed to go. No story should ever be written this way, with this kind of character, or this kind of turn. They were things to be written out, edit away. So that the real story, the good story, could emerge from their absence.

And so the work had begun, and would continue, until the right ending came.

19

Amber

It's not so much a commute home as a race that begins as the workday ends. My step out the door is a sprint and I aggressively dodge traffic as I speed down the highway, ignoring my headache and trying as hard as I can to ignore the frustration caused by other drivers. By the time I park on the street outside our apartment I'm already jumping out the door. Feet on the pavement, then the lawn. My laptop and my satchel swing at my side, but I hardly notice them. I've become a woman of singular focus.

David.

A few bounds and I'm up to the first storey. The key goes into the lock with surprisingly little fumbling, given my state, and this time I do thrust open the door. Not my style, but I do it anyway: full bore, strong swing. I want to see him, all at once, to share what I've discovered and to know what he knows. To find out what it is that's taking place between us, and how it's connected to the story at the river.

But the door slams against our corner cabinet and the noise echoes through an empty kitchen. I want companionship and solace; instead, I've arrived to an empty home.

It takes me ten minutes and a glass-and-a-half of a poor South African Zinfandel to calm myself. Marginally. I haven't been this exercised in as long as I can remember, and there's only so much that wine can deaden the anticipation.

It's 6.42 p.m. when I glance at my watch.

That mundane reality mingles with expectation and starts to slow my pace. Six forty-two is late enough that if David were coming home as usual at the end of the day, he'd have made it here already. It's one of the reasons he works a shift that starts earlier and ends at 3.30 p.m.: the commute from San Francisco back to Santa Rosa at the end of the workday is deadly, and San Fran proper was the only place he was able to get a pharmacy to pay him enough for an assistant's role. The downside is that traffic at the end of the workday never makes it up to the pace of a crawl, so if he's had to stay late, he'll go for the norm and stay late enough that the rush has passed before he hits the road. Doesn't happen every day, but it's far from infrequent. David's a hard worker. Late nights come with the territory.

I command myself to take a few deep breaths, and another long drink, finishing off my glass. Calm will come, I insist to myself, by force if necessary.

I call for Sadie with a little whistle, hoping canine companionship might help. She swivels around my ankles for a few minutes, shoving her wet snout into my knees and absorbing my coos and 'good girls' like they're drugs; then, fluffed enough to satisfy her ageing frame and happily in receipt of a milk bone I toss her from a jar on the counter, she wanders to the edge of the room and flops back onto her belly. She'll want a walk later, but that's something to be saved for David when he gets home, not for me. Sadie's trained us well. I do the petting, David the walking, and she the content lollygagging.

So it's another glass of Zinfandel and a decision to let more alcohol help quell the little freak-out I've been experiencing throughout the day. The bottle was already open, cork pushed in loosely and positioned at the front of a little trio of bottles on the counter, when I got home. Inviting. Another one of David's routine kindnesses, always thinking of me a step ahead, knowing what I'll want or need.

I sip the wine in draws that are too long. *For God's sakes, Amber, get a hold of yourself.*

I'm upset at being so easily thrown off balance. I'm a grown woman. My emotional state should be stronger. But the wine has started to soften my thoughts, and within a minute or two I'm less concerned with age or expectation. Wine will do that to you. The magic of the grape. Just let it rot long enough to become magical in the bottle and . . .

I giggle. I actually giggle, which startles me, then annoys. Only women who never giggle know how annoying the trait really is. It's far too girlish for me, in any case, so I do the sensible thing and immediately blame it on the drink. It may be crap, but the wine's apparently got a kick. And suddenly, I feel I could do with a lot more of it.

I grab my glass and the neck of the bottle in a single hand, my handbag in the other, and head upstairs.

My laptop is out of the bag and on my knees within a few minutes, my body settled into a piece of furniture that David and I have never been able to agree on identifying. It's either a chair (his opinion) or a beanbag (mine). Ikea calls it a *Snorfelbörg*. But it's comfortable, whatever it is, and I'm in the mood for comfort.

The wine is diminishing swiftly in the glass to my left. I'm more at ease, now, that sense coming swiftly. I feel I can sort through my emails without an overload of stress, waiting for David to come home.

It turns out that Chloe did, indeed, send me a few more materials she was able to track down on the Emma Fairfax murder. Despite having no memory of seeking her help, pulling in the aid of a fanatical detective fiction fan was clearly a good move. Chloe appears to have taken delight in proving her investigatory prowess. Her latest email to me contains three attachments. The first is some regional paper's write-up on the discovery of the body, based on various police reports and calls. I'm impressed Chloe searched long enough to find it; there are a thousand regional newspapers in northern California, and this is from one even I have never heard of – and I work at the periodicals desk. Chloe may look the ditsy ever-child, but she's done the greats of her mystery genre proud.

And all for me. Without my even knowing I'd asked her for it.

I swallow more wine. The report that Chloe's sent indicates it had been updated at 4.48 p.m. this afternoon.

LOCAL POLICE CONFIRM DISCOVERY IN RUSSIAN RIVER, SONOMA COUNTY, OF THE BODY OF ONE MS EMMA CHRISTINA FAIRFAX OF SALINAS, CALIFORNIA. MS FAIRFAX, AGED 40, WAS UNMARRIED WITH NO KNOWN CHILDREN, HER SOLE NEXT OF KIN BEING AN AUNT RESIDENT IN PHOENIX, ARIZONA, WHO HAS ALREADY BEEN INFORMED OF HER NIECE'S DEMISE. MS FAIRFAX WAS EMPLOYED AS A RETAIL WORKER, HAVING A FEW YEARS AGO CHANGED CAREERS FOLLOWING A LENGTHY STINT AS THE OWNER OF A SMALL-SCALE HAIR SALON. POLICE CONFIRM HER DEATH IS BEING TREATED NOW AS SUSPECTED MURDER, AND THOUGH THEY HAVE RELEASED FEW DETAILS, OFFICIALS HAVE CONFIRMED THE CAUSE OF DEATH AS STRANGULATION, WITH THE MURDER WEAPON SUSPECTED TO BE A ROUGH

ROPE OR DOG LEASH MADE OF SYNTHETIC RED FIBER. PRESUMABLY IT HAS NOT YET BEEN LOCATED BY OFFICERS, GIVEN THE POLICE DEPARTMENT'S PHRASING, BUT NO FURTHER DETAILS HAVE BEEN FORTHCOMING FOLLOWING OUR QUESTIONS.

Regional paper or not, this write-up is decently robust. The beginning traces of a personality are there, together with more details of the woman's actual death than I'd been able to find before. God, what a way to go. Strangulation. And with a rope.

I have a profound craving to know more, but the article ends there. 'No further details have been forthcoming.' The kind of comment that pulls at you. I've come to learn we're wired like that, all of us: the moment we know something's been hidden from us, there's little we desire more in the universe than to know exactly what it is.

The second file attached to Chloe's email is a screenshot snapped from some sort of chat session. 'Got this from a friend who worked at the bookshop before you came on. He's over at the *Berkeley Gazette* now,' is her only annotation, and I don't recognize the 'KL29906' that's the chat nickname opposite hers in the image.

KL29906: Yeah, saw a picture of the body on a cop's desk when I went to interview them at the station this morning. Kinda snuck the glance when eyes weren't on me. Shouldn't really even be mentioning it, you know.

Chloe_LUV32: Come on, hon, you know I'm always up for finding out if real-life homicides are as catchy as the ones in my books. I'm sure you can tell me a little about the woman.

KL29906: Just that she's a looker, or was. Nice hair, pretty face.

Chloe_LUV32: Online it says she was just under forty.

KL29906: Doesn't look it in that photo, can tell you that much. Would take her for early thirties, tops. A stunner. Looked really peaceful, even with all she'd been through.

Chloe_LUV32: That all?

KL29906: Well, unless you want to chat about lunch tomorrow and—

The screenshot cuts off the conversation from there, and I smile slightly at the thought of why. The wine is making my belly warm.

There's a picture forming in my mind. This woman, Emma Fairfax, is no longer simply a name and a collection of vital statistics. She's apparently beautiful, younger than her years. Pretty enough to be captivating, even to someone seeing a photo of her snapped in the morgue after a rope had been wrapped around her neck and her body deposited in a river. For a few seconds, I wonder what that kind of beauty could look like.

She has no family, but she works with others. Not on the exalted plane of a social worker or teacher, perhaps, but still – running a salon is people work, and even a cashier chats over the counter. My mental portrait of her expands to frame in a chatty, friendly young woman (I emphasize the 'young' in my mind, since as she's older than me by a year or so, this implies only encouraging things about my own age). Maybe I'm starting to like this Emma. She's sounding like the sort of woman that, despite myself, I might have wanted to know.

The final file in Chloe's email is an image. I double-click and a moment later a nearly full-screen window appears. The image is a satellite photograph, the logo in the corner marking it from Google Earth, and Chloe's annotated it with a big, bulky red arrow and a single, square-pixel word: 'Here'.

It's zoomed into a tight scale, and I don't recognize the landscape except for one feature that's unmistakable, snaking through its centre. A river, treed in on both sides, the water a greyish-green rather than blue.

And I know what 'Here' means. Just as I've begun to get to know Emma Fairfax, I've been led to the site of her death.

I stay with my computer for another hour. By the time the facts I'm able to chase up are starting to blur together, the bottle of wine is mostly gone. A coincidence, I'm sure. It's clear that it's time to call it a day. The clock above me is perilously close to chiming nine and David still isn't back, which means I ought to start thinking of supper without him. I'd shopped for a whole box full of organic veggies earlier in the week, thinking a nice stir fry might be fun; but I'm worn out, now, tipsy, and the thrill of cooking just isn't the same when you're only doing it for yourself. I'm pondering a frozen lasagne and a packet of microwaveable broccoli as I pry myself out of my seat and head towards the bedroom. Before anything, I need to free myself from a few of the more enslaving garments of the day. I'm wearing shoes that look fantastically better than they feel and a bra with an underwire designed by a masochist, and I'm anxious to be out of both of them.

I step into our walk-in, Loralees already off my heels and dangling from my toes in an awkward little dance all women learn at birth. My balance isn't perfect with this much wine in me, but I kick them into what is roughly their place along one of the walls, then set about unbuttoning the muted orange blouse that I've had for – damn, I can't think how long I've had it. A long time. Old-fashioned, not today's style, but I love it.

The buttons are undone with a few finger-flicks, and I toss it towards the hangers, and —

— and that's when I spot it. There, where it shouldn't be.

David's briefcase is in the closet.

Where it never is.

Oh God, my heart is stopping. No gentle transition of emotion. No whats or wonderings, just my pulse's immediate threat to abandon me entirely.

The briefcase is oddly positioned in a little space that's

been fashioned behind his shoes, which is even stranger. A pair of gym shorts is clumsily draped over it.

Despite the tipsiness, I immediately notice the trajectory of my thoughts. The shorts 'are draped' over the case, which is so very different from saying 'he draped them' over it, which in that instant is something I don't want to think about.

Because David doesn't hide things from me. He doesn't conceal. He's open, and loving, and caring, and the man I trust more than any other in the world.

And he doesn't hide his briefcase in the closet.

20

Above the inconspicuous den of torture was a quite ordinary kitchen. This is a lesson for life, as well. That even in a kitchen, evil can be born.

'The kind we want you to bring, they can't be the kind from good homes.'

Savage words, camouflaged by their outward simplicity.

'Why not?' *A girl's voice answers, uncomprehending yet sassy at the same time.*

'If their ties to their parents are too close, then . . . you know. They might be listened to.'

'You mean, if they talk?'

A nod, nothing more.

'But I thought you said no one was gonna talk,' *the girl's voice protests, pouty, with the confidence of a practised know-it-all.*

'No one will. We've been good about ensuring that.'

A harrumph.

'You *haven't* talked, have you?'

'Of course not!' the girl objects. 'But that's 'cause you, like, you know . . . you give me good reasons not to.' There's a stylish portable CD player clipped to her hip, the headphones dangling round her neck, and she runs her hand over the obviously new device.

'Exactly. We know what sort of things help you keep your thoughts to yourself.' The words come with a paternal, warm smile, though there are also unspoken threats – voiced in the past but now simply recycled in silent glances – of darker gifts to be given if ever she would turn the other way. But for now the girl seemed happy, but her quizzical look soon returned.

'So, why don't you just find them yourselves?'

A hesitant silence. A brow folding up in contemplation of how much to share, how much to keep hidden.

'Let's just say it's better if we leave that to you. You bring them here, and there's a reward for each one. Something to spice up your life a little.' A nod towards the CD player.

Then a big grin over dental braces, each tooth's equipment wrapped in a different coloured elastic band.

'But like we said,' the man's voice continues, 'none from strong families. You've got to do a little studying before you pick 'em. Make friends. Find out about their life at home.'

'Like, whether they're all hugs and kisses around the supper table.'

A knowing smile. 'Exactly like that. And if they aren't . . .'

'Then bring them by.'

'That's all there is to it.' A pat on a shoulder, kitchen chairs sliding over linoleum and a scuffling back to standing.

'You do that for us, and we're good to go.'

And the devil smiling, his power over man never more absolute.

21

Amber

I know there are a dozen different ways I could react to my discovery. I could calm myself, that's the most obvious. Call it no discovery at all. It's just a briefcase, and my suddenly spiked tension is an overreaction – the after effects of too much wine and a long day.

But I have have the distinct feeling I'm beyond that option. I could ignore what I've seen – that's a second choice. Pretend the briefcase isn't there, or that it doesn't matter that it is. Why should I take any notice, after all? It's a shared life and a shared home. David can keep his things wherever he likes. Yes, he's consistent in his ways, but none of us behaves in exactly the same way all the time. I look over at my shoes, lying helter-skelter on the floor. They're sort of in the place that I usually kick them, but not precisely. Variety is normal.

God, the word feels awkward in my head.

Normal. Normal. Normal.

The cover of an issue of *Variety* magazine flashes into my mind. Some comment about it being the spice-rack of life. But then, that's not quite right . . .

I force the odd silliness aside. There are serious issues in front of me, and it's strange that I should feel playful in their presence, even with wine inside me. Ignoring reality isn't going to work; and pretending this situation isn't odd would be precisely that – ignoring what is self-evidently real. David is spontaneous in so many things: he'll swerve the car across two lanes of traffic to screech it to a halt at a roadside flower vendor, all in order to buy me a dozen yellow tulips (always my favourite flower, so much more delicate and beautiful than the showy over-doneness of a rose); he'll say he's taking me out for a snack at the diner round the corner, only to produce two tickets to *Les Misérables* or *Wicked* or some other show I've been longing to see down in the city. Yet around the house, with his daily routines, he's absolutely predictable. Socks are always on in the morning before trousers. Brushing the hair always comes before switching on the electric razor. He always hangs his brown jacket on the second peg by the door; never the first, never the third.

All of which mean that his briefcase, here in our closet, can't simply be written off as an act of spontaneous variety.

No, no, no. Not normal at all.

The realization causes my thoughts to swirl in a pattern that is surprisingly colourful at the backs of my eyes.

Damn, my head really hurts.

I stare at the gym shorts hanging loosely over the briefcase's frame, suddenly feeling more like a foreigner than I ever have in my own home.

I realize there's only one thing I can reasonably do. No, I won't say 'reasonably'. I'm not sure I'm having any reasonable thoughts at this stage; everything's foggier than it ought to be. But there is, nevertheless, only one thing I *can* do.

I reach down, toss the shorts aside, and pick up the case. Two brass flip locks are positioned aside the leather handle, like always.

Locks I've never before undone.

The fact that David thinks I don't know the combination to his briefcase is one of the tender signs of trust between us that I cherish. He's never told me how the six dials are meant to line up, and we've had more than one discussion about the reality that privacy in this regard is essential to our relationship. When we were first married I think he was concerned I'd find the idea troubling, that I'd be resentful of some corner of his being that wasn't wholly exposed to my scrutiny. Honestly, I don't know when the men in my life started being more feminist than I am. We're husband and wife, not a hybrid being. Even if we do it side by side, we still both occupy our unique sections of life.

So maybe I did feel it was a little condescending when he 'took the time' to explain to me, twice, that *some of the paperwork I bring home from the pharmacy, in order to file the insurance claims and that sort of thing, it's confidential. I know we're open with each other, but some things have to remain off limits, and so I'm going to keep the combination to this case to myself.'* I remember the discussion. I was pondering the order in which I might rack the next day's papers in the shop while he spoke, that's how little my emotions were tugged at by the idea that his briefcase combination wasn't going to be posted on the refrigerator with the shopping list. He said it with such purpose, though. Sweetie.

Still, predictable.

There are six dials on the case, their shiny metal now reflecting the ceiling light back into my eyes. Mathematically, this makes for a lot of possibilities. Significantly more than I'd ever be willing to try at random, which, I presume is why briefcases have six dials instead of two or three.

But the math doesn't matter. I've left the bedroom, walked into another room and set the case down in front of me, laying my right hand over the left on top of it for a brief, contemplative moment. It's not quite a prayer, but I am willing the throbbing in my head to disperse and my eyes, which seem far too wobbly, to focus. The brass is playing with the light again. The reflected beams are far, far too bright.

I unfold my hands. The dials rotate easily, slick from frequent use. I haven't fully exhaled a single, normal breath before I've got them lined up in the only combination I know it could possibly be.

0-7-1-3-8-1.

Or, in its more familiar form: 07/13/81. My birthday. I said David was predictable, sweet, even wonderful. I never said he was clever.

I press my fingers outwards against the two brass knobs next to the dials. With twin clicks, the clasps open.

22

Amber

The earth doesn't shatter.

Big, expectant moments – we're led to believe they'll resolve like that. Definitively. The door to a serial killer's apartment is opened and, *surprise*, there are photographs of his victims pasted all along the walls, linked together by brightly coloured strings. The hotel room of suspected government spies is kicked in and, *voilà!*, there they are, each holding mag lights with stacks of files on the bed. Big reveals. The world halts a second: revelation splinters normalcy.

This moment isn't like that at all. The leather top to David's briefcase opens and the orbit of the earth remains entirely as before. I have no idea what I thought I might find inside. Another woman's lingerie? Drugs? Printed bios from Ashley Madison? There's none of that. Nothing that in any way counts as a shocker. A few manila folders. Cheap plastic pens in their elastic holders. Some envelopes.

What else did I think I was going to find in a briefcase?

The absurdity of my situation suddenly hits me: a woman standing barefoot in her bra and rooting through her husband's things. *There's a good wife.*

Yet I'm tugged by some thread that still won't let me lower the lid. *It shouldn't have been there.* That's the clincher that won't let me alone, and won't let me see nothing in nothing. So I shake the fog from my head, remove my fingers from my lips where I have subconsciously been biting at my nails, and reach a hand inside and pull out one of the folders. It's the one right on top, all but ready to be plucked out and examined.

I slide a finger under its cover and leaf it open. Inside are an array of documents, some loose leaf and some paper-clipped together. I examine the header of one of the single pages: 'LEVOTHYROXINE PATIENT ADMINISTRATION INSTRUCTIONS – UPDATED PHARMACIST GUIDELINES'. I flip to one of the bundled documents. Its cover page speaks of contents even more mundane. 'REORDER QUOTA GUIDELINES FOR OPIOID PHARMACEUTICAL SUPPLIERS IN NORTHERN CALIFORNIA'.

It's precisely the kind of thing I would expect in David's briefcase.

Of course.

But I keep going, nevertheless. I remove the folder and set it aside. Beneath it is another, which I in turn flip open to find more of the same. Then another. Beneath that, I can feel there are even more.

But I can also feel something else. As I lay the folders aside, one by one, the stack remaining in the briefcase gets thinner, and lighter. And starts to bend. Or rather, starts to wobble. The folders aren't lying flat, I realize now. There is something beneath them that's creating a little rise in the middle.

It's a curiosity, hardly suspicious. But I've come this far.

I reach my fingers around their edges and remove the remaining folders all in a single pull.

And here, at this moment, the world does halt. Just for an instant.

Beneath the folders, wrapped into a coil, is a rope.

Not a rope, a leash. Sadie's leash. The one David always uses to walk her.

It's red. It's always been red.

I'm not sure if I'm breathing as I reach down to touch it. And then I'm certain that I'm not, as my fingers press against its rough fibres and feel moisture still bound within them. Sadie's leash, wet, and through the tears forming in my eyes, I can see dirt and sand and grime along its length. And I can smell the outdoors, and a river, and . . .

A face flashes into my sight. The same face from the car. Black hair. Porcelain skin.

She looks peaceful.

My stomach curls and tightens. My fingers wrap

around the wet leash. The woman's face won't leave my vision.

It's the face from yesterday, the face that nearly forced me off the road. The face that caused me to say that word – that *name*. Emma. And deep within me I know, with every instinct I possess, that this rope in my hands is the one the police are after. The one mentioned in the paper.

The rope that killed the woman in the river.

Whether it's the cosmos that begins to fall apart in this instant, or just me, I can't be sure; but the pieces of my world are breaking, and that seems as cosmic as anything else in creation.

Her.

The memory of David's body going cold and firm as I'd whispered the woman's name into his ear.

Emma.

And this horrible reality I now hold in my fingers, extracted from his briefcase. A reality that links him to her in a way I can't fathom. My David, with our Sadie's leash, such an innocent thing. But innocence nowhere in the air.

David. David . . .

I'd rushed home to tell him of my discovery. To tell him about my story. To tell him about *her*.

But he already knows her. God, he knows her. And God, my head hurts.

This leash, hidden away. His case. His locks.

He knew her last night. He knew her before I'd said anything at all. He knows her now.

And he doesn't want me to find out.

PART TWO

TWENTY-THREE YEARS AGO

23

David, Aged 17
With The Counsellor

I always hate these sessions. It's been so many years of them already. Too many. Always the same nonsense, too. Like dealing with dirty hair or dirty clothes: rinse, repeat, rinse, repeat – only you never get any cleaner.

'Did it upset you when your parents died?'

The typical kind of question. Can't think of how many times this guy's asked it. As if parents dying ever doesn't upset someone. Even when you don't particularly love them, and they obviously don't have the time or the inclination to love you. You don't have to love someone to be upset by their sudden absence.

'It was a boating accident. There wasn't anything that could be done.'

I know the man in the sweater isn't interested in the details of the accident, or really even in my response to it. We've covered all this territory a hundred times before. Dr Williams is after Evelyn. Always, always after Evelyn. He can't let her go. Guy hasn't been as successful as me in putting her out of mind after all these years, and you'd think that's pretty much the thing he's still getting my parents' money to do.

'Neither of 'em talked about what'd troubled Evelyn,' I blurt out. 'Not after she offed herself, and not till their deaths. They just didn't care.'

I may only be closing in on eighteen, but you don't need a lifetime's maturity to know how to read that. I know it now. I knew it back when they were still alive. Neither of them were worth the space they took up on the planet, and they sure as hell made clear to Evelyn and me that they felt the same way about us.

Hell of a way to raise your kids.

Dr Williams scribbles down something on a notepad. Therapists. Never known one who doesn't do that. Living stereotypes, all of them. I can see the muscles in his face tighten, though the old man tries so hard to appear emotionless. *Can't pull it off, jackass.* Not quite cunning enough. That kind of deception takes commitment.

'Do you think it's really because they didn't care?' he asks. He doesn't look up.

I shrug. 'Don't know.' But then, 'Yes, yes I do. If they cared, they'd have said something. Have paid at least enough attention to their own daughter to notice something was wrong with her before it got bad enough for her to . . . you know.'

'Maybe they wanted to know what was wrong, but didn't have the answers.'

'Maybe, maybe, maybe.' I don't say more. We've been down this road so many times. Trying to rehabilitate the fallen. They didn't care, that's the simple fact. My parents barely did more parenting before their death than after, and what they did was rough. I'm tired of therapists trying to convince me they were really after the best, deep down inside. But this one's definitely of the time to always aim in that direction.

'Maybe they actually were deeply concerned and simply didn't know—'

'Damn it, Doc, can't you just let it go?' I lean forward, my annoyance peaked. 'Just push it aside, man. It's over. Long, long over. I was twelve, and now I'm about to go off to college. They weren't good folks. You're not going to make them into that now. Just let the dead rest.'

'You were twelve when Evelyn died, but you were sixteen when your parents were killed. That's not exactly that long ago, David.'

'It's in the goddamned past!' I slam down a fist on his posh glass coffee table. I could never afford therapy in digs as elegant as this, from a man who charges as much as Dr Williams, but my parents' will had contained a clause reserving a segment of their assets for a trust 'to provide ongoing counselling for our son as he deals with the aftereffects of the loss of his sister'.

Damned hypocrites. They never gave a good goddamn

131

about her, or me. Thought they could just shovel a little cash out to take care of me, even after death.

But I shouldn't think like that. Not the remark about them – that's accurate enough. But I should watch the swearing. Even if it's just in my own head. Evelyn wouldn't have approved.

'And my parents weren't killed,' I suddenly feel compelled to add, sinking back into the sofa. 'It was a boating accident. I don't know how many times I have to say that.'

'Right. I realize it was an accident. But still.'

Still nothing.

'You've never really wanted to talk about any of it, not in all these years,' he adds. As if this weren't perfectly obvious to us both.

We moved here a few months after Evelyn died, not so far from my father's sister's place, as my parents were too 'sorrow-ridden' to stay in our home. Had to rob me even of that – the familiar sites she and I had known together. I can't think they had any real grief at all, nothing that required them moving to console themselves. Evelyn had always been a burden to them. Their mourning move was just a chance at new scenery, and maybe to be close enough to my aunt that they could pawn me off once in a while. They'd even found this shrink to 'help' me, together with a few others now and then. It had all been counterproductive from day one.

I don't need to talk about her. Or them. And that's all this is. Talk, talk, talk.

I need to forget.

Not the good stuff. I'll never forget that. How happy Evelyn had been. How beautiful. It's not just a mourning brother's rose-tinted memory, either: Evelyn had rosy cheeks, a delicate face, deep eyes. A doll, alive and vibrant.

But a doll who wept, and too often. A doll they tortured. And I can't keep remembering that. I can't. I just goddamned can't.

Just goddamned can't.

24

David
With The Admissions Officer

'What is it about the UCLA pre-med program that interests you, Mr Penske?' The man who is interviewing me has a slightly condescending tone, but it's a friendly rather than disturbing one. I can tell he's been through a number of these interviews already today.

I sit upright and attempt to appear well-kept and eager. 'Like I put in my essay, I have a desire to understand how the person . . . works. How the pieces make the whole. How the whole can function better.'

'Yes, we liked that answer.' He nods. 'A good, nicely articulated motivation.' I'm pleased that he's pleased. I feel the interview is going well.

'But it's also a bit of a given,' he adds, and I feel something within me tense. 'We hear similar kinds of things from most applicants. Yet we all felt – the admissions panel, and me personally – that you had something more to you than just the stereotypes.' He pauses. 'You indicated in your forms that you have . . . personal reasons for approaching this major.'

I squirm slightly. I don't remember having written that in my application, but must have done. I don't particularly want to discuss my personal story with this stranger, any more than I wanted to with the shrink for all those years. It was only when eighteen came and I was no longer a ward of my aunt that I was finally able to send him packing.

The whole point of college is new beginnings, right?

'Every guy has challenges in life,' I say, trying to keep my tone energetic while deflecting the conversation away from my own situation. 'Everyone has struggles, problems. I think that's safe to say. I've had a few. So I can either wallow in them, or get moving towards something that has the ability to be different. A field in which I could help people.'

'So you feel medicine can lead you to that goal, to be able to help people?'

This seems to light a spark in the admissions officer's eyes. I try to fan it.

'Absolutely. Helping others has to be the end goal, right?' He gives a slight not. 'And it's not just pre-med that interests me; I'd like to maybe double it with chemistry, something along those lines. Dig into that whole side of things.'

'That's a pretty heavy combination.'

'But the two go together, don't they? If I'm going to go on to med school later, it'd be good to have the pair. Medicine and chemistry are kind of like synonyms.'

He seems interested by this comment. 'You're thinking of med school after your undergraduate degree?'

'It's a possibility, yeah.'

It's not a lie, either.

He smiles. 'It's encouraging to see such an altruistic streak in such a young man. That is, unless you're aiming for a medical career just for the money.'

A wink, and I know it's a joke. Predictably, he's laughing at his own stale wit. I smile and laugh back.

Old people.

'I'd normally say you should just take on one major at the beginning and think about a combination as you go, David,' he says, 'but your school records are impressive. You're obviously smart. Math and science scores are in the top fifth percentile nationally. The chemistry angle should be a breeze.'

I nod, pleased he recognizes this. Studying has always been my best therapy. Shove your head into a book and there's no need to think of other things.

'Which is another way of saying,' he adds, 'that I think you'll be very happy at UCLA, and will excel in our programs. You'll meet new people, make new friends. I think it will be good for you, son.'

And I catch the words. *Will be,* not might be. And I know I'm in.

The first truly good news of my life.

25

David

What can I really know about my future? What can anyone? I'm eighteen, nineteen in four months, and all I can really say is that I know my past and I've had enough of it. Evelyn's dead. Mom, Dad, dead. It's been tough – no, it's been shit. And it's hurt, and it was evil and all that. But it's over. They're all gone.

From my life, and from this moment, from my head.

I wasn't lying to UCLA's blazer-clad admissions officer yesterday at my interview. I really do want to go the pre-med line, and maybe even chase that chemistry trail into pharmaceuticals and drugs. Lord knows I've seen plenty of examples of why healing needs those tools. Talking just doesn't cut it. Dr Williams was wrong from day one until the last, with all his attempts at 'therapeutic conversation' and digging through the past. Remembering doesn't help. Dwelling on emotions doesn't help. It doesn't help a thing.

What helps is letting go. Pushing the past back into the past where it belongs. I've learned that lesson, and learned it well. When your life is shit you don't learn to come to grips with it. You let go of it, let it disappear. And if I can help someone else to do that, someone else who's hurting, then maybe I could actually do some good with my life. More than I was able to do when I was a kid.

Of course, Dr Williams would say I'm falling into some pattern of self-perpetuating punishment. He was fond of phrases like those. Convinced I was unable really to let go of anything. He'd probably say I'm going into medicine because it will keep me in the world of suffering I've grown used to. Keep me exposed to people in pain, where I feel comfortable. Maybe even hoping to find those whose pain matches my own, who know what I've been through, so I can commiserate – if only by proxy. Even predicted I'd go into counselling myself, seeking out the types behind my pain; but as I've said before, the man knows nothing. Counselling doesn't interest me. Nothing he said does.

So I'm starting at UCLA at the end of summer. UCLA. Not a bad beginning to whatever's going to come next. And I will make something of it, that much I'm completely committed to. Because the one thing I am willing to remember about my sister, about her death, is that I could't help her. I was young, I had no understanding, no tools.

But that's not going to be my future.

PART THREE

THE PRESENT

26

To deal with the man's body was not an easy task. It was not a question only of the weight, though this was significant. His mass was twice what the woman's had been, even with the water logging. But emotion, it seemed, weighed heavier than flesh.

The deepest challenge with him wasn't physical at all. The silver-haired man's life had ended, like the woman's; but what had to follow could not be the same.

This was a fact on which everything rested. Because the man was gone, and that was right; but the sun and the moon now seemed forever off their proper course, beaming down that nothing would ever be as it should be again. Not in the way it once had been.

But it could go on. It could get better.

It could be cleansed.

27

Amber

My thoughts fire like a cannon as I hold Sadie's red leash in my hands. Never before has something so innocuous seemed do damning. This length of rope has led us through walks in Muir Grove, along lakesides, through cities. It's been linked to so many outings and so much joy. But at this moment it has become something else entirely.

The moisture in it stinks of stagnant water. I can smell algae and mud.

Emma Fairfax, found along the river.

He knows, her, somehow. David knows her. This is proof, and proof that can't be controverted.

Though actually it isn't, I chide myself. We can't possibly be the only couple in existence with a red rope leash for their dog. Christ, there must be dozens of them in our little town alone.

But he knows her. I just feel it, like a rock in my gut. *David knows her.*

But then, I do, too. Somehow, even if only intangibly. The two facts collide within me, each equally incomprehensible. Her name had come to me in the car. David had reacted, but I'd known it. I know this isn't the same thing as really knowing her – I'd been reading about her all day. It could have been simply distracted focus. Details I'd forgotten I'd learned until the heat of the moment. It's not the way David knows her – the way this damnable length of rope makes clear.

I see her face . . .

It's there again, in my head. A phantom's outline, as if she's coming at me through the air. Accusing me, because I'm married to *him*, to the man who has *this* in his house, in his briefcase, in his —

I drop the dirty leash as trembling takes over my hands, and it falls to the floor and bounces off my feet.

There is no explanation for why David would hide this here. Having it – no problem. Everyone with a dog has one, and we've got several. And David's the dog-walker, so they're pretty much his kit. Sadie's trained him well. And hell, there's water around here, and mud and dirt, and there are a dozen reasons the leash could be in the state it's in.

But not the place.

In the midst of the wreckage of my emotions, I know it. There is no justification for David locking it away beneath files. We have a hook by the kitchen door. The leash lives there. It sure as hell doesn't belong with his paperwork.

'*I know we're open with each other,*' I remember David saying to me. The words come crashing into my head, a memory that demands to make itself known at this moment. I can't remember how long ago he said them, but their sound is fresh in my skull. '*But some things have to remain off limits, and so I'm going to keep the combination to this case to myself.*'

'Off Limits.' The words sound vile now. This sure as hell isn't an insurance document or medical form requiring spousal confidentiality. This is a goddamned murder weapo—

No, I can't bring myself to say it. Even to think it. Not with such directness. The full reality of this moment is too much. David is a pharmacy assistant, for heaven's sake. A man who fills prescriptions and sorts pills into little orange bottles. He doesn't take Sadie's leash and wrap it around some woman's neck and turn it into a . . .

I look down at my feet, my pulse bashing away like a drum in my head.

He doesn't take something good, and transform it into something so . . .

Then, as my eyes linger on the red coil at my feet, I notice something else.

And with it, the strength in my legs evaporates.

28

Amber

Of the next moments of my life I have only the vaguest of perceptions.

I want, with everything in me, to disregard everything I've found. I want, I need, to believe that the leash in David's briefcase means nothing, just like I wanted to believe the briefcase even being in the closet meant nothing. Potentially normal things, both of them. But I'm well, well beyond anything being normal.

I love my husband. Deeply. Madly. He's the most sincere, gentlest, kindest, scrupulous—

But the rope is at my feet, and beside it . . .

My vision is slightly blurry, and I strain to see. I've drunk far too much wine, and on an empty stomach. I think I'm having one of the worst migraines of my life.

But something's there.

I'm teetering on my feet, my suspicions fired to a

degree I'd never have imagined possible until this moment, and there's a voice whispering from somewhere in the air:

He's lyyyyyyying.

I know it. The voice is right.

I try to bend down to look at whatever it is I've spotted near where the leash has fallen, but I can't seem to keep my balance. The whole world angles off to the side and threatens to slide away. I reach out for the front of the desk and force my bare feet further apart, commanding the world to stop fucking around and be still. It takes a few moments to obey, but it gradually comes to a trembling halt.

The way I'm positioned, my eyes are facing directly into the footspace beneath the desk.

It's in the spot where David normally slides his briefcase when he isn't using it, but that case is now open on the desktop above me, its contents strewn about it. Yet something is where the case ought to have been. My brain has spun upside down in my head, but I still know it's unusual for something else to be there. It's brown, almost the same colour as leather, and yet it isn't. I try to focus.

Cardboard, the word at last flashes into my head. Cardboard. A box.

I slide it out, slinking myself into a crouch, propping a shoulder against the desk's front drawers to keep the world from going all wobbly again. I gaze at this little box. Looks like it was once for shoes. There's print on it, but my eyes are past making sense of letters.

Maybe he's gone and got me a present . . .

And, shockingly, I almost forget entirely about everything that's happened to that moment. The thought of a gift, of David's smile and that lovely look his eyes take on when he surprises me with something he knows I'll love. Like yellow tulips or tickets to *Les Miséra*—

I don't want to wait. *Impetuous little thing*, I chide myself, though it's my mother's voice that's doing the scolding, of course. Shrill and impatient and always harsher than the words suggest. But she's gone and she doesn't matter any more, and I have a present despite her. I almost giggle again, but control myself.

I lift the lid off the box.

It doesn't contain flowers or tickets or a new pair of shoes. Instead, my mother's voice is back in the air, and so is David's, and I can hear Sadie's barking and feel the Marin Headlands wind on my face, and I hear wedding bells, and taste warm tea, and the whole world is swirling around me as it all begins to collapse and disappear.

The box is stuffed with a wrinkled, white t-shirt. It's filthy, stained with something rust-coloured. There's dirt, and mud, and sand, and I can smell the blood even more vividly than I can see it.

I try to lean down for a closer look, but my eyes cross and I can vaguely sense my body collapsing to the floor as I hear David's beautiful voice from somewhere behind me, above.

'Amber, oh God, you weren't supposed to see . . .'

29

David

I was positive, from the instant I walked into the house on a quick pass back home after Amber left for work, that she hadn't drunk the smoothie I'd made for her this morning. She's a sly creature. Tries to hide the fact that she skips out on my little gifts, but I know her far too well. At best she takes a sip, two if I'm lucky, before the rest is sent down the drain. Her attempt at pleasing her man, despite hating what she's being given. Got to give her that much.

She thinks I don't know about her little manoeuvre, too, and that's almost endearing. Maybe it's innocence. Maybe naïveté. At least she's keen to play the part of the doting wife who's happy her husband is concerned for her health. The traditions of a marriage form in strange ways, and this little cat-and-mouse game has become one of ours. And it's okay. Games are a part of life. A pleasant part, I've always thought.

We simply have to find other ways to ensure things get done.

I had just enough time on my little trip back to the apartment to put away the washed glass she'd left in the sink, tidy up the countertop and anticipate what was to come later in the day. I'd been planning to be home before her. Theoretically, it's a possibility, and I enjoy the earlier shifts in the city. Nice to beat the traffic home if I can, and I can always do some of the paperwork from the house. Insurance documents can be scrutinized from anywhere.

Besides, I like being in the apartment when Amber arrives. She always makes a slow entrance at first, almost timid; but then her soft blue eyes meet mine and joy covers her face, and she suddenly bounds in with energy. I know that not every man genuinely, passionately, rapturously loves his wife, but I have to confess, that's a fact I simply can't comprehend. There's nothing in this world I cherish more than Amber. Every day with her is one to cling to.

But not every day goes according to plan.

I arrived home this evening, far later than intended. Work sometimes does that, though what had occupied me today had been something heavier than work. Still, back home things at first appeared ordinary. Mostly so, at any rate. There were no signs of dinner having been made – not that I'd expected she'd have gone to the trouble of leaving something for me, late as I was; but I did assume she'd have cooked something for herself. The counters, however were just as I'd left them at lunchtime, the tea towel still hanging over the curved tap where I'd left it.

My first motivation had been for a drink. Something to help me shake off the shock of the whole day. Ever since last night my mood had been sour and tense, and the events of the day had made that radically worse. I glanced at the niche by the microwave where our Krups coffeemaker has its permanent home, and noted there was nothing but dregs left from the morning. Good. The fact that the native tea drinker has adopted that habit of mine is something I've consistently put to effective use. It's become predictable, and from predictability comes control.

I wasn't motivated enough to brew a new pot, and drinking those particular dregs was out of the question, so I opened the refrigerator to pull out a bottle of microbrew IPA instead. There were no noises from upstairs. My watch read 9.20 p.m., so it was just possible Amber had opted for an early night in. I glanced over to where I'd set out a few wine bottles earlier, one of them appropriately prepped, and saw that it was absent. That prompted a satisfied sigh. Amber can do justice to a whole bottle of wine by herself, and that one certainly would have knocked her out cold. My smile broadened. The quiet in the apartment was no longer a mystery.

I sat for a few moments at the side of the table. I wasn't quite trembling as visions of the past few hours cycled through my memory, but I was suddenly grateful for the beer in my grasp. I took a deep swill, the bubbles tickling my throat – probably more than I should have tried for in a single mouthful, and fizzing drops trickled out the sides of my mouth.

It was as they ran down my chin that I heard what I'd thought I wouldn't hear: noises from upstairs. I glanced back to the bottles on the counter, just to reassure myself, but the important one, the one from the front, was still absent. I hadn't invented that. If Amber had drunk it, she should be all but immobile.

But then . . . movement, again. In an instant I knew something was wrong. My beer went down on the table and I strained to listen, keeping my body as motionless as I could.

The noise wasn't coming from the bedroom. It was creeping down through the ceiling from a different direction and a higher storey.

My office.

With that, I cringed in panic, and my body thrust itself towards the stairs.

To permit Amber to discover that box . . . it's an inexcusable oversight. And God, the leash. Still wet. She was never supposed to know about any of this. Especially not today. She's not up for it. Amber is a woman constitutionally built for things to go according to plan.

She's so perfectly trusting that the carpeting of my home office has been all but untouched by her feet since we first converted the former upstairs sitting room. A few visits early on, a bit of familiarity, but that's all. She has her space, I have mine. She's never pushed those limits. I've hidden things from her there before, more times than I can remember. She's never discovered them. Never crossed the threshold to even being tempted to look.

In this instant I realize that had made me over-confident. Too relaxed. Of all the stupid mistakes. You can plan for a lifetime, but things can all turn on something so small.

Though maybe it isn't entirely my fault. After all, I'm hardly in this alone.

When I walked in, as calmly as I could after bounding up the stairs, Amber was barely able to stand, already on her knees and wobbling even there. At least she came upon things in the right state of mind. Thank God. I'm not sure she fully recognized who I was.

Had she been wholly lucid, I don't know if we could recover, or if I could keep her safe.

But the dose from the wine bottle had been strong enough to do the job. I'd seen to that at the start of the day; after the previous night, there was no point taking chances. One of my usual preparations, innocent and loving and predictable, and Amber had drunk far more than expected. I'd barely said two words after I entered the room before she collapsed on the floor, entirely out.

I gave her another shot, anyway, after I'd tucked her into bed, just to be safe – the old-fashioned way, the needle so fine it never rouses her from sleep.

With so much in her system, there's the chance she might wake up remembering nothing at all. At the very least, her thoughts will be disturbed. I'm confident the drug will have its intended effect. Memories dwindle, turn to fuzz. Reality drifts into a haze at the edges of one's vision.

My breathing has slowed a little. I don't have to panic. Things are under control.

But she saw more than should have ever been put into her head, or pulled out of it. Damn it. I really wish I could have prevented her that. How the hell did she get into my briefcase? How did she even spot it? I woke up a mess after her revelation last night. Maybe I didn't stash it away like I should have. Maybe I —

But there are heavier questions that assault me before I have time to analyse the path of my day. What must the sight of the leash have done to Amber?

She can't possibly understand what it really means.

Though I'm not certain she'll have to. I'm still not sure, even after all this time, how much the drugs can mask.

Worst of all, she saw the T-shirt. *Damn it all, she saw the t-shirt.* I knew it should have just been thrown away, tossed into the trees. But then another might be needed, and cheap as they are, one doesn't want to leave a trail any larger than one has to.

When death is so rampant, you can't always be in control.

THE MORNING

I've taken care of the office upstairs. Packing my case back up took only a matter of minutes, and the room as a whole was tidy again after a few more. No sign Amber had ever been in there.

The box and the t-shirt, though, were going to be a problem. I know my wife. When she wakes, her head will spin. She'll blame her memories on the wine – she's always been prone to drink far too much of the stuff, which is such a helpful trait – and the rest to an overactive imagination. But the box, the t-shirt, these are unusual enough that they might push their way through. If any memory does survive the drug, she'll want to verify. She's an inquisitive person, despite her shyness. The memory of a box beneath my desk will prompt follow up.

So a box needs to be there if she goes back to check on things. It just needs to be . . . different.

The box she actually found is no longer present, its contents out of sight and, as far as certainties will ever go, out of existence. There's a new shoebox under the desk now, as similar as I could find to the other, stuffed with an old white UCLA t-shirt that until about fifteen minutes ago had been folded among my other clothes. It'll work perfectly. Red lettering, blood – a drunken mind could make the leap.

My briefcase is coming back to work with me. The leash, too. I'll find a way to make sure that disappears forever, and can buy a new one on the way home. Maybe even that will slip her mind. Maybe that perception can be altered.

My watch squeezes at my wrist. 6.15 a.m. If I leave any later than this, another day's pattern will be at risk.

There's just the matter of putting the finishing touches on the usual routine.

The smoothie today will be peach-banana-pineapple. I haven't tried that one on her before, but Amber has a history with pineapple, and part of the tradition is her bemused willingness to let me 'expand her horizons'. But I know this won't be the magic combination she chooses to embrace. At this point that would almost be counter-productive. I punch the blender to high and the noise shatters the quiet of the morning. I'm confident it won't wake her.

The fruit dissolves into a swirl of colour. As it blends, I lift off the top. The final ingredient, always at the last moment. I extract the small bottle from my pocket and twist open the black cap. I notice, as I seem every day to do, that it has no smell, even in its pure, concentrated form. I waft the dropper, already full, past my nose – a little motion of reassurance – then raise it over the blender. Fifteen drops. If she drank the whole thing she'd be in a coma, but I know she only takes a sip or two. Need to keep the dose high for that.

And then it's over to the coffee pot. I've had my cup

already, another poured into a silver thermos flask and ready to go. A little less than half the pot is left. I slide the carafe off the heating pad, flip back the lid, and raise the dropper once again.

Five drops into the coffee. She usually takes a good cup of that, so this is more than enough. She needs to remain functional throughout her day, just not . . . whole.

A moment later and the carafe is back in the unit, the little bottle back into my pocket. I force myself to breathe. I pat down my suit, ruffle my hair.

Relax. This situation can still be saved.

30

There were three men involved in the ring. A trio, and a carefully calculated number. Larger, and there was too great a risk of sprouting a leak and things getting out. Just two, and one could get cold feet and turn his back on the other. A third kept them honest and held the whole group to account.

So that's how it was. Three men, with the power to destroy worlds.

They were ordinary men, as outward form went. Dutifully employed, two of them for over twenty years at the same jobs. Family men with wives and relatives, who still cooked a traditional Sunday roast and came out with blankets and coolers to picnic in the park on the Fourth of July. Who frequented their local restaurants and knew the staff on a first-name basis.

Who, in the moments when the world that loved them wasn't looking, ate away at its very core.

Men who killed without ever taking a life, who found their satisfaction in souls being crushed, and who smiled paternally when their fun was done.

They hadn't organized themselves into a hierarchy. No one was the leader. They worked together, with a child cheaply bought and ritually effective in doing what they asked of her. Their helper. They never had to stalk; only to receive, and do what they wished with what was brought to them. All for the price of a bit of pocket cash and some toys.

If the devil had tempted Adam and Eve with something as trivial as an apple and the whole world had fallen into his grasp, it didn't seem out of place that they could follow the same pattern, and to the same ends.

So their world bent to them, and there was no end in sight.

There were always more apples.

31

Amber

Every morning, my eyes look out from the mirror and taunt me.

I feel like this is how my day begins. Really. This is how it's supposed to start. I lean over the bathroom sink, the vast mirror looming closer to my nose, peering with increased intensity into my own face.

There are facts here that are supposed to gel in a comprehensible way. I sense that, but I can't seem to make them obey. I grope for the solidity of what's in front of me.

My eyes.

They're blue, not amber. They don't match my name. *So the fuck what?*

A blur of anger, just for an instant, unexplained but ferocious. It comes from nowhere, and then it's gone – instantly. It was never there.

My face remains in the mirror, but now the world is gentle, just like that. Outside, I feel the sun must be shining; and here, inside, in the midst of it all, my eyes jokingly tease me in their customary way. The anger is now gone, simply evaporated away. I merely shrug and smile.

I'm used to this. The thought echoes through my head.

In the next instant, I'm in motion. My morning ritual, automatic, performed without pondering. *They're a well-honed routine, the actions of each minute tuned to fit—*

The internal narration freezes. My hand is mid-motion, light brown mascara wand halfway to my left eyelash.

Mornings are well-honed. The thought reemerges. My hand doesn't move, stuck in mid-air. *I've done this before. I always do this.*

In the same moment, I begin to feel something deep within me. Whether it begins just then, or whether I only now become aware of it, I'm suddenly overwhelmingly uncomfortable. I feel it at first somewhere in my chest, then deeper, and then everywhere. Something within me is upturned, like all my organs have been removed and put back incorrectly, nothing fitting as it should. There is no specific part of me that hurts, precisely, yet nothing feels right. I focus again on the sight before me, and it too is wrong. I'm an improperly assembled version of the woman in the mirror.

But it's not actually true that nothing hurts. I have a splitting headache – the reality announces itself with glaring swiftness. My head is pounding. Throbbing.

162

And then, *Drink*. The word chimes in my mind and a memory flashes into the present. I remember a strong wine, though not a very good one. Vague, swirling images of an overly colourful bottle. My chest unclenches. *Shit, that would explain this. Another of those nights.* I've had them before – too much of the booze, in whatever form is handiest, with its welcome numbing power and ability to rid me of unsettling emotions. *God bless the stuff.* Whoever thought up the craft of letting grapes go sour and rot before bottling them has my eternal thanks. I've been the beneficiary of the power of a bottle of wine on more than one evening, to the degree that—

To the degree that my current state shouldn't shock me. Instead, I'm now being scolded by another memory. The too-familiar voice of my mother, somewhere out of the past. *Only fools drink to excess,* she says, and she smells of orange blossom hand soap and annoyance, even in the memory. *It's a sin with its penance built right in.*

Then her voice fades and autopilot switches back on. I have the tools to shake away my unease. The landscape changes. Back into the known.

Within a few moments my face is done and my hair brushed. I'm all polished up and ready to go.

My feet are already moving towards the kitchen, speeding me along to the next motion of my normal day.

Like they've lives of their own.

In the kitchen things are a portrait of normalcy, as I suppose I should only expect them to be. The formica is peeling at the edges of the counter, like it has been since we moved in, and the fourth leg of the table is still a quarter inch shorter than the others. Everything looks like it needs dousing with a good swath of bleach, even though I'm pretty ruthless about keeping it clean. You can only scrub the thirty-year-old surfaces of a cheap apartment up to a point. Beyond that, you have to admit defeat.

There's a vase full of yellow tulips near the sink, a sign that David must be in his customary cheer, and that can't help but make a person smile. Even me. And it's not even a vase, really: it's a cleaned-out jam jar with pebbles in the bottom, David not having been entirely successful in getting all the label off the side. Something about that pleases me immensely. Who needs crystal when glass and stones say so much more about the love of another person?

Near the flowers is a large glass, filled with something thick and hideous and yellow. A groan is already on my lips. I lean forward, lower my nose to the surface – so very much wishing it would smell like tulips – but instead am rewarded by some combination of banana, and something citrus, and pineapple. God forbid, pineapple. David is so forgetful.

You'll love it, the memory arrives with the scent. Our honeymoon, at one of those fake but lovely seaside resorts. He's laid back on a beach chair wearing only his swimming shorts, sand in the hairs of his chest sticking to oil with the scent of coconut, the sun beaming down.

Between us is a small table onto which the overly Caribbean waiter, who must have attended a class in order to become so stereotypically Jamaican, has just deposited two drinks David had ordered. They both have umbrellas, which is ridiculous.

It's pineapple, David, I'd answered. *I can smell it from here. Smells revolting.*

I remember he smiled at me – that devious, tender smile of a newly-wed on a honeymoon, still sorting through learning his lover's tastes.

You just think *you don't like pineapple*, he answered, teeth gleaming in the seaside sun. *There was moisture on his shoulders. But you haven't tried it like this. It's all in the mixture.*

I must have smiled back, because I remember him laughing. And I remember lifting the drink to my lips, driving the umbrella out of the way with my nose, pretending with every ounce of my own newly-wed's passionate intensity that I didn't want to vomit all over my shiny new husband.

And now . . . the counter, the smoothie of the day. And a little note. *Remember the beach? Maybe this is the combination I've been looking for all these years.* –D.

I'm smiling again. Damn it, he does it to me every time. Makes something he knows I'll hate and still he has me grinning like a schoolgirl.

I lift the glass to my mouth, sure I'm going to hate it but still willing to give it a try – but I'm right. It's putrid.

All the gelatine-esque revulsion of a pureed banana, accentuated with that fermented fizz that makes pineapple so loathsome. I can barely swallow.

I manage to get the mouthful down with two gulps of trying, but I'm already overturning the rest of the glass into the sink as I sidestep towards the coffee pot. Thank God, David is at least that aware of reality. This morning, the coffee is a necessary mouthwash, if nothing else. At this stage I'd take rubbing alcohol.

I down half a cup in three quick swallows.

And then the pictures start.

I don't know what triggers them. I have the carafe in my hand, refilling my cup. There is nothing to spark memory, nothing unusual, but I suddenly have images in my mind.

Though they're not images. That's not the right word. Images are vague, amorphous things, while these are crisp. Vivid. Like photographs. Physical things that I see, perfectly clearly, in my head.

The jolt of their appearance is so forceful that I slam the carafe down on the counter. I want to examine the scene, see if I've broken the glass; but the images are still there, shining out of a radiant, white light. No more coffee pot, no more kitchen. Just – vision.

There's a woman, waterlogged and still.

My stomach becomes a knot.

The woman. Emma Fairfax. *The river*. I can see the texture of her skin.

And I remember David's briefcase – the sight pours

out of somewhere within me. The briefcase concealing Sadie's wet leash, and despair, and . . .

. . . a box. Oh God, a box, with cloth and blood, and—

It hits me, all at once, that these are memories from last night, and they explain the odd feelings that have been pulsing within me. Something happened last night. I saw something. *I saw these things.*

Before I know why or how, my feet are once again in motion. My hands have let go of my coffee and my legs are steering me towards the stairs, up to the heights of our rented home.

Like they've lives of their own. *Like they've lives. Like they've lives . . .*

32

Amber

I'm at the door of David's home office in fewer strides than the trip normally takes. I'm in a state, the memories gradually emerging, each hazy and inarticulate. My chest is fluttering, my breathing is short and rapid. I'm utterly confused, yet simultaneously, inexplicably horrified of what I'm going to find.

I push open the door, and in a reality that shouldn't surprise me, I see absolutely nothing out of the ordinary. Everything looks just like it always does – at least, the few times I've ever been in here.

There is no briefcase. Of course there isn't. David's already gone to work.

I step over to the desk, though, and my belly trembles. The wood grain is the same as in the image bouncing in my memory – the sheen surface that was covered in files I'd sifted through and set aside. A tangible connection to the strange memories that began downstairs. I feel a powerful recognition at the swirl of the lines and the striations of colour in the fake panelling. But there are no files here. No signs of disarray. Everything is in its place, tidy and presentable.

I feel like a madwoman. This has got to be the greatest damned overreaction to a bad pineapple smoothie in the history of—

But then the memories ambush me again, this time with almost physical force. The briefcase is back, and the leash, and I'm consumed by the absolute conviction that there is something else terribly, horribly out of place. *Right here, right now.*

The box.

The sudden image of it almost blinds me. I don't believe in divine revelations, but it's almost like that: a flash of light, a vivid image. Solid knowledge.

A small shoebox, under the desk, filled with blood and horror and guilt and, oh God . . .

I dive under the desk. It's really a dive, almost perfectly head-first, catching myself on the balls of my palms. I feel a sharp pain in my wrists as they meet the dense carpeting, but then—

Shit.

There really is a box.

Even though I'm now on all fours, I feel myself go off balance as I see it. I wasn't expecting it actually to be there, I realize that now. Despite everything. My avalanche of memories and visions over the past minutes have each taunted me, but then they've each been proven wrong. There is no case. No leash. Just anxiety and suspicion.

But the box is really here. The reality of it is like an assault. The harsh fact that it actually exists means this isn't all just emotional confusion or leftover drink. There's a box, right where memory said it would be. Small. Cardboard. The right shape.

And it's going to be filled with impossibility and horror . . .

I feel as if my insides are dissolving, but I pull myself closer and force myself to drag the box towards me. I've never been composed of so much dread. I know what's inside. *I know.* It's horrible and indefensible, and I realize my world is going to fall apart the second I open it.

But I have to open it, and I do.

The churning emotion stops. I've reached that point of emotional overload where it simply doesn't register any more at all. I tear the lid off the box and am an indistinct, undefinable mass of nothing.

The lid hits the floor. I blink, and then I don't know whether to scream or to laugh.

My expectation is fulfilled. I see what I knew I would see; but at the same time, I realize that I don't. Not at all.

There's white cloth inside the box, just like I remember it in my head. And it's spotted with red. Red in the very folds of its fabric, glaring and crimson. But the red isn't blood. *Of course it isn't blood! You paranoid wreck!* Instead, the bold UCLA lettering of David's *alma mater* twists in rusty crimson across the folds.

I am so relieved I can barely breathe, and yet I'm furious with myself. *Damn it, Amber, stop with this bullshit!* I simply don't know what the hell is wrong with me. What sort of dream or drink possesses a woman this way? Is the quiet monotony of normal life really getting to me this badly?

I put the cover back on the box, ashamed of myself, forcing resolve to take shape within me. I will get over this – this spectacular nothing that bears testimony only to my fragility and stupidity. I'm a grown woman, not some child afraid of monsters and visions.

Then, as I start to slide the box back into its former position at the back of the footspace beneath the desk, my sides quiver. A goose somewhere loses its skin as its bumps rise all at once across my back.

There's something else there, beneath where the box had been.

A streak of red stains the beige carpeting. It's rusty, and I reach out my nail-nibbled fingertips to run them across it.

Something has dried into the fibres. Something that crumbles at my touch.

Everything in me wants to cry out *blood! It's blood. You knew it was blood from the very beginning!* But I simply can't keep wandering down the path of mindless dreams and hungover visions. I won't allow it. This could just as easily be mud. It's beneath a desk, after all. It's where feet go.

I slide the box back into its position, directly over the stain. *It's nothing.* This is all nothing. I will not make it into anything more.

There's a beeping at my wrist. My watch scolds me. *You have to be at the bookshop in thirty minutes . . . What the hell are you doing under your husband's desk?*

I right myself, readjusting my hair and blouse after my little adventure.

Ridiculous creature.

And my feet are pulling me back down the stairs, towards the kitchen, the door and the car beyond.

With just enough time for another cup of coffee to go.

33

The act of dealing with murder is not as difficult as society makes it out to be. Physically, it takes a bit of effort, of course, depending on the means one chooses to employ. But of the great moral crises that plague human consciousness with guilty soul-wrangling and despair, of these I have experienced absolutely none.

Sometimes, things just need to be done.

Yes, a life may be taken. Something that cannot be given back. But the idea that this is a bad thing is only the romanticism of a too-compassionate generation. Calling life an inalienable right and all the rest – surely, that's just emotionalism at its most absurdly poetic. Life is a gift, and if you make yourself unworthy of it, you deserve to have it taken away. Simple. If you go further, and make it into something sinister, then relieving you of what you've perverted is no evil at all.

I look down at this one's mouth, his final breaths already departed, and I can all but hear those last wheezing moans, seeking compassion and forgiveness. But no guilt wracks me. There is no wobbly uncertainty of virtue or righteousness.

Only memories. Memories of how this life was used. How it's brought me here. What it's given and imposed.

What it's taken away, and what it, now, will never take away again.

34

Amber

It's 8.15 a.m. when I arrive at the shop, and I'm into my sheltered corner amidst stacks of newspapers, magazines and shipping invoices without much fluster. The morning has convinced me that something is off balance inside me. I can't think of another explanation for my extremes of tense suspicion and overactive imagination. Or hell, of what's amounted more or less into a descent into fantasyland. It's not stress at home, of which I've never felt any at all, and Lord knows a bookshop is the antithesis of a fierce work environment. And I don't think I tend to have strong emotional tendencies in general. Maybe my hormones are off balance. Maybe I'm pregnant.

Oh shit, maybe I'm pregnant.

The thought brings tingles to my spine, customers mingling in the spaces nearby with coffees in hand and passing glances at the papers I've laid out. David and I haven't exactly been aggressively trying for children – no timing of cycles and fertilization-promoting postures or the like – but we haven't been doing anything to upset the possibility, either. We'd both like kids, and we've talked about it often before. David will be a great father. As for me, my comic side generally teases that I'm mostly interested in children for the opportunity to fuss over and embarrass them as they grow. Terrible pity I'm not Jewish. Being a stereotypically overbearing Jewish mother has always sounded a real treat.

I can feel my lips arc into a smile. It's probably nothing, but I make a mental note to pick up a pregnancy test at lunch all the same. It would be a surprise if it were true, but a brilliant one. Both David and I are quietly growing tired of people expressing muted surprise that we're rounding forty with no children to our name.

Then the smile sags. Half an hour ago I was on the floor beneath my husband's desk, wondering if he was concealing blood-stained clothes – this man who's never been anything other than charming and open and honest. This man who in the present moment I'm thinking of as a father.

Shame on you, Amber.

'Got you your tea, as usual, neighbour.' Mitch's voice once again arrives in the bubble of my personal space before his body catches up. 'But, Amber . . . well, I don't know how to say this. You were late, and . . .'

He's tapping his fingers together in mock worry, hands empty, but there's the edge of a grin at his teeth.

'What happened to my drink, Mr Tuttle?' I'm ashamed of my inner emotions, so I force frivolity into my voice to compensate. The question comes out in the mustered tone of a displeased schoolteacher, catching a student without his homework.

'Well, it's kind of got all,' Mitch feigns a struggle for the right word, 'drunk.' He reaches to the side and a Peet's paper cup appears in his right hand, which he promptly overturns. Not a drop spills through the lid.

'Mitch, you bought me tea, and then you . . . drank it?' I'm trying hard not to smile. An actual smile, not a forced one. The exchange is comforting, and the normalcy of Mitch's humour soothing.

'Didn't seem right to let it go to waste. Wasn't sure if you'd make it in before the tea went iced.' Another toothy grin, and Mitch walks away.

His voice is almost immediately replaced by another.

'Well, I'll be damned.' Chloe's nest of hair becomes visible over a magazine rack where she'd been hiding until our boss was out of sight. 'Sounds to me like, oh, I don't know, a bit of flirting going on over there in the land of Mrs "I never flirt".'

I face a moment of apprehension as I decide how to respond. I'm not trying to dodge her, as I was yesterday. There are times when everyone needs a little dose of crazy to make the madness around them feel sane, and Chloe is good for that if she's good for anything.

I'm apprehensive, instead, because the memory of my last conversation with her fills me with a vague shame.

I think I half accused her of lying, and I remember I was abrupt. I don't know what to blame that on. Maybe the hormones. Hell, if it turns out I'm pregnant, she'll forgive all. And I don't want to sit in my corner today in silence, feigning solitary confinement.

'How's life on the other side of the Great Wall?' I ask, ignoring her comment to me but sugaring my words, nodding at the magazine rack still between us.

'Oh, so I exist, too, do I?' Her head rises more fully over the shelving. 'Even if I don't bring you tea and sweets?' Sarcasm like butter spread thickly on toast.

'Mitch never brings me sweets,' I push back. 'At least, not yet.'

That's it – just the right touch of provocation. 'Yet.' It opens a world of possibilities that I know Chloe will be all too anxious to anticipate.

'So you *do* flirt with him, you ditsy little liar!' She's wholly upright now, breasts pressed against a shelf, leaning on it with a devious look. The eyeshadow of the day is tangerine orange and her lashes are mascaraed into spikes that ought to have a safety warning attached.

'You know we're both happily married,' I say back, though I'm smiling broadly. 'He's just a genuinely good guy.'

'Not saying you're not happy at home, love. Just good to know you're not dead to the rest of the world.' She at last steps around the magazine rack and pats me on the head like a pleasingly attentive puppy. 'It's an important part of true awareness and the embrace of your illumined self.'

I can't hold back a sigh, bemused as it may be. Chloe was a 'deeply committed' Hindu a few months ago, then for a few weeks profoundly Buddhist. Yoga and self-enlightenment are the current focus of her spiritual energies, which seems only appropriate to the Californian stereotype, and when she isn't talking sex or gossip she's taken to ruminating on the power of the inner heart to expand into eternal oneness.

'My inner self thanks you for your concern,' I answer. The words are tongue-in-cheek, but Chloe appears gratified at the recognition of her current spiritual prowess. Thank God, we have such an extensive spirituality section in the shop; there's a nearly endless supply of enlightenment resources to hand.

I am calmed further by the fact that this singularly odd exchange is so very normal for her, and for us. The world has not, in fact, flipped entirely upside down.

I break with the theme as I look up at her. 'Chloe, thanks again for your help yesterday. I know I was a little off form, but I'm really grateful for your interest. And for your email.'

Another contented nod. It's not a difficult chore to gratify someone whose main interests in life are to be noticed and appreciated.

'Hells, hon,' she says, gushing, and I don't even mind the nonsensical accent, 'I ain't one to hold a grudge.'

Chloe, the most well well-practised grudge-holder I've ever known, means this in all seriousness, and it looks like she's contemplating reaching out and wrapping me in a hug. Wishing to prevent this, I rise up and peck a friendly kiss at her cheek, hoping that none of the glitter sparkling there will rub off on my lips.

'I may have something to stir up the thank yous again,' she adds as I sit back down, 'that is, if you haven't seen it already. Or maybe heard it on the drive in?'

Today my mind was full, and the radio in my car had stayed silent.

'Heard what?'

'Your body along the river. Not the only murder of the week, any more.'

My ears tingle.

'Pardon me?'

'Get yourself online and you'll know the same details I do. But as of this morning, northern California's scored another dead body.'

So the riverside killing is now a duo. Chloe, as usual, was melodramatic but not wrong, and within a few minutes of powering up my laptop I have access to morning headlines and reports that recount the discovery of the second body. Too fresh to have made it into any of the papers around me; but a suspicious death makes the online newsfeeds more or less instantaneously.

This one wasn't by the river, but in a residential neighbourhood in a town south of the Bay. It was found in the early hours of the morning by a cleaner with a key to the house, who'd discovered something more than the usual layer of dust that needed tending to.

The blogs were already drawing connections to the Emma Fairfax discovery of just over two days ago, despite the difference of circumstance. Murders in northern California just aren't as frequent as down south. With the exception of San Francisco and Sacramento, almost everything north of Los Angeles is a small town or farming community, and bodies being discovered at all is a rare occurrence. Two in so short a span is unheard of, and so even these outwardly different cases were inevitably going to be linked in the public's eye.

Right from the beginning, though, I was consumed with the differences.

Apart from the location, the most notable difference was the sex. This body was male, which immediately suggested a range of quite different motives for suspicious death. The age, too, was disparate. Emma Fairfax was reported by the police as being thirty-nine, but the man's body – no name or age was yet provided – was described as having grey hair.

And there was a different cause of death. While it it had taken a while to be made public, it was now widely circulated that Emma Fairfax had been asphyxiated; while the man's cause of death, by contrast, was made known immediately. A stab wound on his left side, a few inches above the hip. Other signs of conflict there, too

– scrapes and tears in his skin – but the cause of death was unequivocally stabbing.

Reports also indicate that he was well dressed, his clothes suggesting the budget of someone who wasn't exactly living off welfare handouts. Not a shop clerk. Not a hairdresser.

All of which I absorb as I read various articles, with an attention that becomes so focused I can no longer hear the beeps from the till at the door or the murmured tones of visitors among the aisles. I'm pretty sure Chloe has long since stopped speaking and moved on to other things, but she could be standing at my shoulder shouting into my ear and I don't think I'd notice her.

I want, I really want, my world not to start dissolving again. My irrational reaction to news of Emma Fairfax's discovery had led me in every direction except the reasonable; but I don't want to be that woman – the woman who worries and fears and speculates and suspects. I want to be the rational woman that I know I am. That I've always been.

But I'm not sure how much we can control just who we actually are. As I sit at my computer, jotting down facts and figures onto my Hello Kitty notepad and bookmarking websites, the edges of my vision are starting to go white. My pulse is taking on the thrash of a heavily pounded drum, and my blouse is gluing itself to my back.

35

Amber

I want to go home. Two days running, work has been an environment that catapults my inner world out of control, and I don't feel I can bear it any longer. I just want to be in my kitchen with my dog at my ankles, my husband beside me, and nothing at all beyond that beautiful bubble. And it doesn't take much longer for me to realize that there's no real reason I can't be precisely there.

It's coming on noon. For a few hours I've been caught up reading reports on the new body. Chloe seemed to sense my interior distraction, because she did what is relatively uncharacteristic for her and came over to help me through my morning obligations. Boxes unpacked. Papers racked. Pricing, done. Sorting, accomplished. A good friend is a good friend, and today she's stepped up to the plate, seen me through my chores, and enabled my little obsession. God bless her for it.

My normal lunch break kicks in at 12.30 p.m., but I don't see any reason not to push it up and make a day of it. I can't exactly take the rest of the day off, of course; even a low-stress job has standards of performance. But that doesn't mean I can't make up an excuse.

I rise from my desk and walk over to the small L-shaped counter near the entrance that constitutes Chloe's world. The iPad-based till has, as is often the case when she isn't actively scanning a sale, been converted into a chat browser, and Chloe is masterfully demonstrating her ability to make it look as if she's actually working while she chatters away with anyone willing to type back. She has a pair of white wireless headphones stuck into her ears and, between bursts of typing, she's applying what can't be less than the tenth coat of varnish to her fingernails. It's the same shade of tangerine orange that decorates her eyelids.

'Chloe,' I announce to no response. I reach out and gently tap her shoulder. 'Chloe, you have a second?'

The nail varnish brush gets dropped into its tiny jar and a headphone – only one of them – is plucked from her ear.

'What is it, hon?' Spiked eyelashes flutter.

'I think I'm going to head out a bit early, take the afternoon off at home for a bit of a lie down. Can you tell Mitch I'm away, if he asks?'

'You not feeling well?' Chloe's eyes suddenly beam concern.

'No,' I say, honestly, though I make a motion towards

184

my stomach that hints at indigestion or something un-becomingly bowel-related, which is less honest. I don't want to talk about what's hurting in my head.

'Gotcha,' she acknowledges, nodding. 'Don't worry. If Mitch comes questioning, I'll let him know you're unwell.'

I pass her an appreciative look, tuck my notepad and computer firmly under an arm, and head towards the door.

'Maybe it's just your age, love,' I hear Chloe announce behind me. 'I hear a bit of bloating is normal with the onset of menopause.'

I pause and turn back to face her. 'Screw you. You're going to get to this age one day, too, you crazy bat.' But Chloe is all grins, and for one blissful moment so am I.

I'm in the car, somewhere near Fulton, when I ring David. My Ford Fiesta predates Bluetooth call integration by about a century, but David got me one of the little earpiece options for my mobile a year ago. It's in my ear without my really thinking about it.

I don't know why I call him, either. An impulse. I just want to talk, to be with him; because my vision is swooning again, and my headache is nearly too strong to bear. There's no reason to think that David can help with this, but I still want to hear his voice. I feel the edge of an abyss drawing too close to the balls of my feet, and I want him with me.

Another body, to go along with hers. My innards tighten. The abyss. *Another corpse. Another death.*

At least there are no mystical visions in the car this time. No faces or names, just a deepening dread.

The line buzzes in my ear, and after a few rings David answers.

'Hello, love.' His voice is warm. 'This is a nice surprise.'

I'm trying to keep the road in focus, working not to let the pain between my temples force me to close my eyes.

'I'm on the road, David. I'm going home.'

A slight hesitation. 'Working lunch?'

'I'm taking the rest of the day off. I don't feel well.'

Another pause, longer.

'Is there anything I can do for you? I don't think I can get away from the pharmacy early, but I could pick up some soup on the way home this evening. You need anything from here in the shop? Or maybe . . .' there's a change to his tone, which becomes suggestive, 'or maybe just the promise of a little physical attention when I get there?'

'I'll be fine,' I answer, completely ignoring the innuendo. 'I just need to lie down, I think.' I'm not sure lying down has anything to do with it. 'When you come home, I want to tell you some things.'

There's an unidentifiable shuffling noise at David's end of the line. A second later his voice returns, slightly quieter and with no romantic suggestion lingering.

'Tell me things? What sort of things?'

'I've got to talk to you about something I read in the paper. A girl's body was found along Russian River a couple of days ago, and today the police found another body. Down in Felton. A man's. I don't know why, but the whole thing is really weirding me out.'

The words flow out of me spontaneously, and David doesn't say anything back. He's normally chatty on the phone, but right now he's stops and starts. Mostly stops. Then, after a long pause, his voice finally sounds again in my ear.

'I want you to drive straight home, Amber.'

Odd. 'I am already, David, I told you.'

'Don't make any stops along the way.'

I'm not in the mood for stops, my thoughts answer. *Not feeling like this.*

'I'll be home as soon as I can,' he continues, 'within an hour or two tops, and we'll talk.'

'I thought you couldn't get off early,' I mutter.

'I'll be there. You just lie down and wait for me.'

I have such a loving husband. Willing to bite into his day like that, just to care for me.

'Lie down, wait,' he adds, 'and don't call anyone els—'

It sounds like he cuts himself off. Not sure, but I think I catch a whispered profanity slanted against the line.

'Have a cup of coffee when you get back,' he returns in full voice. 'Nuke it from the counter, it'll taste fine.'

'I don't feel like coffee.'

'Just drink half a mug.' Audible impatience. 'It'll calm your stomach.'

Odd, I always thought coffee did the opposite.

'And keep to yourself, Amber.' His voice is steadier now. I think it might be calming. Sturdy.

'Whatever you may think,' David continues, 'remember this. Absolutely nothing happened.'

36

Amber

I arrive home in one piece. For a while, I had my doubts. My phone call with David ended and my head was spinning as much as I can ever remember it doing. Definitely not safe for driving, but I was already mid-highway and there wasn't much to be done about that. Thank God, it was the middle of the workday and traffic was slight. I made it home alive, and so did everyone around me.

My key is in the foyer lock with only a few slips at the slot, and I drag my ever-heavier feet up the stairs to our landing. Another key in another lock and I'm through the entrance and into the kitchen, which some star of a junior architect must have thought would make an appropriate front room. Its lights flicker like they always do, and when they finally snap to attention their white glow feels like it physically stabs at the back of my eyes.

Sadie's not in the kitchen. It's not the first thing I notice, but it doesn't escape me long. She's somewhere else. Her leash isn't hanging on its hook, either. I'll have to go find her in a moment. I'll enjoy a little snuggle.

David's voice is back in my ears.

'Have a cup of coffee when you get back. It'll calm your stomach.' The advice even now strikes me as absurd. 'Churn a little acidity into your burdened entrails' doesn't seem like the most common-sense counsel I've ever received.

But the invitation is still tempting. I'd never gone through with making myself a replacement for the cup of tea that Mitch had drunk on my behalf this morning, and going from the start of work to lunch without so much as a cup after leaving the house is unusual for me. I crave tea, but David's right: there's still a bit of coffee left in the pot on the counter, and the microwave is faster than the kettle.

I approach the countertop. The cold coffee, black and thick, sloshes around the bottom of the glass carafe with my handling. I draw it up to my nose, inhale a long whiff of its scent – but the coffee's cold, and the scent is more stale than inviting.

The man in Felton, stabbed in his house. His story is back in my head, too. No images of him, but I envisage his body lying prone on the floor. *I wonder if it looked peaceful, as the woman's had.* At least, as I presumed she had, based on the image I'd formed in my head from the way Chloe's chat-interlocutor had described her. *Her eyes open, gazing at the sky.*

The online reports say the man had grey hair.

Grey. Older. Something different.

I stare down at the carafe in my hands.

Screw this. I want nothing to do with the coffee. My appetite is entirely gone. With a little thrust the carafe is back on its pad and I'm turned towards the staircase. The having-a-bit-of-a-lie-down portion of my plan is still inviting, and the bedroom calls to me from its usual location up the steps. A three-storey apartment. Dear God, it's just an absurdity.

I wish I knew where Sadie was.

On the third or fourth step upwards, Emma Fairfax is back in my head, just as the man had been. All the details I'd hoped I'd forgotten, lingering in my attention.

I can't forget this. Not any of it.

The details of the memories mingle together. As they do, the staircase seems abnormally white, almost phosphorescent.

Oh, God. It's happening again. My vision blurs, and I can't focus on the not-exactly-lotus-blossom patterns that line the staircase wallpaper. I grab for the handrail, suddenly unsure of my feet.

David's voice is back in my head, displacing everything else, and my spine goes solid as I hear him speak.

'Whatever you may think, remember this. Absolutely nothing happened.'

For the first time since he said them at the end of our phone call in the car, the full weight of my husband's words falls upon me.

191

Nothing happened.

He can't have said that. He can't, because if he did, then I have the final proof that my memories – the brief-case, the desk, the leash, the box, the things swirling in my head – they aren't my imagination. Something *did* happen, something real, and something my husband knows about. I'm not mad. *I'm not mad.*

I'm racing up the steps, tears suddenly filling my already blurred eyes.

I have only one target as I ascend the stairs past our bedroom and take the few extra that lead to our minimalist uppermost storey. There is only one place here that has the potential to make sense of all the strangeness colliding in my mind.

I reach the upper floor and within a few steps I'm at the door to David's study. I pause before I slowly slide it open. I need to breathe. Focus. Then move, and pray for some calm to prevail in what's coming.

The room looks exactly like I'd left it this morning. Exactly like it always does. I step towards the desk with my stomach turning over and David's voice assaulting my memory.

'*Whatever you may think, remember this. Absolutely nothing happened.*'

And I remember another singsong voice, one I'd heard in the closet at our bedside when I'd discovered his briefcase there yesterday. *He's lyyyyyyying . . .*

The surface of the desk is tidy, organized with David's

customary efficiency. But this time, the tidiness seems fake. Fabricated. That something unusual took place here yesterday is no longer something I'm willing to relegate to fantasy. I'm sure of it now, and it means only one thing.

I try not to envisage David clambering to gather up the files I'd strewn about the desk. The leash. Planning where to hide it all away from me again. Instead, I look towards the footspace beneath the desk.

As before, there's no briefcase there. But I expect to see the cardboard box, and I do.

My head has resumed its swirling, though I manage to keep my balance under control as I lower myself down onto my knees once again. I reach out and lift the lid, finding inside it precisely what I remember. I stretch out a finger to touch David's white t-shirt with its crimson UCLA lettering.

This morning I'd been so certain that it was going to be blood, but it wasn't anything like that. *Yet there was still something, something here.*

Not in the box, beneath it. The memory resurfaces. A stripe of something rust-coloured, ground into the carpeting. Mud.

But now I'm horrifyingly certain that it wasn't mud at all. *It was blood, like I thought from the very beginning.*

There's one way to find out: I can fetch a flashlight and get a proper look. I'm not a forensics type, and I know *CSI* is mostly myth, but I think that under bright enough light I could probably tell the difference. I have to hope so.

I slide the box out of the way, and I freeze.

Beneath it, the carpeting is pristine. There is no smudge of anything, dirt, blood or otherwise.

Vertigo threatens me even from my stance on my knees. This isn't right. I'm sure I'd seen it. I'm . . . absolutely . . .

I lean forward. I don't know what possesses me, but I bow down, almost prostrate, until my face is millimetres from the carpet. I imagine my eyes are microscopes, capable of seeing at close range what I must have missed from a few feet away.

But it's not my eyes that make the discovery, it's my nose.

The scent of chemicals is overwhelming. Faux pine and ammonia and aerosol, so strong it burns my nostrils. I bring a hand forward and feel the spot beneath my face. It's wet, and my fingers come away from the carpet with the same scent.

'Oh my God.' The words come out aloud, as I realize with deadened certainty that David had been here after I was. 'He's cleaned the floor.'

It's hard to know how to react when you suddenly become certain your husband is deceiving you. Not in general terms, the way most women wonder at some point whether they're being cheated on or marginalized by another love interest, but in concrete, factual terms borne out by evidence that literally clings to your fingertips.

As the chemical scent of the carpet cleaner sticks to

194

my skin, I'm made firmly aware that David has done everything my unreliable mind had suspected him of since last night. He's hoarded away our dog's red, rope leash, made of the same course fibres the police say marked out the weapon that killed Emma Fairfax. It was wet, and sinister, and he tried to keep me from finding it. But I did, and now he's covered up the fact that it was ever here; and he's scrubbed up the stain beneath his desk, which means that it definitely wasn't mud. He wouldn't have made time to deep clean the carpeting for a scuff of dirt. He was evidently concerned enough about my seeing the blood stain that he'd have had to come back home after I left this morning, just to address it.

'*Absolutely nothing happened.*' His words echo more and more loudly within me.

My honest man is lying. I can't stop the tears rolling down my cheeks.

Then David's odd command rolls into my consciousness.

'*I want you to drive straight home, Amber.*' A tightening in my chest. '*Don't make any stops along the way.*'

The chemical smell wafts through my nostrils like an accusation. I'm starting to feel cold, the chill emanating from inside.

'*Lie down and wait for me.*' Then what has suddenly become the most ominous instruction of all. '*And don't call anyone else.*'

David had clipped off the end of the phrase. It had struck me as odd even in my state, but now I can hear him swearing at himself as he realized he'd said something he didn't mean to. Something that had slipped out anyway.

Never in all of the years I've known him have I ever feared my husband. From our first collision, to his seeking me out at the inn that night, to the romantic wonder of every moment that followed once we were back in civilization – nothing he's ever done has put the slightest hint of dread into me. But in this instant, crouched on this floor, I'm terrified. Terrified, and possessed of only a single thought.

I have to get out of here before he gets back.

37

Amber

'I'll be home within an hour or two, tops.'

There is nothing comforting about the timeline David set out on the phone. His willingness to alter the statement he'd made only moments earlier in the same call – one minute saying he couldn't get off work early, the next announcing he was heading this way – compounds my anxiety.

He's worried. What I told him, spooked him. He's upset, and he's racing here to find me.

For the first time in my life, I don't know what David will do when he sees me. And for the first time since I've known him, I'm afraid to find out. Rational or otherwise, my chest fills with panic.

I glance at my watch. It's 1.19 p.m. I don't know exactly what time it was when I'd called him from the road, but it was likely near on an hour ago. Given that he'd have had to come home sometime today to take care of the floor, I can't even be sure where he was when we spoke. Was he all the way back down in the city? Somewhere closer? God, he could be here any minute.

I'm on my feet again, leaving David's office and rushing down the few steps to the bedroom. *Get out of here. Get out of here!* I don't know where I'll go, or entirely why I'm going there, or how long I'll be away, but I have to obey that inner voice. It's time to get the hell out of this place.

I glance around our room. It's so familiar, yet in this moment feels foreign and unoccupied. I didn't make the bed before leaving this morning. The place is unkempt. The closet door is ajar.

I'm in no mood to scold myself for my domestic failings. Obviously, I had other things on my mind this morning, whether I fully understood them or not.

I stride over to the closet, trembling with an anxiety that has more or less extended through all my limbs. I have a yellow duffel bag inside, I think, tucked away somewhere in the back, and a plan quickly forms to stuff it with a few pairs of underwear and socks and at least one full change of clothes. Wherever I go, that'll get me through until I can figure out what's really going on.

I swing the wooden door fully open and shove aside my hanging clothes. Behind them, a general jumble of odds and bobs is stacked in a mess at the back, one on top of another without any semblance of order. I have to shuffle through the mess for a few seconds, but eventually

I see a familiar, lemony shade of yellow, just visible beneath a triplet of loosely folded sweaters.

With a few more manoeuvres I've exposed the duffel bag I'd remembered was there, and I grab it and fling its crumpled shape onto to the bed. It takes only a few additional seconds to sift through my drawers and gather up my underthings. I'm back at the side of the bed a moment later, and I drop them into a small well of space between the bag and the balled up wad of our comforter. My breathing is getting away from me and I try with all my will to control it, but I'm on autopilot now. I'm anxious, but I'm moving. I'm off to somewhere safe.

I set the yellow bag upright and slide open the zip that runs crookedly along its top. With both hands I pull it open.

I get no further than that.

As my face goes numb and the whiteness at my eyes overtakes any hope of sight, the interior of the duffel bag just has time to burn itself into my vision. It contains only two items. A white t-shirt, caked in blood, and a knife, its blade coated in crimson.

PART FOUR

TWO-AND-A-HALF
YEARS AGO

38

David

By the time Emma Fairfax was finished telling Dr Marcello and me what she'd done, there in that interview room in the ward, I despised her. I can't say I'd seen everything yet in the short decade following graduating from UCLA and then med school in San Diego, but I'd seen a lot. Sat beside this very doctor as he'd dealt with a lot. But I'd never seen anything like this.

This was the first time I'd come face to face with a monster.

It wasn't just the things she said, the things she'd done, that made her such a shocking revelation. It was that after all these years and a life surrounded by the kind of tortured souls that reminded me of childhood and my sister, I'd at last found one that had been in that same world – in the same kind of tortured hell as Evelyn had been. Though their stories would always be different, and this woman's so much more grotesque and vile, I nevertheless felt that I had encountered someone, for the first time, whose life was linked to the kind of terror that had consumed my life as it had taken my sister's.

My pen had stopped moving across my page as she spoke. Dr Marcello was an older hand, conditioned to these things. My mind, on the other hand, was trained to think of prescription options and dosage ratios, not to hear words like this woman was speaking.

Though I'd heard them before. From another perspective. That was the whole point.

Christ, it was all so repulsive.

She spoke for almost an hour, opening up about her past in sickening detail. Marcello grilled her, dispassionately toned but with the force of law behind him, and probed every corner of her story. It wasn't really his place to judge – she'd already been in a courtroom, already beneath the gavel – and yet knowing the full details of her story was part of the process of mental treatment and care.

Because that's what we were meant to do. Care. God help us.

In the end, I did what I'd never done before, and never done since. I lingered a moment after Dr Marcello left the room, just to take a long, uninterrupted stare at this creature. Emma didn't respond to my sustained, probing gaze. Then, without a word and trying my best to conceal my inner world of utter disgust, I turned and stormed out of the room, slamming the door in my wake.

My heart was bursting.

I had never been so disgusted, and yet I couldn't believe what a gift I had received.

I was back in the room two days later, as Marcello met her for his first follow-up and I was on call to see if the prescription we'd assigned forty-eight hours earlier was having any effect – the state's desire to embrace 'holistic, team-based approaches' to patient care meant we often visited together. But in reality, I was there to learn much more than just the efficacy of the drugs. Secretly, of course. I couldn't let Marcello or anyone else know about the thoughts that had overtaken my attention. This Emma Fairfax was suddenly everything to me, and yet I couldn't permit myself to show even that slightest hint of it.

She was led to her spot opposite the doctor, as before, and while the orderlies saw her into her seat and signed off on their instructions, my mind swam. It was disgusting to me that someone so vile as this could be responsible for bringing my sister's memory back to life, and so powerfully; and yet it was hardly a surprise that she had. Their lives were sickly linked, in the way that every victim is in some way linked to every abuser, whether it was her own abuser or someone else's. The spirit of such agony is universal. That was the whole tragedy.

My sister had been beautiful. All these years later, I can still see her face so clearly. Evelyn was the kind of teenage girl every other teenage girl craved to be, and the shape of girl that every teenage boy wanted to have, and she knew it. Didn't care about it, but knew it. She had the odd ability to know she was a looker, and still find herself ugly. Crazy, but totally true. Took me years to figure it out, too; though I'm not sure if, even now, I really have.

When news came that Evelyn had killed herself, my first reaction was silence. I mean, what does a boy say when he's told his sister's swallowed a fistful of pills and that the only place he'll see her face again is in a casket and in his memories? I went numb, and dumb. For a few moments, I wanted pills myself, just so I could follow her and be with her. But that passed. Maybe because I was strong enough to resist such escape. Maybe because I was simply too weak to follow her example.

What I remember most about the last months of Evelyn's life, before the suicide, was the look of emptiness she wore around her like a shawl. It was there whatever expression her face took on – when she was pensive, or smiled, or even when she laughed.

How is it possible to laugh and be empty? I ask the question now with the same bewilderment I had as a boy. It seems senseless. Impossible. At least, until you know the reasons.

'*Why do you look like that?*' I remember asking her. Little brother to older sister; the questions were allowed to be direct.

'*Like what?*' Evelyn had seemed disinterested.

'*Like you're far away.*'

I was only twelve, and not exactly eloquent. Evelyn

had turned right to me. There was kindness in her face – she was always loving to me, a bond we shared in response to the fact that neither of us had ever really felt loved by our parents – but she still looked far away.

'*It's because I'm hollow,*' she answered. '*I'm all emptied out.*'

I'd read *The Wonderful Wizard of Oz* and heard of hollowed out tin men, but I sensed that this wasn't what my big sister was talking about. In honesty, I didn't have a clue what she meant, and I think she knew it. She patted my head and fluffed my hair, an act she knew I 'hated' but secretly loved. She walked away.

That'd been six, maybe seven months before the pills. In those months, she broke down a little more day by day, and she did finally tell me why. Never told the parents, because she said bad things would happen if she did. She looked afraid as she said it, too, like someone might overhear her. So she just told me. As if I could bear that burden.

But it wasn't her fault. Christ, it wasn't her fault. The things they did to her, those sons of bitches, and to the rest of them. To gut her like that, so there wasn't anything left of the sister I loved . . .

And then, here, a connection.

The little room was antiseptic and the glow of the lights harsh, and I tried not to recoil from the sight of this woman. Even Dr Marcello's normally unreadable look was a shade harsher than before, and Emma Fairfax seemed marginally happy with that. Contented by it. At least someone knew what she'd done and hated her for it, even if it was only the two of us. Sometimes even monsters know they're monsters, and there are times when we're all comforted by another person understanding our reality, however terrible it is.

'You realize,' Dr Marcello finally said, 'that I'm going to have to write up everything you told me in an official report. Even though we're chiefly here for care, and as much as you may have been a victim yourself, we'll do everything we can for you, the details are going to need to go into your record, all the same. There might be repercussions, beyond your current incarceration.'

'Thought you might talk,' she answered, defiance in her voice, but not anger. 'It's why I told you. I'm done keeping secrets. Can't do it any more.'

The fact that you feel guilt doesn't exonerate you of anything! I wanted so much to shout out the words, to throw aside my clipboard, leap up and throttle her. Evelyn's face smashed into my vision, and I had to blink it away to see Emma again. I'd never been so repulsed by another human being.

She leaned towards Dr Marcello, boring her gaze straight into his. 'I ain't looking for *exoneration*, Doc. I'm telling you, I can't live with what I've done any more.'

He stared back at her for what seemed a very long time, simply letting her heaving breath echo through the room. Then there was the scribble of a few words on his pad, his face inscrutable. Perhaps he was pondering her wrongs; perhaps seeking vulnerabilities behind her defensiveness that may have led her to be taken advantage of. They were both routes I would expect of him, and, normally, of me.

He was about to ask another question when a small beep sounded at his hip. He had been in this line of work too long to feign apology when he reached down to examine his beeper, and as his brow rose I knew there must be some issue elsewhere in the facility that required his immediate involvement. My suspicion was confirmed a second later as he rose.

'I'm afraid we'll have to continue this a little later, Miss Fairfax,' he said, turning towards the door. 'The orderlies will be here in a moment to return you to your room.' Then, to me, 'It's a patient I'm looking after with Thompson, so I won't need you. I'll catch up with you at our next appointment.'

A second later, he was gone.

And we were alone.

39

David

I could have followed Dr Marcello out of the room, but I didn't. I stayed in my seat, glaring at Emma. I controlled my breathing as best as I could, but with only marginal success. The orderlies would be here soon, and it wouldn't strike them as odd if I stayed to await them. It provided an unexpected moment.

'What you . . . did,' I finally managed, wholly aware that protocol didn't allow me to speak directly to patients at all and that this was a severe violation that could see me censured, or even sacked. I didn't care. 'Why is it . . . bothering you . . . now?'

It was hard to piece the words together.

'I've bottled it all up for a lot of years,' Emma answered, 'like I said.' If she had any suspicion I wasn't meant to be talking with her, she didn't let on. 'But I'm haunted,' she added. 'Haunted by all of it. Every day.

Can't get away from what I did, however many years go by. I've had enough.'

You, haunted? I tried to feign compassion, some part of me might even have genuinely wanted to find it, but it was an impossible attempt.

And then, 'She haunts me.' Emma's utterance was sudden, direct. 'Out of all of them, she haunts me.'

There was a look of agony on her face, just then. Apparently, there was more to her internal torment than what she'd yet revealed. A personal dimension. She'd just said 'she', not 'it'. A reference to a person, rather than an act.

'Who haunts you?' I asked. My heart rate was increasing. In all Emma had said before, the girls had been referred to as an undefined mass. 'Victims' in the anonymous collective plural. However many of them there'd been. This was the first time Emma was singling out an individual.

'She wasn't like the others.' She was narrating to herself, now. With remarkable swiftness I'd become an invisible presence, no longer in her world. 'She was so . . . kind. Just a child.'

For a moment I thought she might be talking about Evelyn. I straightened, anticipation filling my body. Evelyn had been a child when they did what they did to her. She had been kind. She . . .

I brought myself back to the moment, keeping my breath controlled. Evelyn hadn't been in the same area as this woman. I couldn't permit their stories to get that intermingled in my head.

'You said they were all children,' I responded. 'You were barely more than one yourself.' The disgust was thick in my voice, and I didn't attempt to conceal it.

'But she was different,' Emma continued. 'I can't explain it. Like a flower. Saw everyone in such happy terms, even though she came from a shitty background, near's I could tell, just like all the rest of them. Absent father, overbearing mother, a fist or an open palm never too far off down the road of possibility. Nothing too happy, that's for sure.'

My stomach curled in knots. I could see Evelyn out in the woods behind our house, filled with light. Back before it had started. Like sunshine, dancing on the leaves, bringing me into her song.

'Fact that things were crap at home,' Emma continued, 'made her an ideal candidate.'

She said the last word so casually. It turned my skin to fire.

'No, she wasn't just ideal, she was perfect.' Fierceness, now. 'So bright and cheery, despite everything. Why couldn't she just be broken, like everyone else!' The accusation gathered rage, and Emma repeatedly beat a curled fist against the arm of her chair.

I wanted to throttle her, then. It felt entirely justified. All my years not knowing what had happened to Evelyn, not really, and then to come upon a woman who'd been part of exactly the kind of group that had destroyed her. Only this girl hadn't been abused. She'd been a friend to the abusers. Not just a friend – a helper.

And the demon has the gall to raise her voice against someone who suffered and—

My anger swelled, almost overtook me. I hadn't felt that sensation in decades. A lifetime of pushing away those memories, those emotions, and suddenly they were all back in my chest like an avalanche.

Emma took a few breaths, restoring her stillness, and I forced myself to follow suit. Despite my rage, I couldn't lose this moment.

'It's what made it so awful,' she eventually continued. 'That girl went in happy, despite the troubles she'd faced at home in her little teenage life, all the unpleasantness it created. All the reasons to be dark and upset by life. She kept shining, never mind all the shit. And . . . and . . .'

Something choked in Emma's throat. She couldn't get the words around the guilt lodged in her neck. I prayed to a God I didn't believe in that she would choke on that guilt, that I could watch her gag and turn blue in front of me.

'And?' I finally prodded.

'And the kid didn't last a goddamned day.' The words gushed out, wet and sticky. 'I brought her to them on a Friday afternoon, late, just like always. I think it was about four o'clock. There were three of them in there.' There were tears streaming down Emma's white cheeks as she spoke now, but all the convulsions of her skin had stopped. Her face was stone. The light in her eyes had long ago left the room.

'They brought her out forty minutes later, maybe. I'd

215

stayed in the foyer, like I was told. To keep watch. But this was the first time, the first time . . .'

I leaned forward as far as I could go. 'The first time . . . what?'

Her breath scraped across her larynx, rasps echoing in the little room.

'The first time they brought a girl out dead.'

I gaped at Emma in silence. This woman had confessed her part in crimes heinous enough in their own right; things no human could fathom, and most certainly couldn't stomach. She'd been brought here on more innocuous grounds, but I now knew the reality behind them. Emma Fairfax, the tool girl for a group of men who had abused . . . the Lord himself only knew how many victims.

Like other groups, and other men.

And other girls.

And one of them had been mine. Christ, the things I now knew they'd done. Things Emma had revealed. Things that went so far beyond what Evelyn had told me . . .

The fire was back in my spine. I heard the blood coursing through my ears. Just like the day my parents told me she was dead.

Dead.

I straightened. Evelyn had been raped, abused. But she hadn't come home dead. She'd killed herself.

The pills, after we fought and I called her a bitch in a childish taunt I could never take back . . .

I focused anew on Emma, who had hardened into a mountain in her chair. I didn't know how long I had until the orderlies arrived, and I suddenly felt a panic at the thought of losing the moment. Emma was still breathing, there was the stilted rhythm of it in my ears, but she now seemed a solid fixture. Her confession had de-animated her, sucked out whatever spark of life may have been keeping her going. The woman in front of me was a shell.

'The girl,' I forced out of my lips, my own voice creaky with the attempt not to let it turn to flame, 'she was . . . dead?'

A little electric charge shot through Emma Fairfax's skin. Her head snapped to mine.

'Not literally.' She shook her head. It was the wrong word, and she was visibly unhappy with it. 'Not *physically.*' A nod. That was better. 'I mean, she was still breathing and all. They'd never have gone so far as to actually kill anyone. That would have brought down all kinds of shit on 'em. Fuck sakes, they weren't idiots.'

Tears suddenly welled in Emma's eyes and rolled over her lower lids. The demon she'd become was replaced by the child, tortured and horrified, wallowing in the trauma of having become a beast herself.

I had no compassion to share, not with this person, and so I simply stared on in silence.

'She wasn't dead,' Emma finally continued, her voice little more than a whisper, 'but she sure wasn't alive any more, either. And she never was again. Poor thing never came back to life. They'd groomed her through me, made a connection, and then made sure she knew there'd be repercussions if she didn't come back when I told her to, or mentioned anything to anyone. That's what they always did. And believe me, they could be . . . convincing.' Emma peered at me, as if this should be obvious. 'And they had her come back many times. That was usual, too, when it was someone they liked. Someone pliable. Quiet, after they'd invested all that work in it. And she never said a word. Never confided in a schoolmate – they always had me on the lookout for that. God knows she never talked to her parents. Must have threatened her real good. Maybe beat her around some. Or maybe she was just done for. You know, inside. She just . . . switched off.'

My pulse was escaping me. Like the woman Emma was describing, Evelyn never spoke to our parents. She barely spoke to me. She had, to use Emma's godforsaken words, just switched off.

'That girl's life was over, and we did that to her.' Her eyes were veined and red. '*I helped* do that to her.'

You goddamned bitch. I couldn't control myself any longer. I could feel my muscles tightening, ready to throw me over the table to wring the life out of the monster's hideous frame.

Then, in a heartbeat, Emma's emotion vanished. The spark that had momentarily returned to her soul departed, and her whole frame sank itself in the chair.

'Emma,' I leaned forward, 'this girl, I want you to tell me exactly what happened to her.' Thought I heard

218

footsteps outside, in the corridor. I needed an answer.

There was a twitch in her shoulders. 'Just did. Don't tell me you weren't listening. This is, like, heavy stuff.'

'Heavy stuff', like she'd been discussing a tough break-up and not the cruel destruction of multiple lives. I bit at my lips.

'In the end,' I offered in clarification. 'If you didn't kill her' – and for a terrible instant, I almost thought it would have been merciful if they had – 'then what happened? Where did she wind up?'

I have to know. I have to know. I have to . . .

Emma's twitch expanded, spreading to her neck, up into her cheeks. Her eyes moved, shifting uneasily from side to side.

'Emma, don't think you can say what you have, and then not tell me what eventually happened to—'

I didn't even pretend to be objectively professional now. I couldn't control myself.

'What the hell are you talking about?' Emma was suddenly animated again, her face pointed back at mine. 'Is this some kind of sick psychotherapy joke?'

'Don't try to change the subject.'

'Seriously, I'm not here to play about.'

'This isn't a game!' My temper spent, I slammed my fist down on the table. The thunder echoed through the little room. 'What you did was unspeakable! Don't think you can hide the fate of the victim you've already told me plagues you the most. Tell me what happened to my sister!'

I conflated them again. This woman hadn't known my sister, but I couldn't separate my thoughts.

Emma's expression changed from scorn to incredulity as I exploded.

'Your sister?' Shock, then she drew back in her chair. 'What the hell does this have to do with your sister?' And then a moment of dawning recognition. 'No, wait, don't tell me your sister was abused by—'

'My sister was killed by people like you!' I shouted back. I simply couldn't help myself.

All her torment. All her pain.

'Me? I've never killed anybody!' Emma shouted out. She didn't understand. Didn't realize that suicide can still be murder, and once you help one abuser, you're part and parcel with all of them. It didn't matter whether Evelyn was abused by the same men Emma had worked with. She'd been abused, and I wasn't prepared to hold Emma innocent of her fate.

Her face was white.

'Tell me exactly what happened to her!' I demanded again, pounding down my fist a second time as spittle flew from my lips. 'To the girl you've been talking about.'

Not my sister, not my sister. But it didn't matter.

'Fuck, don't tell me you don't get it,' Emma finally answered, shaking her head. 'I mean, you can't not understand.'

My chest was heaving. 'Understand *what*?'

'Come on!'

I slammed my hands into the edge of the table in

frustration. I was standing, then, towering over her, letting my nostrils flare and sensing that the skin of my face was a bright red.

'What the fuck sort of game are you trying to play here?'

'The girl!' she almost shouted back, almost laughed, though she cowered beneath my presence. 'She's right fucking here!'

'What the hell is that supposed to mean?' My question flew at her as an accusation.

'In the building!' Emma shouted with all her strength. 'Christ sakes! You assholes lock me up in here, and you're keeping her four doors down the goddamned corridor! You've made the girl I've spent my life trying to forget into my goddamned psych ward neighbour!'

40

David

My conversation with Emma Fairfax continued another ten, perhaps fifteen minutes. I don't remember how it ended. I don't remember her being taken away by the orderlies. I just remember that she was there, and then she wasn't.

And I remember what she said. Every breath of it.

I remember everything else, too – all the pain, all the guilt, all the sorrow of my life – it all came flooding back in full force. Like an ocean unleashed into my head. Far, far too much to take. I could feel the current sweeping away every facade I'd built there over the years: each retaining wall, each barrier. All the emotion that I'd thought was gone, was back. It had never really left at all.

Turns out that shrink back in my teens may have been right, after all. You really can't bottle things up forever.

And you never really escape the things from which you're trying to run.

There was another woman, there, in that facility, who knew what my sister went through. Who went through it, too. And who, unlike Evelyn, survived.

For the first time in as long as I could remember, I felt something other than anger, or guilt, or dread, or deadness. I felt hope.

My feet were moving before I really had a chance to think matters through. I left the treatment room, having extracted from my unexpected conversation with Emma Fairfax only one detail that mattered in that moment: the name of the woman whose suffering had so affected her. I headed straight towards Admissions to seek out a file and a room number. The motion in my legs was energizing. If Emma was telling the truth, I'd be able to set my eyes on her opposite in a matter of minutes. On a woman who is the only echo of my sister's innocent suffering that still existed in this world.

Her file, however, wasn't at Admissions. I learned this from Mrs Albertson, the elderly attendant who'd been perched behind the intake and filing desk as long as I'd worked there, with a nest of nearly fluorescent hair that she dyed afresh on a weekly basis. That day it was a ridiculous shade of yellow. On any other day, I'd have been distracted by the sheer weirdness of that, in a woman who could easily have been my grandmother.

'Sorry, that file's out on rounds,' she said after I'd

given her the name. 'Dr Marcello took it with a handful of others this morning. You doing a pharmaceutical consult on her case as well?'

I shook my head and almost released the simple truth, 'No', but recognized that asking for the file of a patient for whom I haven't been requested for medication analysis would be highly irregular. Beneath that bright yellow coif was a woman who knows how things work around here. 'I was just asked to cross-reference her meds, for inventory,' I answered, concocting a response that felt reasonable-sounding. The next question was harder to ask, since it wouldn't normally be relevant to inventorying a patient's medications. 'You don't happen to know what room she's in?'

There were a few taps on a surprisingly noisy keyboard before Mrs Albertson grabbed a sticky note and a bent ballpoint and jotted down a number.

'She's resident here.' A number was circled on the pad in dark ink, designating a room in A-Bloc. 'But Dr Marcello is having his sessions today over here.' Another number was added below the circle. 'You might try both.'

I nodded my appreciation and took the little slip of paper. The A-Bloc was only a few minutes' walk from central administration, and I saw no reason not to go there immediately.

Curiosity can be an overwhelming force.

A series of interconnecting corridors led me to a door that was the same as those found on all the other residential blocs: heavy metal construction with a Plexiglas window reinforced by internal wire mesh. A video camera mounted high above registered my presence as I approached, and a flash of the credentials hanging around my neck provoked the loud buzz that came with the lock being remotely released. I grabbed the heavy door before the buzzing stopped, opened it, and passed through.

The corridor on the other side looked more or less identical to the one I'd just left. A-Bloc was just like the rest of our establishment: apart from the locks on the doors that were only operated from the outside – a feature for patient safety rather than anything else – it looked much like any hospital ward would. Only D-Bloc housed patients with violent tendencies and had the extra security features to match. Here, things were more septic and institutional.

I counted off the doors. It was only forty or so yards to room fourteen, the first number on my little slip of paper, and I halted momentarily before I turned to gaze through the window. I realized, in this instant, that there was something truly bizarre about what I was doing. The woman inside wasn't a patient I had any business approaching. I wasn't assisting her doctor. I wasn't supplying her meds. I had no connection to her at all, save for the statement of a woman who was admittedly psychologically disturbed. But in that moment I wasn't acting on behalf of the healthcare system, or the justice system. I was acting as a brother whose heart ached for his sister, who'd been told a patient here knew more about her pain, and the pain it had inflicted on me my whole life, than anyone else I'd ever known.

I spun on my heels and stared through the hazy window moulded into the door. The room contained what almost all there did: a metal-framed bed; a wall-mounted washbasin and plastic mirror; a little desk with a round stool fixed before it, bolted to the floor, for those who might try to use a movable chair to inflict violence on themselves; and recessed lights set into the ceiling with protective Plexiglas between them – no graspable light fixtures, to remove the suicide-ready temptation of hanging. A small metal toilet unit stood in the corner. For a moment, it looked far too much like a prison cell.

But it had no prisoner. Or patient.

I glanced down at Mrs Alberton's paper. Since this room was empty, chances were the woman was in the other location indicated in her penmanship. Consultation Room 22A. I swung my legs into motion again.

I hesitated even more significantly as I approached the consultation. If there was a session taking place, interrupting it would be an abnormality of protocol of the highest order. I couldn't possibly disturb them. I couldn't make myself known at all.

But I also couldn't stop. I couldn't do what I knew I should: simply turn around, walk away, and wait until her session was over and she was back in her room. Then I could have passed by and got the glance I for whatever reason felt so compelled to steal.

No. I had to see her now, immediately. The drive was a possession. My sister's memory was calling me.

I stepped forward cautiously, rolling my feet from heel to toe to keep them from echoing on the tile. I halted before my body came to the inset window and angled my frame towards the wall, placing both hands on the slick paint to support myself. I leaned in, slowly moving my head to the window.

Finally, I stopped. One eye – that was enough – was able to peer through the glass.

And I saw her.

Dr Marcello's back was to me, seated in his customary position at the table. Opposite him, the woman sat facing in my direction. She wasn't speaking. She was a statue, yet in that first glance I realized that she was absolutely the woman Emma Fairfax had spoken about. In that statue I saw a woman haunted. Dead. Empty.

And as her features came into view, I thought I'd found my sister all over again.

She didn't look like my sister, nor did she captivate me physically. Her skin wasn't remarkable, though she was far from unpleasant looking. She didn't have Evelyn's build, or her skin type, or her sense of style. Her hair wasn't done up. She was of relatively plain appearance, though her eyes were a beautiful, deep blue.

But their colour wasn't what grabbed me. Through the window, what I saw first and foremost was pain – and in that, she was like my sister through and through.

227

More than pain, too: absence. With one eye I was glancing into a psych facility treatment room, but with the other, with the whole of the rest of me, I was seeing my childhood. I was seeing Evelyn in those final months.

'Why do you look like that?' The memories burst back into my head. Christ, how I'd tried to kill them. But there was my childhood voice, back in the air, wafting toward's Evelyn's sorrowful features. *'Like you're far away.'*

And my sister's voice. *'It's because I'm hollow. I'm all emptied out.'*

Now, beyond the Plexiglas window in front of me, was another hollow woman. Not my sister's features, but my sister's soul. This woman was carrying her experiences.

You stop my breath. I could feel my heart weeping. *You look like a part of my soul that was ripped away.*

And I felt I knew her. Emma Fairfax told me what happened to this woman, and if the vileness of what she endured can upset even a monster, then I knew precisely why the woman in this room was empty.

And I didn't want my sister to die again.

I sidestepped away from the door and walked quietly back down the corridor. With each step, I felt my life changing. It was going to be intertwined with this woman's. I was certain of it.

I would ensure it.

This woman about whom I knew only two things: her

torment, and her name. Her torment was the same as Evelyn's, the torment of a woman whose life was no longer hers.

And her name was Amber.

41

David

Amber Elizabeth Jackson.

The name on the chart, when I was eventually able to get my hands on it, was exactly as Emma Fairfax had said. She'd even remembered the woman's middle name.

Amber's case file read like nothing I'd ever seen before. I'd been working in pharmaceuticals in our secure wing of this rehabilitative psych care facility for a while, but a pharmacist isn't exactly a doctor. I didn't always get exposed to the nitty-gritty, especially of the extreme cases. I was brought in now and then, when a doctor wanted someone in the room to assess drug options on the fly, but not usually for the long haul. Not to hear the full stories of what brought people to this place.

And I didn't normally read their whole files. Not that I wasn't allowed to handle them, just that there was usually no need. But this one . . . Christ. Amber's life had been lived in realms I just couldn't imagine. The details amassed from multiple hospital stays at multiple facilities were almost surreal.

She came from a broken home: perhaps a classic starting point. Her father, Peter, was, by her admission in counselling sessions years ago at a hospital upstate, distant ninety percent of the time and aggressive the other ten, not afraid of swinging a fist or a bottle when the mood struck him. She described her mother, Judith, as 'overbearing to the point of agonizing, like having a taskmaster always at your back'. She said other things about her as well, in different flavours of resentfulness and bitterness, recorded throughout her file. Clearly, her mother was the dominant power in her childhood, however gruff her father may have been. That both of them had died before she was twenty-five didn't seem entirely like something to lament.

My own parents' faces were suddenly back in my head. John and Katie Penskie had always struck me as amongst the worst parents a boy could have. God knows, 'love' was not a sentiment they either conveyed or engendered. But next to Amber Jackson's parents, they didn't feel quite as awful as I'd so long remembered them. I wasn't willing to let them off the hook for treating Evelyn and me like we were leeches burdening the freedom of their lives, but I don't remember them ever beating me. Not beyond the random smack now and then. I mostly remember their distance. Their coldness. Especially to

Evelyn, whose presence in their lives they seemed to resent even more than mine, since she was the more troubled of us and therefore intruded even more into the time and energy they clearly had no desire to shell out on such burdensome distractions as children.

Amber Jackson's home life was at a different level entirely. But the truly horrifying reality of her story was that Amber's home situation had been the least tragic dimension of her childhood.

By her own admission, dispersed through fragmented conversations in counselling reports that spanned the last several years, her world had started to crumble when she was fourteen.

Fourteen. Just two years younger than Evelyn when she'd died. Maybe she'd been fourteen, too, when her torture started. I had no way of knowing.

Amber had been befriended by a girl at her school who'd talked to her openly, and more than some others (she couldn't remember her name, and a red-inked note in the margin of her file reads 'repressed memory'). They hadn't just shared ages, but experiences. Bad home, bad parents. Bad lives. An immediate connection.

Amber and this other girl had entered into a friendship of sorts, with bags of pot and cans of booze being thrown in to secure its intensity and longevity. To a child who had few friends, this one had seemed a lifeline. But the line was to drugs, to escapism, to the darker corners of life. And then, one afternoon, to a visit to a neighbour's house 'for something a little different'. Amber hadn't known what this was about, but she'd had no desire to go home, so she'd agreed.

'The girl showed me up to the door once we got there,' Amber had said in a report emended to her case notes by a counsellor with different handwriting. 'She rang the bell and then started to walk away. I was confused. I asked where she was going, but it was like she'd become someone else. Her face wasn't friendly any more. It was hard, like she was mocking me. She just snorted and said, "I've done my bit. Sorry about this."'

Sorry. It was hard to be made aware, when I first read these records, that such a conciliatory word could be filled with venom. Especially as I knew what Amber didn't: that this girl's name had been Emma, and the woman she'd grown into was in a room just across the property.

Precisely what happened next, and over what precise span of time, is hard to determine from the file. Bits and pieces have been acknowledged in different sessions, in different clinics, over many months – but never the whole. There are notes indicating Amber loses memories from one session to the next. One day she weeps through the memory of an act she says happened all on a single day; then the next day she doesn't remember speaking of it, or that it ever took place at all. And then in the next session, it was a series of events, over several weeks. It's impossible to sort through all the details.

But those that can be made out are enough. She was met at the door by a man who drew her into the house. Either one or two other men were present inside – her recollections on this point aren't consistent – and she was coaxed downstairs, into a basement den. In some memories, this happened the same day; though in others there are flashes of a more likely story, of weeks passing, with multiple visits and stirrings of civility – friendly gifts being pressed into her hands, pizzas consumed around the television and the external appearance of familial care and concern. But the stories always end in the same room. A den with peculiar locks on the door, with a fold-out bed, already unfurled. And the men telling her she couldn't tell anyone what was going to happen, and—

I slammed closed the file as I read it the first time, cold sweat pouring down my chest. Disgust racked my body. It took another two attempts before I was able to make it through to the end.

When I finally did, I felt I knew my sister better than I ever had before. And I no longer wondered why Amber Jackson's eyes were hollow.

'What's her condition, now?' I'd set up a meeting with Dr Marcello a few days later, under the guise of wanting to ensure her meds were in balance and having their desired effect. Parts of that story were even true. I've never been much for deceit, but I've always thought a good lie doesn't stray too far from the truth, not if it's going to retain the air of believability.

Dr Marcello was pleasant, professional.

'What you see on her face is pretty much what she's

got inside,' he answered. 'She's been in and out of counselling and treatment for years. Every time, her memory's been a little more piecemeal. Like a gradual, extended breakdown.'

'Is it depression? Psychosis?'

'A bit of both.' His tone was professorial. 'But her case has been particularly characterized by an increasing post-traumatic amnesia. She remembered much more about her childhood trauma three years ago than three months.'

'And now?'

'Now? Now it's down to almost nothing. We had her admitted because a neighbour called the ambulance after finding her more or less catatonic in her flat. The first month here she didn't make a sound. Barely moved. We tracked down some of her former doctors, the ones she'd opened up to in that file.' He pointed to Amber's case folder on the desk between us. 'But it had no effect.'

'How has she got by this long?' I asked. 'Her abuse, it was more than twenty years ago, but she hasn't been institutionalized until now? If she's being found in a catatonic state by neighbours, how has she managed to live on the outside?'

'The catatonic states are a recent development,' he answered. 'There are no records of her having them before. They only began maybe five or six months ago, probably pretty minor at first. But her state has been deteriorating rapidly, and the mental blocks growing dramatically.'

'Caused by?'

'You tell me,' Dr Marcello answered. 'That's what we're working on at the moment, but even with all we're doing I'm in no position to give you a definitive diagnosis. Probably the effect of a lifetime of repressing what was done to her.'

His words made me go rigid.

'You can only repress the past for so long,' he added. 'It breaks through eventually. Miss Jackson seems to have done that repressing very well, but that only means that the collapse is all the more powerful.'

I remembered the floodgates of emotion that had broken within me a few days ago, as Emma had revealed who she was. I had followed the path of repression as well. And it had sure as hell failed in the end.

'Is it getting worse?' I finally asked.

'She's started to come out of it over the past two weeks,' Dr Marcello replied. 'Little by little. A word here, a phrase there. Right now she's conversant a few minutes of each day. That's about it, though I'm hopeful the trend might continue and we'll eventually be able to release her back out to as close to a normal life as this woman is ever going to have.'

'So there's progress.'

'With a distinctive catch. When Miss Jackson does speak, she appears to have no memory of anything from her past. It's like her slate's been wiped clean, again. There's today, and before – nothing.' He hesitated, reflecting. 'Which means she's coming through this particular breakdown, but doing so by repressing her memories again. And eventually, that's going to fail, again.'

Dr Marcello said this with a professionally formal grimace, as if it was the kind of mixed news, mostly unhappy, that we had to be prepared to encounter in this kind of work.

But I'd listened to his words. I'd heard her story, and in a radiant, glimmering moment, this news didn't sound bad to me at all.

Given everything I now knew, the normal course of action would have been to take everything I'd learned to the police. We had in our halls a woman who'd been horrifically abused, repeatedly, by a group of neighbours who had made a science of their perversion, just up north along the coast, right in the heart of NorCal tourist central. And we had, in another room in this same building, a woman who was involved in that ring – the bait who'd only too willingly been used to lure victims in. There were the pieces here for an investigation. A bust. The legal righting of a grievous wrong.

But I was too captivated by Amber to do that, because I also know exactly what would happen if I did. If I filed a report saying what I knew about Emma Fairfax, what she'd admitted to me, Amber Jackson would never be left alone. A woman who'd been completely broken would be forced to face the girl who'd led her to her ruin. She'd be made to relive, again and again – in police

237

interviews, legal depositions, court interrogations, probably even the media – every detail of the gruesome acts that destroyed her. She'd be resurrected, only to be killed anew. The hollow woman would be gutted and drained of even the life she no longer possessed.

And I wasn't prepared to let that happen.

Amber Jackson was not my sister, I knew that. I really did. But I never had the chance to save my sister.

Maybe there was a balance to life, after all.

42

David

It felt something close to an abomination to permit Emma Fairfax to be released. It happened, though, five months later. The term mandated by her sentence. Even with what she'd admitted in Dr Marcello's presence, the administration didn't feel there was enough evidence-based grounds to appeal for re-sentencing. She was troubled, and probably always would be; they'd done the bit that the courts had required of them.

Of course, she'd admitted far more to me. And while there was no conceivable defence for this creature ever to be unleashed back into society, I, like every other member of the group-care team, signed the release paper-work when it came. Not every choice made in life is made in terms of a legal framework. I had my own reasons for determining that Emma's release was a necessary evil, and those reasons outweighed everything else.

She appeared as surprised as anyone when I saw her at medical distribution after she'd been told the news.

'What the hell do they mean, they're letting me go?' Even her practised self-assurance couldn't mask her genuine confusion.

'Just what I said, Miss Fairfax,' I answered, drawing her into the pharmacy's consultation room. I kept my voice low. 'The paperwork's gone through today. Your court-mandated term is over. Barring any unforeseen complications, you'll be released tomorrow afternoon.'

'But . . . but the things I told you. I didn't think I was ever getting out of here.'

I didn't break eye contact with her. She was right. That's how it ought to work.

'The things you told me,' I drew out my words. It was important that she understood what I was about to say and what I meant by saying it. 'They didn't make it into any reports.'

Emma's breath was as slow as mine, but her stare was blank.

'I don't believe you. I confessed to—'

I didn't permit her to complete the sentence. What she'd admitted to was not to be uttered again. Not here. 'You're clearly a disturbed woman, Miss Fairfax. Depressed. Addicted to booze. You misuse the drugs you've been prescribed, and I've made a strong recommendation that you no longer have them made available to you without strict controls. But it will be the doctors, and the courts, who ultimately decide those things.'

'*That's* what concerns you?! That I misuse my prescriptions? Christ sakes, that should be the least of your interests. I told you I—'

'Emma,' I cut her off. My eyes were fire. 'Our time together is finished. You need to accept that.'

She looked like she was about to react, but no words emerged from her open mouth. She leaned back into her chair, her expression lingering on mine.

'I . . . I don't get it,' she finally said. 'Why are you doing this for me? Why aren't you out for blood?' There was a momentary appearance of genuine agony, something I'd seen on her features before. 'You *should* be out for blood! I mean, you told me things, too.'

I tapped my fingers across my lap.

'What you told me,' I said, my words conspiratorially quiet, 'is beyond my power to comprehend.' I paused, and felt bile on my tongue. I did comprehend it. That was the fucking nightmare of it all.

'How can you not care?'

'It's not that I'm not appalled by what you've done. Be clear about that, Emma. Your life, your choices, they're . . . beyond words.'

'Then why don't you report all this?' Her voice was barely above a whisper. 'You know as well as me they'd throw away the key. Whether I was a "victim" or a "vulnerable personality," or any of that crap, I'd still end up one of them bitch demon women you see on the news. Who threw away others for her own ends.'

'Because, Miss Fairfax, you're not that important to

me.' I opted for honesty. She was hardly going to report the affront to polite propriety. 'Someone else is.' *Someone else's redemption matters more to me than yours.*

I caught myself, just then. I didn't need to tell her any more. She didn't need to know the details.

There was nothing left to say. Emma stared at me, and I couldn't tell if she was grateful or upset. Part of her must have been relieved she'd walk out of here; but part of her had wanted, I think, to face justice for all she'd been a part of.

I leaned forward. 'Just don't think, even for a single second, that this amounts to forgiveness for what you've done.'

You'll end up in hell soon enough, my inner voice wanted to cry out. *And it will be my prayer, every day between now and then, that you suffer until you do.*

I got up and turned my back on Emma. Whether or not I'd ever encounter her again, and what I might do if that occasion arose, was something that had to be left to fate. I was done with her, and good riddance.

Now, the path before me felt both secure and unknown. An odd mix. I was a man with more questions in his head than answers, and I sensed that feeling was going to be with me for a while.

But I was certain about one thing. I hadn't been able to bring justice to my sister before she'd ended her life. I hadn't been of any help to her at all. But I'd now met

Amber Jackson, and Emma Fairfax, and I knew the story of the men who tortured them.

Revenge wouldn't do much for Evelyn now, but it'd sure as daylight feel good to get it done for Amber.

PART FIVE

THE PRESENT

43

Amber

My day doesn't start with blue eyes staring back at me. It's the first one in the longest time that doesn't. Nor does it proceed through a well-timed ritual of morning preparations, or involve a drink left on a countertop or a drive along the highway to the bookshop.

My day begins abnormally, in a hotel room in Calistoga, tucked between the steep, mountainous rises on either side of Napa Valley, my head thrashing in spasms of what I'd insist was a hangover if I didn't know perfectly well that I didn't have a thing to drink last night. So different from the night before, with nearly a full bottle of wine inside me then. Last night was dry, sober, and paranoid.

The new day has started on a thick mattress that's far nicer than the one we've got at home, clearly chosen to cater for the comfort that visitors to Wine Country crave.

But it's begun alone. I'm staring vacantly at an unfamiliar ceiling with a thought in my head that I'd never have dreamed could ever live there.

I don't know who my husband is.

The man to whom I've been happily married for just over two years is not a man who does the things I've witnessed him do over the past days. He's straightforward, honest as they come, plainly plain and straightforwardly simple. Nothing if not completely sincere, an open heart always ready to open himself up to mine.

The man from whom I fled yesterday afternoon – though 'fled' isn't really the right word, 'avoided' is more accurate – this is someone different. This is a man who offers me drinks in the morning and hides bloodied garments and murder weapons in our house in the evening. Who assures me nothing's happened after I tell him about a body stabbed and left to bleed out, then conceals a blood-stained knife in our closet. A man who hides, who lies, and is so very different from the one I've held in my heart.

I'm not sure how long I've been lying here, in the calculated comfort of the hotel decor, contemplating this unknown man David has shown himself to be. Long enough that the physical headache has gradually started to wear off, though the mental one is only growing. I don't know what that translates to in real time: maybe a few hours. Maybe many more.

Long enough to know I don't want to lie here any

longer. This mulling over impossibilities isn't going to bring me any relief, and it's certainly not going to bring me answers. The facts of the past twenty-four hours leave me with only one option.

Nothing is going to make any sense until I can find out who my husband really is.

Somehow, by a force in me that exceeded the strength I expect of myself, I managed to stay in motion after my discovery in our bedroom yesterday. Wobbling into collapse and staying that way for the remainder of the day would have been understandable, but I kept myself upright after finding the knife, managed to plant one foot in front of the other and get myself out of the apartment. I'd started out intending to pack a supply of clothes, but in the end took nothing with me except my handbag, snatched off the kitchen table as I rushed by. It meant I had the usual stash of things I kept there: my laptop, wallet, pills, keys and the like. That was it. I walked out of my home, and my life, with nothing more than the contents of my purse.

In the car, all I could see was that knife and the bloody shirt, hidden away in the yellow duffel. Everywhere I looked, they were square in my vision. I don't know how I finally managed to force them to disappear, to get about the physical tasks of driving, but somehow I made it away from home. The familiar lanes of Highway 101, and then the winding, two-lane ascent into the hills to cut across into the Valley, flash through my memory.

How I managed to drive those forested bends is a complete mystery.

I was pulling into the Comfort Inn in central Calistoga before I'd consciously thought much else. My only stop was at an ATM somewhere en route, and I'm only really certain of that because I paid for this room in cash, and there's still a pile of it on the desk. Once checked in, I stumbled my way to this room and collapsed. I don't recall the time, I don't remember any conversation with the front desk clerk on my arrival. Just a keycard in a digital lock, tossing my handbag onto the overly bleached white of the hotel bed coverings, and flinging my body onto it afterwards.

Then this morning. Waking. The textured ceiling.

Suddenly, I think of my phone. I haven't thought to look at it till now, which is another oddity, I suppose. I ruffle a hand through my bag until I feel its familiar little shape. A second later I'm holding it above my face.

Fourteen missed calls.

I blink. The phone wasn't muted – I've never seen the point of having a cell phone if you're going to silence the thing – and the extent of the calls I hadn't heard ringing surprises me. One is from a central San Francisco number I don't recognize; but, unsurprisingly, all the rest are from David. I realize, with an unhappy certainty, that the last thing I'm ready to do is call him back.

Not until I have the faintest idea what I could possibly say.

252

The first time in our relationship, I didn't know how to speak to the man I love.

And it's not just that. I'm becoming aware that I don't want David to know my whereabouts, either; not until I've got a better grip on things. That means I can't be going into work this morning, as the bookshop is the first place he'll think to look.

A quick phone call to Chloe, invoking the unique power of the 'best friend super swear', reassures me that my boss will be told I'm 'feeling a little unwell,' and that if David rings to ask after me he'll be told that I'm 'out on a supplier relations visit for the day'. Just that. Though however things play out, this is going to cost me. After pledging her to keep my whereabouts concealed from my husband, there's no way Chloe will ever believe I'm not having an affair.

So no office, no home. They're firm decisions, and though they don't exactly bring me comfort, they do at least give me a sense of resolve. I force myself to continue in that determined vein, stepping into the Plexiglas-stalled shower as an act of necessity rather than desire. Perhaps the water will wash away the remainder of my non-hangover headache away. It's something to hope for. But as soon as I'm under the hot running water, I'm happy I'm there, for more than just practical reasons. The shrink-wrapped soap smells of lemon and lavender and the mini-bottle shampoo foams up more nicely than I'd have expected. The scents, the warmth – there's something rejuvenating about them all. I linger under the water.

When finally I emerge, pat myself down and face the fact that I have no other clothes to put on than those I'd taken off, I'm nevertheless refreshed. There's the littlest spark of gusto that's somehow found its way back into my psyche.

Last night I was crushed; but right now I don't feel completely powerless. I have my laptop and my phone with me, and with a WiFi connection live in the hotel room, it's really all a person needs. It's time I take reality into my own two hands.

My first thought is to return to the two victims. In David, if in nothing else, the two are connected. He'd hidden Sadie's leash, of the same type that was used to kill Emma Fairfax, and the knife in our duffel bag at the flat definitively connects him to the man found yesterday. In this context I'm well past entertaining coincidences. Besides, it's not like a bloody knife in a closet ever has a good explanation.

It's hard to bring myself to acknowledge, even internally, what this really implies. How has my husband gone from perfect man, whose greatest fault is that he makes shit breakfast drinks, to two-time killer in the span of under a week?

I choose not to try to answer that directly. *Focus on the victims*. I gather together everything I can about them, drawn into parallel.

Emma, female; man – obvious. Emma, my age plus a year or two; man, significantly older. Emma, retail worker; man, successful enough to be wealthy. Emma, strangled at a river; man, stabbed.

What could have drawn David to these two people? To these acts?

That knife, coated in blood. Christ, it was like I'd been drawn to it. Like David's acts were beckoning me, calling me to discover what he, what he . . .

I'd reached that can't-quite-bring-myself-to-say-it point again. Not of the man who brings me flowers and takes me for walking holidays on the coast.

But if he's done this, then obviously he's been hiding a hell of a lot from me. Concealing so much of himself. I am ashamed with myself for having been so blind. There's a guilt that comes with being gullible.

But it doesn't help me to understand. Maybe, though, others have seen more. Maybe some of David's friends have noticed something different about him. Something that might offer me a clue. It's a prompt. A call to action.

I have to talk to his friends.

And it's following that, that I realize I know of only one. Chad Markiez, David's friend who works over in the Sacramento Police. Only now, in this moment, does it strike me is so terribly strange, that after years of marriage, I can name only one of his friends.

A man I've never even met.

The Sacramento Police Department's number is publicly listed on the Internet, and with a few keystrokes I have the non-emergency contact listing on my laptop, and a few finger presses after that I have a number dialled into my cell phone. I'm determined to find this friend I've never known, and discover what he can tell me.

'Sac Police, District Three Central, how can I help?' A man's voice answers, businesslike and efficient. By the sound I would place him in his late thirties or early forties.

'Good morning,' I say in response, trying to sound equally professional and not like a crazed woman convinced her husband is an emerging serial killer. 'I'm not sure who I should talk to. I'm trying to get in touch with one of your investigators there.'

'Which department?'

'Homicide.'

'Just a sec.' There's typing on a computer near the telephone, and a moment later the man's voice returns. 'Okay, I've got the directory up here, ma'am, though I trained up in homicide myself, so can probably help you directly. What's the officer's name?'

'Chad Markiez,' I answer. 'Not entirely sure of the spelling.'

There is a brief pause. Only a touch longer than I would expect. Then the typing resumes. The man's voice, when it returns, is less solid.

'I just wanted to check to be sure, but it's as I thought. We don't have anyone in homicide by that name.'

I try to swallow, but can't.

'That, that can't be right,' I fumble. 'He's been one of your homicide investigators for several years. He's a close friend of my husband. He's mentioned him to me several times.'

'I don't know what to tell you, ma'am. There's no one here by—'

'Maybe try a different spelling? An "s" instead of a "z" in the surname?'

'I can try if you like, but I can already tell you what the result will be.'

'Please, just do it.' And there's typing again, the clicks echoing over the line. The wait is a little longer this time.

'None,' the man finally says, 'and before you ask, I just searched the whole database. We don't have a Chad Markiez, or Markies, or a Chad anything-at-all, anywhere in the Sacramento Police Department. And we never have.'

The only friend of David's whose identity I can name, doesn't exist. He's a myth, a puff of air, and nothing more.

Rather, it seems, like reality itself.

44

Amber

I've been staring at the wall since my phone call with the desk agent at the Sacramento Police Department ended, I don't know how many minutes ago. Ten? Fifteen? Outside my hotel room, the sun shining through the blinds is of the midday sort, rather than morning. So maybe it's been hours, then, gazing at the commercial-grade paint, wondering what part of my world isn't collapsing.

Why would David lie to me about his closest friend? What's there to be gained by it? I have no connections in Sacramento, I've never even toured the Capitol. Why such a deception?

But lies and deception are all I seem to be discovering about David, and this latest one only urges me on in my desire to talk to someone, anyone, who might know more about what's been going on in his head lately.

Perhaps not just lately. He told me about his friend Chad shortly after we met. The math isn't hard to work out. That was more than two years ago.

A long time to be lying about a friend that doesn't exist.

I shake off a sudden chill. I can't lose my resolve. If it's not going to be possible to speak to David's friend, then I can try one of his colleagues. If anyone is liable to have seen a change in his behaviour, something that might account for whatever the hell is going on, or at least help explain it, it would be his co-workers at the pharmacy. He's there at least nine hours a day. They spend almost more time with him than I do.

I pick up my phone once again and scroll through my contacts, and it's then that I become aware of another fact that, until this moment, had never struck me as particularly odd. I don't have a work number for David. Just his mobile. It's never seemed necessary that I should have anything else, since he's never without his phone.

Today, the fact seems suspicious.

But this is a problem easily enough solved. I wake up my laptop and return to the browser, readying myself to type calmly. I just need to pop in the name of the pharmacy and—

My fingers freeze, hovering over the keyboard. David's worked at the pharmacy since we met. Down in the city.

But I can't remember its name.

Baycrest? Bayview? Something to do with the bay, I remember that much. He told me the name, once, but it was years ago. Since then it's always just 'the pharmacy' or 'work'. *Shit.* I remember he told me it was some little place, tucked away in a residential neighbourhood. Near the sea.

Which describes most of San Francisco.

Then I remember my pills. In my purse, in one of the side pockets – the three prescriptions David brings for me each month, two for my blood pressure and one for my thyroid. Little bottles, orange with white lids. And labels.

I race from the hotel desk to the bed and grab my handbag. Within seconds it is overturned, contents spilling out over the bed's surface. I reach inside the now vacant space and unzip the side pocket, then give it another shake. The three pill bottles fall to the bed.

I grab the nearest one, my head in a rush, and then freeze. It's my prescription of course, but the label is from CVS Pharmacy, one of the largest chains in the country. And David doesn't work for CVS.

I grab the second bottle, and then the third, but the logos on the labels are copies of the first. All from CVS, and I cannot for the life of me understand why David would get my prescriptions filled at a chain store when he works in a pharmacy and could simply pick them up from his own counter. It makes no sense.

I stop myself. David's behaviour isn't normal, but no, I can't actually say it doesn't make any sense. Not in this instance. It *does* make sense, if what you're trying to do is keep your wife from knowing where you actually work.

My heart is racing again. *Why would he hide something so basic from me?*

I collapse back into the desk chair. I can feel my will deflating. It seems I don't even have the most basic of information about my husband. What can I find online, or anywhere else, when in reality I know so little?

But then, there is one thing that I do know. A second later, my fingers are dancing on the keys. It's about the only option I have left.

I've never logged into our Wells Fargo account on the web before. David always takes care of the banking. This presents me with a certain problem, since in this moment the screen in front of me is asking for a username and password, and I don't know either. But I have said before, and I remind myself again now, David is a witty man, and caring, but not necessarily clever.

It takes me only two attempts to guess the right combination. The numerical passcode is my birthday again, just as the code to his briefcase had been, and the username he's chosen for online access wasn't the dog's name, as I guessed first, but 'TheHowells'. David always takes such delight in referring to us by our collective name.

I start to scroll through our accounts online. We have two with the bank: a savings and a checking, and the former has almost no activity except a few deposits scattered over the past months. I switch to the checking account, which has, as makes perfect sense to me, a great deal more activity recorded in the register. But as I scroll through the entries, I don't see anything unusual. Nothing in the lengthy listing looks suspicious or out of the ordinary.

What, really, did I expect to find here? What secrets is a bank account really going to hold?

As I scroll through the list, less and less interested in what I am seeing, I come across three consecutive payments to CVS Pharmacy. The amounts match what I would guess my prescriptions cost, but otherwise provide little insight.

I am just about to close down the window when a line at the bottom of the screen catches my eye. Another payment, and the 'Category' field is marked 'Medical / Healthcare' just as my three prescription payments had been. Only this one isn't made out to CVS.

The 'Payee' field reads, in boldface font, 'Bayside Inland Pharmacy'.

Bayside Inland. That's it. I remember it coming off David's lips now, years ago. A conversation that had once been and never repeated. I remember. *I remember.*

Heart thumping, I open another browser tab and type 'Bayside Inland' into Google Maps. A second later, its pin is on the map in front of me. A small shop, in a residential neighbourhood, in a part of San Francisco only a few blocks from Ocean Beach.

It's the place. I'm sure of it. And its listing has a telephone number.

I can't punch the numbers into my stupid phone fast enough. The San Francisco number goes through when

I hit Call, and the line seems to ring forever before someone finally answers.

'Bayside Inland,' a female voice says. She doesn't exactly sound bored, but from her tone of voice I'd say it's a safe bet she doesn't find answering the telephone to be the greatest thrill of her life. 'How can I help?'

In this instant I realize that I haven't actually thought through what I'm going to ask of David's colleagues. My attention has been too absorbed in simply trying to find out where he actually works.

'Could you connect me to the pharmacy desk, please?' I ask. 'To anyone other than Mr Howell.'

Shit, that's not exactly a customary kind of request. But it's out there. I can't suck it back in.

The woman seems puzzled, if only by her silence, but a moment later the line clicks, clicks again, and then a man's voice replaces hers. I tense at the first breath of it, terrified it will be David, but force my shoulders to relax when I realize the voice isn't his.

'Pharmacy,' the man says simply and efficiently.

'Hello, I'm sorry to disturb you,' I begin, commanding timidity out of my voice, 'but I'm really stuck here. I hope you can help.'

'If I can help, miss, I will.' His voice becomes a shade friendlier.

'This is Amber Howell. It's about my husband, David. He . . . he hasn't been himself lately, and I'm getting concerned. I'm wondering whether you might be able to give me any information. About his behaviour. His mood.'

The pause that follows is long. I can sense the man's discomfort through the line.

'Sorry, miss, but I'm not sure what you mean.'

'I mean,' I sit forward, trying to make my thoughts take a more concrete shape, 'he hasn't been acting like himself. His mannerisms. Turns of phrase. They're not . . . usual.' That's going to have to be enough. I'm sure as hell not going to tell his colleague about the wet leash or the bloody knife.

'Miss, I'm sorry if your husband's behaviour is unusual, but I don't understand why you're calling here.' The man is beginning to sound mildly agitated.

'Because I thought you might be able to tell me if you've noticed anythi—'

He cuts me off. 'Are you under the impression that I know your husband?'

My skin turns cold. *No, no. This can't be.*

'Of course I am!' I almost spit the statement into my phone. 'He's been your co-worker since before we were married. At least two years, maybe two and a half.'

'And his name is?'

'David!' I cry. 'David Howell! Your counter assistant. He's there every day. He's probably there right now!'

Again, the long pause.

'Miss, I think you have the wrong number. We don't have an employee here by that name.'

Ice, travelling through my body.

'That can't be true,' I answer. 'He always comes in early. Stays late, to miss the traffic back across the bridge.'

264

'I'm telling you, I don't know a David Howell.'

'You're lying!' I can't stop the accusation coming. The tears welling in my eyes have already broken over the lids.

'Listen, lady, all our employees are listed on our website. Take a look for yourself. And don't call here again unless you want a prescription filled.' No more words, and the line dies.

I slam down the phone, almost cracking it on the hard surface of the desk, and wipe the tears from my eyes. A sweep of the touchpad and the laptop is awake again, and I call up Bayside Inland Pharmacy's website from its Google listing. Three clicks in, and the 'Meet our Staff' page loads in front of me.

A listing of five names beams into my face.

And I suppose in that moment, I'm not actually surprised that David's isn't among them.

45

The third body was predictable. It didn't feel a shock now. There were no surprises in this move down the line. His features, too, were those of a man who would be found in this situation.

He looked, indeed, like the portrait all humanity carries of him. Fat, not pudgy, beer belly protruding over trousers belted far too tightly around his midriff. Balding, with a terrible comb-over, thin hair so greasy that even the struggle didn't displace it from his scalp. His shirt was plaid, or maybe a fake tartan, with edges in the darker tones of a garment that wasn't regularly washed.

In the symphony of life, what is really lost by the omission of a note such as this? Does the song really suffer?

46

Amber

The thought that torments me as I continue to stare at the pharmacy website's employee listing, David's name absent, is one I can't bring myself to vocalize, even mentally. My world is disintegrating, melting away, but I still can't say it.

I simply have to be on the wrong track. The scene in front of me, with all its apparently definitive dimensions – it can't be leading me to the actual conclusion. I *know* David after all. Know him more intimately, more thoroughly, than I've ever known anyone else. To think he's been lying about the most fundamental aspects of our lives . . . no. He's just not that convincing a liar, at the end of the day. He's too blundering and sweet to maintain a ruse for long. He's tried once or twice, for reasons of romantic surprise. It's never worked. I've always managed to find him out. Now this same man is suddenly a deceiver so masterful that he can hide entire dimensions of himself from me, and for years? It's nonsense.

But a panic has long since set in, and won't be rationalized away. David has lied to me about his best friend, who doesn't exist. He's lied to me about the pharmacy, where he's not actually employed and where no one has ever heard of him. What else has he been lying to me about?

Everything in me goes rigid. I can't stop the thought. It's taken on a power of its own, and my fingers are already moving. The phone is back in my hand, Chloe's contact is up on the screen, and my thumb is on the green button.

I hold the phone to my ear as I rise from my seat at the desk and start to pace the not-too-posh, not-too-scrappy hotel room that's been my campout for the past night. By now David's got be truly frantic over what's become of me, however guilty or innocent he may be.

Guilty or innocent.

A vision of my yellow duffel bag flashes back into mind, the blood-caked knife secreted away within. The way I'd walked up to it, so cavalier. My stomach tightens even further.

Chloe finally answers, and sounds of fumbling fingers draw my attention her way.

'Hallo, Ambs?' she asks, excited. It's a nickname almost as bad as Amby. 'That really you?' There is gum smacking between her teeth.

268

'It's me,' I answer, trying to keep the dread out of my voice. I'm impatient. I don't want a lengthy conversation. There is only one reason I'm phoning.

'Was beginning to think we were going to have to call in a missing person report on you,' she teases. 'What's this, day two of The Great Amber Absence?' She pronounces the words with emphasis, like the title of a Hollywood blockbuster.

'It's only the first full day.' Breathe in. Calm. 'Yesterday was just balking out after lunch, remember?'

'So does that mean you're not coming in today, either? Because I've got to tell you, I'm not sure how many more excuses I can make to Mitch about your—'

'Chloe,' I interrupt, my impatience past its threshold, 'please. I need to ask you something.'

A pause. 'Ok, hon. Ask away.'

I take a breath. There is no way to ask this but bluntly. 'Chloe, what's the name of my husband?'

Silence. Longer than the ten seconds I'd experienced with her a few days ago. A record-breaker. I think it might never end. All I can hear is my own pulse.

'Amber,' Chloe finally says, 'what's got into you lately? You must be more sick than you were letting on.' She sounds worried. Deeply, presciently, worried.

'I'm fine,' I snap back, too hastily to be believable. 'Just tell me my husband's name. Say it. You do know it, right?'

'Of course I know David!' she says, 'I've known him since—'

269

Her voice trails on, but I can't hear it. My relief is so powerful it deafens me. Someone, at least, actually knows David. He's really there. He's really my man.

I snap back to attention and cut Chloe off mid-sentence.

'What do you know about him?' Chloe goes silent at the question, so I persist. 'Concretely. What do you know about David?'

She stutters, but full words don't come.

'Is he really who he says he is, Chloe?' I finally give voice to the question that's been tearing away at my innards all morning. 'Tell me just that much. Is he really the man I know at all?'

There is only silence on the other end of the line. My question has driven Chloe mute. She either can't answer, or won't.

I don't care which.

I'm in motion again, ending the call and gathering up my laptop and the contents of my handbag from the bed, shoving them back into place.

I am horrified, and I'm a damned sight beyond confused. Yet in this moment I have a plan.

I am going to find out the truth.

Four steps later, I'm out my hotel room door.

47

Amber

The Assessor-Recorder's Office for San Francisco County is located in City Hall, smack in the middle of the city. Its website, examined from my car, lists options for phoned-in records searches, but only with a five-day waiting period after a query is made over the line. Fuck it if I'm waiting for that. In-person response time is listed as twenty minutes after payment, and that sounds good to me. There are other sites that say I can search records online for a fee, but I have neither the patience nor the trust that such 'public service' sites ever really provide what you're looking for. Besides, more time holed away with my laptop doesn't fit with the keep-moving-or-go-insane strategy I know is a necessity right now. A drive into central San Francisco seems like a good solution. Out, but nowhere near work or home. A densely packed metropolis where there's absolutely no likelihood of running into anyone I don't want to see.

I check out of my Calistoga hotel with a few signatures and the handing over of a few more folds of bills from my wallet. Is it wrong that I'm keen enough on staying hidden from David that I impulsively paid for my room in cash? Do I really think he's going to try tracking me through the credit card? Part of me suspects there's nothing positive about my character to be gleaned from the fact this seemed like such an obvious thing to do – that I so easily drifted into subterfuge. Or that I thought David aggressive enough to need such thoughtful deceiving.

It isn't 'aggressive' for a husband to want to know where his wife's gone, I scold myself, *or to use whatever means he's got to try to find her if she disappears*. I've never before felt so aware of how hair-thin the line is that stands between loving and obsessive.

I make the hour and forty-minute drive south along Highway 101 as far as the Golden Gate and the little post-bridge district of Cow Hollow, when I decide to switch to public transportation. Finding parking there isn't exactly a treat, but it's a damned site better than trying to find a free spot anywhere downtown. I eventually slide my car into a free space along the straight stretch of Lombard Street, then walk a few blocks to the nearest bus stop. A few dollars lighter and I'm on the 47 line, heading down Van Ness to my destination.

The journey is unremarkable, save for one fact that I

272

only become fully cognisant of there on the bus. A thought, or rather a realization, so foreign that it actually startles me.

I don't have a headache.

They're so customary, and they've been usual for so long, that I can't think of the last day I didn't feel one grabbing at the sides of my face. Every day, until today. And today seems like the most unlikely of days not to have a headache.

I chide myself. Feeling good, rather than poorly, shouldn't be upsetting me. I sense I'm as close to paranoid as a sane person can get, suspicious of the fact that, for once, I feel physically well in the middle of the day.

No, not well. That's the wrong way to put it. I'm not feeling my customary pain, but I can't help but feel that what's replaced it is far worse. In the place of that familiar agony, a deep hole, buried within me, is showing its shape. A forgetting, sucking pieces of myself into it, leaving only empty space behind.

Less than half an hour after entering the overcrowded bus, I exit through its central doors and make my way the last few yards along bustling Van Ness Street towards the looming edifice of San Francisco City Hall. It's an awe-inspiring building, built in Beaux-Arts style after its predecessor had been destroyed in the great 1906 earthquake, looking like a cross between a French palace and the US Capitol – though its gilded dome rises even taller than the glistening white version in Washington.

I'd been here once before, to go through the formalities of registering my marriage to David. I'd been overwhelmed by the building, and the moment.

The memory is no longer drenched in sweetness, but at least it confirms I've come to the right place. This time I'm here for what is going to be the worst discovery of my life. I desperately don't want to find it, but I'm as certain as I've ever been of anything that I will.

I locate the appropriate door and enter. It's a matter of minutes before I'm at the front desk of the Assessor-Recorder's Office, tucked into room 180 of the massive complex.

'I need to look up a marriage record,' I announce to the twenty-something clerk behind the counter. She's clearly trying to look older than her years, using a loosely knitted jumper and bunned-up hairstyle to effect a moderately maternal appearance. She's wearing make-up my mother would have approved of, if my mother had ever approved of anything, light and not too showy.

She nods at me. 'Good morning. I'll be happy to help you with that.' Her voice is as rehearsed as her gestures. 'Do you happen to have an index reference number for the record you want?'

I shake my head, stopping before the motion becomes too energetic. 'I don't, I'm afraid. I was hoping I could look it up through the family names.'

'Can do that for you, sure.' There is a bit of tapping on the young lady's keyboard. Finally, she peers up at me. 'Could I have the last names of both parties in the marriage?'

'Howell,' I answer. 'The husband's first name is David, and the wife's is Amber.' My voice trembles. *The Howells.*

'And the date the marriage was registered?'

'Just over two years ago, in this building, July the seventeenth.' The date comes off my lips automatically. I'd sat out on one of the granite benches in the corridor, back on that day, while David went into the office to take care of the paperwork. I was as happy as I'd ever been, dreaming of everything ahead of us.

More typing. The woman focuses on her screen. At last she looks back up, dropping her wrists to the surface of her desk. I grab a sheet of scratch paper from a pile on the counter and take hold of a plastic pen shackled to a metal chain.

It's my last gesture of hope that this could still go right. But, of course, it was never going to.

'I'm afraid there's no file in the registry for those names,' the clerk announces impassively.

The words thunder through me as fiercely as if she'd yelled them. Though for a moment my lips stay silent, my physical reaction is immediate. My skin goes cold and my pulse starts to become audible in my ears; yet I can't think of anything to say. *That isn't possible. Of course there's a record!* But then, *of course there's not a record. You knew he was lying. You just needed the proof!*

'I think . . . maybe . . .' I finally stutter, 'maybe you

275

typed the last name wrong.' I have to try every possibility. 'It's Howell, H-O-W-E-L-L.' I can't think of any variation on spellings for my own first name or David's, so I don't add them.

The clerk looks back to her screen, but her head is shaking even before her eyes come to a stop. 'That's the spelling I used,' she confirms. 'And the date was July seventeenth, correct?'

'Yes.'

'Sorry,' she says back. 'There's nothing here. You're absolutely sure of that date? It couldn't perhaps have been another?'

Of course I'm sure of the fucking date! I want to scream at this young woman, grab at the bun at the back of her head and swing her around by the hair until she starts talking sense. *Of course I know the date of my marriage. Don't tell me there isn't a file!*

'Maybe it's not in your electronic records?' I quietly ask, holding back tears and screams, grasping for solutions. 'Not everything's been digitized, right? Maybe you have it in a filing cabinet out back?'

'If a marriage has taken place in San Francisco County since we established this office in 1915, it's in these files, ma'am,' she answers. There's a glimmer of pride in her eyes. 'So unless you're searching for a record from somewhere else, I'm afraid this database is exhaustive.'

The marriage had taken place in the tree-covered Presidio, in a little chapel connected to the old Officers' Club that dated back to the site's life as a naval base, before being turned into a city conservation district. It's there in my mind, vivid and beautiful. A whitewashed wooden structure on a hillside, as Californian as it comes. A moment only for us, hidden away from the world in a quiet corner of a park tucked into the centre of a city.

Hidden away.

I glare back at the woman. A thought has just occurred to me. I don't know about government databases and registries, but I know enough about looking things up on the Internet to recognize that sometimes things just don't get cross-referenced in every file as they should.

'Can you look up records by birth certificate in that same system?'

The clerk lifts a brow slightly. This is more quizzing than she usually gets. 'Sure, it's possible. Give me just a second.' Typing, keystrokes coming out in rapid bursts. 'Okay, I'm ready. What name would you like to search?'

'Look up the husband,' I answer. 'Howell, David. Middle name Joseph.'

She nods. 'His date of birth?'

The detail comes to my lips automatically. 'November fourteenth, nineteen—'

But then my words stop in my throat. I'm unexpectedly mute.

I can't remember the year of David's birth.

The black hole in my mind is suddenly, spontaneously back, and it's grown into a cavern. What I am feeling is so far beyond fear, beyond panic, that I simply don't know how to react. It's one thing to be confronted with the fact that you're being lied to, but when you can't remember something yourself . . . when your own thoughts are leaving you, hiding from you . . .

The woman is peering at me, waiting, but I can't complete the year.

'Nineteen . . .' I stutter aloud again, hoping impulse will do the trick, but no clarity comes – muscle memory holding nothing over the stunning absence in my recall. I look to the clerk, imploring, but she's obviously in no position to help me.

Then, a memory that can. David is four years older than I am. By quick math that makes him forty-two. I quickly subtract from today's date and give the clerk the year.

'Do you happen to know his place of birth?'

'La Jolla, outside San Diego,' I answer. *California born and bred,* David has always said. That memory is still vivid.

'One day we'll visit La Jolla together, hon,' he whispers in my ear, a campfire crackling in front of our toes. *'There's a little cabin, tucked into a nice grove of trees that sits just above the beach, where we used to play as children. You'll love it. Like a postcard. Everything down there's so gorgeous. It'll make me happy to share it with you.'*

To date, we've never gone.

The clerk is typing again, but rather than focus on her actions I'm trying to squash the frog in my throat and force my pulse out of its sprint. Neither act of will is working.

Finally, she looks up.

'I'm sorry, ma'am, but I don't have a file for that name.'

Everything collapses. Inside, all around me. This was my last hope. I now know it's all been a lie. Our life. Our family. Everything.

'You don't have a record of his marriage, then,' I start, simply for emphasis.

'No, I'm sorry, ma'am, you misunderstand.'

I blink as she utters the words. My eyelids scrape their way back upwards.

'It's not that I don't have a marriage record for him,' she continues, 'I don't have any record for him at all.'

I can't react.

'No marriage licence, no divorces,' she continues. And then, 'No birth certificate, no register of death.' She looks into my uncomprehending eyes. 'We only keep in-state records, of course, so he's probably from out of state. But at least from the perspective of the state of California, and according to these files, David Joseph Howell doesn't exist at all.'

48

Amber

My throat has clenched up almost completely. I can barely breathe, and sight is becoming a challenge.

'Are you alright, ma'am?' the clerk asks after a moment. For the first time her tone is something other than automatic and professional, graced with the subtleties of genuine concern.

'I'm . . . I'm . . .' I have no idea how to answer. *According to these files, David Joseph Howell doesn't exist at all.* The statement is impossible. I cannot have heard it correctly.

Suddenly, I slam my palms down on the counter. 'Would you please do a search on the wife instead?'

'The wife? I've told you, we don't have any record for a Mr Howell, and so certainly nothing on any wife such a man may have—'

'Just search her!' I snap. My words are fiery and she

pulls back, so I try to gain control of myself. 'Search, please, for Amber Howell.'

'That's the name of the . . . wife?' The woman asks cautiously, her disbelief ripe and her nervousness around me mounting.

'Search it. Please, just search it.'

'I'd need her maiden name to pull up her birth certificate,' she replies, and though the rest of her thoughts go unspoken I can read them across her face. *Because she has no married name, at least not the name of a man who doesn't exist.*

'Of course,' I answer. 'Her maiden name is Amber—'

And that damned pit leaps up to my toes.

I'm more than shocked by my sudden silence. Beneath me, the great abyss that shouldn't be there. My insides are in revolt. The universe is becoming simply impossible.

I cannot remember my maiden name.

'It's Amber . . . Amber . . .' Whatever certainty I might have possessed fades with each repetition. 'I'm, oh God . . . just a second.'

My hand is in my bag. I'm too frantic to bring any order to my thoughts. *I'm Amber . . . I'm Amber . . .* On impulse I grab for my phone. *I'm Amber . . . Oh God, I need help . . .*

I try for Chloe's number in the recent calls screen, but in my state I can't make the listing display itself. I want to scream.

Frantically, I manage to open the contacts listing and scroll to the 'bookshop' group. My eyes are glassy, and the screen is hard to read, but the first name in the list is Mitch Tuttle's, and I hit dial without pausing. I press the phone to my ear so firmly it causes me pain, and it rings and rings.

Answer!

I'm rocking on my heels, an impulse away from hanging up and trying the next number on my list, when finally it connects.

'Mitch!' I blurt into the phone before he has the chance to say hello. There is an uncontrollable sob that comes with my words.

'Amber, is that actually you? Thank God.' His voice is as warm as always, but drenched in concern.

'Yes, yes, it's me.'

'We've been worried sick about you,' he says. 'Ever since you called this morning and hung up on Chloe. You've had us all rather . . . concerned.'

I don't have time to explain. My brain is on fire and I need to put out the blaze.

'Mitch, I need you to tell me my maiden name.' He is my employer. Maybe he'll remember it from my application.

Silence. Thunder inside me, but silence. The line is quiet. I know my request must sound absurd to my boss, but I can't help it.

My own name! How can you forget your own name?

'Mitch?' I finally blurt out, desperate, impatient. 'Are you there?' *Damn you!*

'I'm here, Amber.' He hesitates. 'Why would I know

your maiden name? My God, you must be in a really bad way. Worse than ever before.'

It's possibly the only thing Mitch Tuttle could have said in this moment to distract me from my distress.

'Than . . . ever before?' I try to wrap my head around the statement. 'What the hell's that supposed to mean?'

'I mean, you've had your moments in the past, Amber, but you've never had lapses like this.'

'Lapses? What the hell are you talking about? I've never had any lapses of anything!' *And for Christ sakes, what's my name?!*

'No, no, of course you wouldn't remember,' he adds, and it sounds suspiciously like he's being condescending. Talking down to me.

'Mitch, I don't know what the fuck you're on about,' I all but scream into the phone, 'but I'm asking you a simple question. What's my goddamned maiden name?'

The clerk in front of me has risen and taken a step backwards. However professional her personal styling may strive to make her, this scene is something her twenty-something years haven't prepared her to witness.

'I don't think I can . . .' Mitch's voice is halting. 'David told us we shouldn't talk about your background unless he was—'

'David told you!' I'm screaming now at full bore. The clerk is backing away, but I'm well beyond caring. 'What the hell has *David* been telling you?'

Mitch mumbles, like he's trying for an answer. 'I'm sorry, I shouldn't have said that. Oh, damn. It's just that he was in here this afternoon, looking for you, telling us things might have got bad, and . . .'

With a powerful impulse I realize I don't want to hear another word from him. Not from anyone, not any more. I've had enough of second-hand reports and bursts of impossible information.

I click the red button on the screen and throw the phone into my bag. I'm already moving towards the exit, even as sounds of 'Excuse me, miss, could we have a word?' emerge from the window behind me. It's a male voice, now. The clerk's supervisor has apparently been called in.

No, you cannot have a word, asshole.

I'm done with being circumspect. This has gone too far. I want to talk to David, face to face. I want the truth, and from his lips. Whatever it is.

It's time to confront the man who isn't there.

49

Amber

I have no memory of the bus ride back to Lombard, only a stop-and-start blur of colours and faces that weave a trail between City Hall and my car. My emotions are simply overpowering, a crowd so brash and noisy I hear nothing besides them.

I'm in my car now, and the familiarity of it calms me fractionally. The plastic dashboard, with its remnants of old tea in paper teacups in the holders, has something reassuring about it. I've pushed buttons on this dashboard before, and those buttons are all still here. They haven't morphed into something different, or told stories about doing one thing while secretly doing another – the air-con subversively turning on the windscreen wipers or the handbrake ejecting the wheels. *They all do what they're supposed to do.* I remember drinking the tea in all these cups. *I remember.*

Things are supposed to remain real even when you're not looking at them, just like this dash in this car. Reality is constant and predictable. Until today, I would have thought it was true of everything; but apparently it's one in a series of dimensions of real life that I've got disastrously wrong for years.

I point the car north towards Santa Rosa and Windsor, and thoughts of what's to come start to fill my mind.

David's face lights up in my vision. Every contour of his skin is bright and vivid. Three days ago my lips were wrapped around his earlobe and my hands wondering across the familiar terrain of his body. We were in love. We *are* in love. And in my mind I gaze into his eyes, peaceful and strong and . . .

And different. The whole image starts to turn cloudy and ominous. There is a different man in that body, a different face that houses those eyes.

I'm shuddering, and I try to shake it off.

I focus on the catalogue of things I need to lay out before David when I see him. There's an overwhelming amount, and some semblance of order is going to be the difference between a conversation that goes somewhere and one that doesn't.

I try not to permit it, but my mind impulsively walks through the scenario of a bad encounter. The worst. I walk into the kitchen at the end of this drive, finger wagging and accusatory.

'You killed her, didn't you?' I demand, storming through the doorway, though I never storm. 'The woman

286

in the river. You killed her, and the man! Just admit it!'
David is at the table with a beer in his hand. He tries
to answer without getting up, but I don't let him.

'And you've been lying to me since we met, haven't
you? About who you are? What, so you could concoct
some shield of a loving marriage to guard you from
suspicion for what you've really been up to?'

'How dare you!' David shouts back. His normally
tender voice is rock hard and he slams his bottle down
on the table. It rattles under the force, and in an instant
David is on his feet. He's got a knife in his hand, the
same knife that was in my duffel bag. It's still caked in
dried blood, and he points it in my direction.

'You just had to go nosing around, didn't you?' he
demands, spittle coming out his lips and falling onto his
chin. The words aren't really a question. He takes a step
towards me, the knife at chest height, his eyes a tired,
diseased red. 'Couldn't keep yourself to yourself. And
now, now you've brought me to this.'

And he lunges at me, the tarnished blade aimed at my
stomach as he extends his arm, and I feel a cold sensa-
tion bite through my blouse and . . .

'No!' I shout the word as I drive. It's not an exclama-
tion made from fright: it's a cry of sheer disbelief. The
scenario I've imagined is absurd. David isn't like that,
whatever else I may think of him. He doesn't use phrases
like 'nosing around' or 'keep yourself to yourself'. I'm
drawing images from films and poorly voiced radio plays,
not anything of realistic substance.

None of that is going to happen.

But I need to be measured. It won't do simply to barge through the door with a wagging finger and an accusation.

I could go directly to the police. This isn't the first moment that option has occurred to me. I still might. Eventually, I'll have to. But when I do, it has to be with more than just scents of carpet cleaner in my nostrils and memories of a dirty leash I can't produce. I'll need evidence, something hard and concrete. The curious blanks in the record of our life together will help, but won't be enough. *I'll need that knife.* And the police will ask questions, of course. What could I possibly say right now? I need answers as much as I need the weapon. A confrontation is the only way.

I sense my fears spiralling dangerously close to out of control, and try to combat them with logic. I won't rush at David. I'll stay near the door, near an exit, so I can turn and run if I need to.

Maybe I should have some kind of protection.

I've never held a gun before, and wouldn't have any idea how to get my hands on one if I wanted to. But there are other means of self-defence. Maybe it should be me who goes into the conversation wielding a knife. I don't have to hold it menacingly. Just have it in my handbag, easy to grab. I could gather it from the kitchen before I face David, just in case. As a backup.

For a moment I ponder the possibility of how a knife would feel in my hand, wielded as a weapon. I've held

288

all our knives a hundred times, but always as a utensil. Something to watch one's fingertips around. I can't imagine how I would wrap my fingers around a handle in reverse, or what it would be like to point a blade at another person.

I imagine it, and I can feel the knife in my grip. I suppose it wouldn't be wholly foreign. A handle is a handle, whichever way it's facing.

No, this is nonsense. I'm not wielding a knife at my husband. I'll stand in the doorway. I'll leave my keys in the ignition of the car and leave the driver's door unlocked. If I need to run, I'll be able to do it without faltering at the last step. That's sensible.

And I'll, I'll . . .

Fuck it, I finally scold myself. *Enough of this. You'll drive yourself mad before you have a chance to do anything at all.*

I realize I'm fumbling through the little indentation in the seat divider, home to the odds and bobs of my daily commute, and I grab hold of the Bluetooth earpiece for my phone. With a few button presses it's paired to my phone and I press it into my ear. I key in the voice recognition with an extended press on its sole button.

'Call David,' I command, and the order is confirmed with a verbal reply in my ear. A few seconds later, I hear the line ringing.

Let the chips fall where they will. I'm not shying out of this.

The line connects.

'Amber! Oh God, finally! I've been trying to—'

I don't let David say another word. For an instant my nerves collapse, and I wonder if I should change my plan, here and on the spot. Suggest to meet him in some open, public place – a shopping centre or a mall. But momentum is a powerful force, and despite it all, my fear melts away. I refuse to be made to feel afraid.

'I'm driving to the apartment,' I announce. My words are emotionless and hard. 'I'll be there in an hour. I expect to see you.'

And for the third time in my life, and the third time that day, I hang up the phone on another human being.

50

David

It doesn't take an utter genius to figure out you're being avoided. When a person doesn't want to be found, who normally wants nothing more than to be close to you, you sense it. Even before the circumstances make it obvious.

Amber has been hiding from me. She doesn't want me to know where she is or what she's doing. And she's trying to be sneaky about it all.

For a brief moment, there was the worry that something had happened to her. Given the fluctuation in the amount of drugs I'd been giving her, there was a chance she'd blacked out somewhere. Fallen, injured herself, maybe broken her phone. God forbid, she could have had a spell in the car. That thought ran through me too late. It may be necessary to concoct a reason for her not to drive any more. I couldn't bear to see her go that way.

I phoned the emergency services, twice, seeking any

accident reports for Highway 101 that involved the plates on her car. None had been called in; and the same was true when I searched the surrounding regions. That particular fear was assuaged.

But she didn't answer her phone, and I haven't stopped calling. Even when it was clear I wasn't getting through to her, and even once I'd figured out she was avoiding me intentionally.

Calling the bookshop was the natural next step. Not only do I need to play the doting husband, but I actually am one. One of her colleagues might have known where Amber had gone. The calls weren't only for show.

I called yesterday, and got stories. She was 'out meeting with suppliers'. She was 'ill'. I knew the second excuse wasn't true. The first sounded implausible. The whole point of her working there is that she doesn't have to do that sort of thing. She can stay in a comfortable place. Familiar.

I couldn't call the police, of course, despite the fact that something was very wrong. So I started my own search.

The next day I called the shop again, got the same stories again, just as inconsistently delivered. Amber had obviously spoken with her friends there, at least the woman. She'd made known she wasn't feeling well and would be out all day – that was it. I even went in and visited in person, but it didn't yield anything more.

They took my visit well. I'd introduced myself to them years ago, when everything with Amber began. The benefit of a small place, locally owned, not a big chain. She needed employment, and they were willing to help me in helping her get it – part of their community-minded ethos and the 'we're not big-business' attitude they tried to foster. Caring for those others didn't want to care about, even as they sold something that modern techno-centrism didn't seem to want. Might not be the best business model, but they were committed to it as a point of principle.

I knew the drugs would occasionally bring about mood shifts and different degrees of highs and lows, so it was useful to concoct a story with her colleagues to help fend off any suspicions. *Amber had a hard childhood, and went through a lot of trauma. Her past sometimes catches up with her, and if it does, it can cause real health concerns. But the doctors say there's nothing preventing her from working and leading a normal life, as long as we leave those things alone. So I'd be tremendously grateful if you might be willing, as her colleagues, not talk with her about her background. Not at all. She may seem inquisitive or gentle about it at first if you do, but it will torment her, and her meds can go off balance if that happens.* I'd even provided a few medical documents, forged of course, to back it all up. And they listened, and were agreeable. Said they were like a family in their little shop, and as I was a caring husband with a wife in pitiable mental straits, they seemed eager to help.

Why wouldn't they listen to me about such tender things?

But the stories she's told them, the stories they've told

me about her whereabouts now, they simply aren't true. Amber isn't ill. And she isn't simply 'out'.

What is a man supposed to do, in a situation like this?

Amber's never liked the 'Find My Friends' app on our phones, so the easiest way of pinning down her location isn't an option. But there are other ways to track a friend, or a wife.

She needs money, whatever she's doing. I've been checking the banking app on my phone zealously since I lost track of her. A credit card trail would have been immensely helpful, but Amber seems not to be using the card. A woman who swipes a card for everything, from topping up the gas tank to purchasing a 65-cent pack of chewing gum – *'It all goes for points, David. How are we going to get a free flight to the Caribbean if we don't collect the points?'* – has suddenly gone credit-card-silent for a day and a half. Only a single ATM withdrawal off the debit card, the maximum daily amount, the afternoon she left.

She's trying to stop me finding her. Clever thing.

And I know precisely why.

Amber's departure from home left little in the way of mystery. She'd already got too close to the truth when she found my briefcase, but we'd dealt with that. A little higher dose, and it all became a haze. Something to be explained away.

But when the knife made its appearance, there was really no turning back then.

I've been trying to control my anger over that. I originally had it tucked away in the drawer in my desk – somewhere I'd normally have thought she'd never venture. But then my nerves had mounted. She'd never *normally* have ventured into my study at all, and yet she'd done that. And stayed there, and broken into my briefcase. If she'd done all those things, then the feeble lock on my prefab desk didn't seem like it would stop her if she chose to go further – and the longer I dwelt on it, the more certain it seemed she actually would go back into the study, searching for more. From being a decent hiding place, it began to seem like the most at-risk spot for discovery of any I could choose.

So I'd opted for a place that seemed totally beyond the realm of possibility. The back of our closet is home to suitcases and baggage. Nothing to do with the present moment. No reason to dig around back there, burrowing through cases and duffels. A decent spot, until I had the time to get rid of things more permanently. The last place she'd look.

You would have thought.

Amber didn't find it at the close of the day, either, when drinking and dreams could be called on to blur away the experience. She found it in the middle of the afternoon, when the concentration of the drug in her system would have been at its weakest.

For a moment, this fact distracts me. Amber's been away a day and a half now. That's a day and a half off dosage, and this is the most worrying reality of all.

Without the drugs, things are going to go south. Radically, and more so with each hour that passes. I haven't been able to get to her physically, and I'm not sure I'm going to be able to get this back in control in time.

She has all the pieces, now. She even saw that t-shirt. Damn it, this woman has derailed my plans. Threw off everything I've been working for.

There's nothing left to do, in these circumstances, but face the consequences.

It's she, of course, who will have to face them. The limits I set have been reached, and breached, and responsibility for that reality rests with her.

God, it was my dream to keep her safe.

But not every dream really does come true. Sometimes blood is the price to pay for peace, and there is a kind of safety that comes only through death.

Suddenly, a buzzing in my pocket.

It takes a physical shake of my head to snap me out of my contemplation, but I focus on the buzzing and the ring, and slide my fingers beneath the layers of denim to retrieve my phone.

I smile.

Amber's face is on the screen. An old snapshot: her teeth wide in an enormous smile. The one that always flashes up when she calls.

Someone is coming out of her hiding.

* * *

296

The line connects as I pull the phone to my cheek. My mouth moves automatically. 'Amber! Oh God, finally. I've been trying to—'

But I can't get out another word. Her voice carves through mine. It isn't soft or sweet in its usual way.

'I'm driving to the apartment,' she announces. 'I'll be there in an hour. I expect to see you.'

I draw in a quick breath to reply, but I'm stopped by the sudden silence of a dead line. Amber has hung up on me. I've never known her to hang up on anyone.

But then, that voice didn't sound like Amber. It was emotionless. Hollow. And I've only ever heard her talk in tones like that once before.

It's the final sign. All that can be done now is orchestrate the end of this well.

51

The actual torture always took place in the basement den, never anywhere else in the house. Just that one room, purpose-crafted to their needs.

Bringing the constant string of girls there posed their most serious challenge, as the snooping eyes of neighbours would surely start to question it if there wasn't some legitimate explanation to be offered. It's why they'd purchased the house in that location, in Santa Cruz, where none of them could claim to be from. Close enough to get to easily, but not a place where they were known to the locals. So when Ross had signed the paperwork and agreed to be the one who would move into the house, they'd also agreed that the young girl they'd lured into helping them would be presented as his niece. 'My brother's little Miss Emma Sunshine,' he'd call her, with suitable familial emotion.

No one could be too surprised that a niece would

come to visit her beloved uncle, nor that she would bring her friends with her. It's what normal girls did.

So Ross would stay in the house, providing them all with the right facade, while the others would play the role of his buddies. Their comings and goings would hardly be noticed. They would be able to access the house when it was needed, coordinated with Emma bringing by one of her 'friends'. And then they could do what they wished.

Downstairs, they'd over-prepared for their first venture into the unknown. Ralph had ripped out the walls and insulated them with soundproof padding, before re-plastering and painting them exactly as they'd been before. The room was a vault for sound. They'd placed a television inside, rented a VHS of a slasher film and cranked it up to its maximum volume, then stood outside, only feet from the wall that rose above the den. Silence. They couldn't hear one fucking scream.

Then there had been refitting the door with something reinforced, with better locks.

And, of course, the bed. There needed to be a place for the action itself.

A bed proper didn't seem right. If ever anyone came by, unlikely as that possibility was, it would be better to have the room look like a den than a bedroom, so they'd opted for a pull-out sofa. Not as comfortable as a proper mattress, of course; but then, they never intended this room to be a place of comfort.

Then the grooming began. The hardest part had already been accomplished: finding their little recruiter. Emma Fairfax was a loner of a kid: no friends, unhappy home life. As Gerald had monitored her from the street across from her school, she had mingled only occasionally with others, obviously not one of the 'in crowd,' mostly drawn to other outcasts, which was perfect for their purposes. She was also obviously poor. Other students burst from the school doors into recess and drew out Walkmans and CD players; Emma had nothing. Even her clothes looked second-hand and tired.

Positively perfect.

Gerald had taken his time with the approach to Emma. None of them had done this before, and so they exercised an abundance of caution. He'd watched her long enough to know that after school she often went and sat in a local park, watching other kids play and fiddled with her schoolbooks. That seemed the most plausible way in. So, a few weeks later, on the bench next to Emma Fairfax on a semi-sunny day, sat a middle-aged man in a comfortable sweater, an undersized dog on a rope leash.

She'd immediately loved the dog. Asked if she could pet him. Took delight in his slobbery tongue.

Two days later, when Gerald was back at the same spot, she asked if she could throw his ball.

The following week, he confessed that his nephew was too old to play with the dog any more, and if she ever *wanted to come by, he only lived a few streets away, and she could play to her heart's content.*

She'd been at the house the next afternoon.

Emma had eventually agreed to play the role they wanted for her, once sufficient 'preparations' had taken place. Grooming, by another name. They didn't let her know what it was all about, of course, though they all suspected she probably had some idea. But a careful balance of bribes and suitably menacing threats, following weeks of increasing familiarity and conditioning, was all it took to convince her to come on board, and to be quiet about doing so. The girl with nothing could have her Walkman and her CDs, and new shoes and adult friends and whatever else they would dangle in front of her. Only she could speak to no one, and if she did – if she ever did – not only would the gifts stop, but they'd blame everything on her. Say she stole it all. Say she was a pervert kid who was doing her own thing in the house – sick, depraved stuff that she'd be shunned for forever – and blaming them out of spite.

The threats they'd give the girls themselves would be far severer. Severe enough that if Emma ever cracked, not one of them would risk supporting her story. Gerald and Ralph had taken some convincing, but Ross had known from the outset that this would mean the need for a touch of violence, some pain, inflicted on each of them the first time they were brought in. Nothing too dramatic, but enough to give their threats credence. It couldn't just be all about their own gratification and fun. They had to ensure they wouldn't get caught. That the girls wouldn't talk.

It was elaborate, thought through, and thoroughly planned out.

They were all on board.

And most importantly, it all worked.

It had been a Thursday afternoon the first time all the gears went into motion. Emma came by shortly after school had ended. She had a 'friend' in tow, and brought her to the kitchen door, as she'd been instructed. She entered with her, to make the experience feel normal. Said she'd meet her downstairs in a second. Ralph, who'd been waiting at the door, offered to show her the way to the TV room.

Emma never joined her downstairs, of course. As the other girl had stepped into the den, Ralph had closed the door swiftly behind her, and the click of the bolt lock was audible.

Two other men were inside. The sofa was folded out into a bed, covered in red sheets.

Gerald was already half undressed. Ross, standing nearest the girl, swung a backhand that landed in her chest, knocking the wind out of her as she collapsed backwards onto the bed.

Gerald was already at her feet. 'Listen, kid,' was all he said, 'if you want to live through this, then for the next twenty minutes you don't make a fucking sound.'

52

The last man's body was slenderer than the other two, barely a bulkier frame than the woman who had started it all. A cancer deep in his bowels had emaciated his flesh, and any signs of happiness had long since departed from his features. Ports for the chemotherapy protruded from his wrist and his side, and the sense of hopelessness was written across him.

But the cancer was not to be allowed to kill him. He had stolen life from the innocent, so his would be stolen from him.

It was the only way.

He died with his eyes open, as if seeking to stare into the heavens, despite the captive space. A final human desire in an inhuman man.

Fingers pushed down his lids. He was to be denied even this.

Peace was not to be this man's end. He was simply to be stopped. And he was.

And the world sang out more beautifully than it ever had before.

53

Amber

The front entrance to our apartment building has never looked as ominous as it does this afternoon. Windsor, our peaceful little town, home to an uninspired edifice that on this particular day fills me with immeasurable apprehension. I stand before it, dreading every brick.

But I'm here, and I'm not stopping now.

I get out of my car and depress the button on my key fob on impulse. The locks close with a chirp, almost as quickly as I remember that this isn't the plan of action I'd decided upon. *Keep an easy, open route away.* It's always in the last steps that a fleeing housewife is caught out in films. She makes it out of the bedroom, down two flights of stairs and through a maze of furniture, only to find the latch on the glass patio doors is locked and she's condemned to face the reflection of her killer in the black glass, just as the axe falls and . . .

Christ sakes.

The paranoia is powerful. But I do want to keep the doors unlocked, and I chirp the fob again. Then, with nothing left to prevent me doing so, I walk.

Within a few seconds I reach the low wall surrounding the front garden. My nose is tickled by its familiar scents. It's an odd thing, to have gardenias fill up your nostrils on your way to what can only be sorrow and grief.

I slide my key into the front entrance, which opens onto the common landing for all the apartments in the building. The hairs on my neck are already at alert. I could admit that I'm afraid, if it wouldn't sap the resolve from me right at the moment when I need it the most. So I don't. There is no fear. Only purpose.

I climb the single flight of stairs to our door and swap keys. Before I insert it into the lock, I decide to test the knob. It's possible David is already here, waiting inside – but the knob holds fast. I experience a swell of relief. I want to stage our meeting the way I think it should go, not have it dictated by his presence.

Of course, he could just have locked the door behind him. The hairs rise again and more anxiety finds its way into my throat. But I'm not stopping.

I shove the key into the lock and turn. I'm not so deadened by my fear as to miss the fact that the world sways as I do. A palpable motion. The edges of my vision aren't clear, either. Sounds come into my ears in magnified form – from the interior mechanics of the lock, which clank like metal hammers, to the scrape of wood against wood as I push the door from its frame. Then wood on carpet, clawing its way slowly along the floor.

I push cautiously. I've often wished I were the kind of person who bursts through doors, energetic and unafraid; but that's never been me. For a moment, though, I have a memory of flinging open a door. Was it this one? Was it yesterday? Did it happen at all? It's a hazy memory, linked to a situation I can no longer recall.

Today I push more timidly than usual. For once, I'm genuinely unsure what I want to see on the other side. Do I want David to be there, worried and concerned? Do I want him to be condescending, infuriated, ready to be challenged?

Do I ever really want to see him again at all?

I feel the pit in my stomach opening up.

I'm only saved as the haze clears and reveals an empty kitchen. *Empty.* I smack a hand against the light switch, and a few flickers later the hospital-like glow of the fluorescent tubes confirms the vision. He isn't here.

My release of breath is so strong it casts an echo off the refrigerator. Sadie catches it from one of the upper floors and I immediately hear the familiar trample of her short legs bounding down the staircase. She rounds the corner and comes at full pace up to my ankles, burying a wet nose in my legs.

Her old leash isn't hanging on the wall. There's a new one there, shiny and never been used.

A vivid, red condemnation.

I so want to reach down and pet her, to do something

so down and out normal as to greet my dog in a mess of orange fur and hugs. *Like every day.* But my stomach is a rock.

'David!' I shout. The word emerges bestially, but there's no response. No sound but Sadie's enthusiastic pleading.

I'm up the steps that lead from the kitchen to our bedroom faster than I've ever ascended them before, Sadie at my heels and certain this is some new game with play and treats at its conclusion.

I want the evidence in hand when David arrives. Too much of my past few days has been the stuff of suspicion and extrapolation. I want concrete reality between my fingers as he tries to deny what I've discovered.

The closet opens with its familiar creak and I have all my hanging clothes shoved out of the way in a single movement. The customary piles of sweaters and other odds and ends are stacked behind, including, in its usual place, my yellow duffel bag. Right where I remember it being.

I rip it from the pile, flinging it onto our bed. For a moment reality wobbles around me. It's hard to separate this moment from my earlier discovery here – from that moment when the bag first yielded the knife and the truth that David had hidden it away from me. The memory and my present seem to overlap, like the blurred lines of an old-fashioned 3D movie's red and blue layers.

I blink a few times, willing the distortions away. My bag is on the neatly made bed, singular and in the present tense. All that's left from the memories is the awful knowledge of what's inside. The one concrete thing that proves what David really is.

I wrap my trembling fingers around the zip and pull.

Tears immediately fill my eyes. I realize I'm not surprised. I'm devastated, but I'm not surprised.

I see no knife. No towels. No blood.

There is nothing in the bag.

David's been cleaning up after himself again. I recognize the antiseptic smell of the same cleaner from before, beneath the desk. It wafts up from my open bag in condemnation.

The tears well more deeply. All hope of David's innocence is now completely gone. My honest man is nothing of the kind. All my dreams are a myth and the love I've known in my heart has been nothing more than the crafted fakery of a man I should never have trusted in the first place. He's been lying to me, and my skin is a pepper of fire and suspicion – a feeling I recognize, in this moment, that I've had before, though 'before' has become such a fog of deceit that I can't pinpoint when.

Eventually, for lack of any reason to remain in the bedroom, I descend the stairs, leaving Sadie locked behind me. Somehow I don't want her to have to witness what's to come. My little ageing ball of innocence – let her go on loving David. I don't think there's any way that I can.

I move more slowly now, a different resolve beginning to fill me as I take the last of the stairs. *I am not the plaything for a liar's games.* Not some memento for a killer to keep on his mantle, stalking victims along a river or through a house by day, then coming home to organic veggie stir fry and a skin-tingling embrace by night.

I'm nobody's toy, and I'm sure as hell not going to be anybody's victim.

I'll confront David, but I'm done living at his mercy. He'll hear what I have to say, and he'll answer. I'll demand it of him. What comes now will go according to my plans, not his.

Back in the kitchen, I select the right position to meet him. I want David away from the door as quickly as I can get him to move. There's only this one way in and out of our apartment, apart from the window fire escapes, and I want a direct line of access kept open. I find a spot at an angle across the table. It will keep distance between us, and a barrier, and the angle should prompt him to move, to come a little closer to face me, away from the entrance.

And screw it, I'm not sitting here without some means to defend myself. I waffled on the question through my drive, but in this instant the decision seems too straightforward to permit deliberation.

David's taken the knife from the bag. God knows what he intends to do with it.

I'm not a victim.

I walk over to the counter next to the sink, our little Krups coffeemaker standing in its usual spot, and slide open a drawer beneath it. I'm not sure which is the right size kitchen knife to use as a weapon. In movies it's usually some great big thing, but I have a feeling that a big knife would be hard to wield. I opt for a smaller one and practise inverting my grip in a way that seems like it would be useful in self-defence. I can't believe I'm going through these motions. This is Carrie shit. This isn't me.

But I am not a victim. I make my grip tight. It doesn't feel entirely unnatural, after all.

Then, in the silence of my preparations, I hear footsteps. They're not canine movements from a dog who's escaped her enclosure. They're heavy, a man's steps on wooden stairs, and they're leading up to our landing. They slow as they approach.

I'm certain it's him, and that means there is no more time for preparations. The knife in my hand will have to do. I sit myself at the table, tucking it under my thigh so I can have both hands free, and I lay them on the tabletop.

In the oddest sensation of the day, I realize that I am calm. For all that it has fluttered and halted before, my breath in this moment is even. My shoulders don't feel like rocks. My vision is clear and open.

A key slides into the lock, the knob begins to turn. David is here for me.

And I'm ready.

54

Amber

The look on David's face is not what I expect. Our kitchen door opens, my husband enters, and I expect to see a visage transformed by the exposure of his true self. I've found him out. This is when Dr Jekyll becomes Mr Hyde, when evil is unleashed and the killer is revealed.

But David's features aren't angry, or fearsome, or fearful. They are surprisingly difficult to read. He looks concerned – a loving husband overcome with anxiety for his wife. It's the same beautiful face I met on the cliffs by the sea. The stubble at his chin catches in the ceiling lights. But there is something colder there, too. Something in the wrinkles at his eyes that speaks of a different, darker emotion than tenderness.

He speaks before I can.

'Amber, I'm glad you're here. You've had me absolutely panicked.' He doesn't look panicked, and the word feels disingenuous; but the emotion in his voice is real, like it wells up from deep inside him.

Hard to fake, but not impossible.

He's about to speak again, and my chest clenches with a sudden jolt. *No*, an interior voice shouts, *don't let him take control of this moment. Don't let him start with the lies.*

I hold up a hand. 'Don't, David. Don't say anything else. I don't want to hear any more stories.'

He doesn't react. There's no attempt to sputter out a kindly 'What are you talking about, hon?' or 'Don't talk nonsense.' David knows exactly what I mean, and he stands motionless. His solidity is disturbing. He holds his bearing like a rock, and I feel smaller and smaller before it.

My questions tumble in my head.

'Emma Fairfax.' Her name simply shoots out of me. Not a plan, just the way things start. With it my mind suddenly goes clear, vacated by the desire to see how David will react.

He appears to freeze solid. He's already been still, but now . . . it's just like a few nights ago. Motionless as ice.

'You remember her name,' I add, given an odd strength by the sight. 'I said it to you before. You went quiet then, too.' He can't deny it, and so he says nothing, though with flexing cheeks and hands that are balling into fists at his sides.

'Who is she, David? Who is Emma Fairfax? I mean, to you.'

His stoicism evaporates. For an instant he looks squeamish, wiggling on his feet. I can see the workings of the Dr Seuss-like machinery in his head that fabricates fantasies and lies. His eyes still look dark.

'I'm not really . . . I don't kno—'

'Before you say you don't know,' I cut him off, disgusted already, 'let's get something straight, David. I saw what was in your briefcase. Let's neither of us pretend I didn't. Sadie's leash, wet and muddy.' The slight shift of his eyes gives away his guilt. 'The same type of rope all the reports say was used to kill that woman. In a river. In the mud. And now there's a new replacement hanging on the wall. So don't go saying you don't know her. I'm just not going to buy it. Be honest, for the first time in your life, and tell me. Who was she?'

I'm trying to keep my voice under control, but I can't help the volume rising.

He's thinking about his answer, concocting some story, before he finally looks straight at me. His stare is startlingly hard.

'I can't tell you.'

'Can't!' My disgusted snort isn't forced. I push down the urge to reach out and slap him. 'Let me guess, David, it's "confidential," like the fabricated insurance paperwork you supposedly bring home to work on.'

I don't expect he'll answer, but I have plenty of words left to throw his way.

'It's not going to fly this time, David. Such a petty lie, but it turns out you're chock full of them. In fact, let's

314

just be totally clear, why don't we? You never bring home paperwork in that briefcase, at least not legitimately and definitely not from the pharmacy in San Francisco. Because you don't work there at all, do you?'

You heartless liar.

He tries to move closer, but I gesture again for him not to close the gap. *The table*, my hand commands. *You can sit there if you want.* He hesitates, the muscles in his shoulders flexing, but then steps towards the chair opposite me. Another foot away from the door. He's almost out of a direct line between me and the exit, but not quite.

He doesn't sit.

'Amber, you don't know what you're saying,' he says. His voice is uncomfortably firm. 'Things aren't what you think.'

'Isn't that the truth!' I shout back. There are tears and sobs that want to get out with the words, but I won't allow them. Not yet. I have to stay in control of this one situation, if nothing else. 'There's a damned good reason I'm not crystal clear on all the details of things. You've been lying to me since . . . since when, David?' I don't even give him the chance to reply before I add, 'Turns out, I can't say it's since we were married, can I?'

For another instant, David appears thrown off balance. His expression morphs in quick succession like a kaleidoscope. Sorrow into worry, worry into fear. Then panic.

Panic. That's fucking good. He's trying to look menacing, I can almost feel it, but I've scared him. He didn't know I'd discovered this little secret. He's still not sure how much I really know.

'I can't say you've been lying since the day we were wed, can I?' I continue, encouraged by the effect my prodding is having on him, 'because, if I've come to understand my position correctly, we're not married at all, are we, David?' I fire all my anger into the glare I project at his scowling face.

With it, David's emotions, whatever they might actually be, puncture him. The tension in his shoulders collapses. His scowl evaporates. His head falls towards his chest.

'That's right,' I persist, 'turns out your lovelorn non-wife can actually figure out a thing or two when the situation warrants it. Never thought I'd have to look into my own life this way, or our life together, but then, I never thought you'd turn out to be – whatever it is you actually are, either. It's all there in black and white, though, once I went to look for it. Or more accurately, it wasn't. No records, David. No birth certificates, tax records, nothing. So much for your story of being Californian born and raised! I have no idea who you are or where you actually come from, but one thing I know for sure: Mr David Howell, who dotes on his "wife" like the very best of the best of men, has never been married in his entire fucking life!' I lean forward, my hands balling atop the table. 'You heartless, unloving bastard. How could you do this to me? How could you make me fall in love with you, all based on a lie!?'

David's eyes are glassy. I think my accusations have broken him, and for an instant he looks weak. But though his downcast face won't directly meet mine, I can see him drawing deep breaths, and with each his features grow harder. Sorrow is becoming resolve. I don't want that to happen.

'I'm not sure how you pulled it off,' I quickly add. 'The wedding service in the Presidio. The vows. It sure as hell felt real to me, David. It was supposed to have meant something! But then, so much that's felt real has proven itself a mirage over the past days. Don't even know if it's an actual memory, or one I've dreamed up, or something you've fed into my head.' It's becoming harder to hold back my emotions. I can see the twin bouquets of flowers on the wooden altar table, smell the Bay air floating in through the chapel windows with hints of sea and salt. But then, we've been there a dozen times. Seen those windows and smelled that air a dozen times. Maybe this isn't a memory, but a story woven out of nothing, a testimony to suggestibility.

'Amber, you've got this wrong.' David's words are barely more than a whisper emerging through clenched teeth. 'Things aren't what they seem to you. I love you, I always have.' He still isn't looking at me.

'Love me? *Love me!*' All my rage erupts. 'The way you loved Emma Fairfax?'

His eyes shoot up to mine. The fierceness that had been brewing there is momentarily displaced.

'Love . . . Emma?'

'Don't think I'm so simple I can't string two and two together, David. What was she, another non-wife on the side? You have an apartment with her somewhere else? A mirrored mockery of the life we've lived together?'

He doesn't shake his head. He barely moves, but his eyes grow wider.

'What fabulous string of lies have you dreamed up to define yourself in that little world?' I keep on going. 'Pharmacist is probably too dull to use twice. Are you a businessman this time around? Maybe a banker? Come on David, what's the story you spun for her?' *You unmitigated, heartless ass.*

The taunts broaden the concern on David's face. He stares at me – not so much as if he doesn't understand, but as if he's trying to decide what to do with my words.

His own are surprisingly steady when they finally come.

'Amber, I was never in love with Emma.'

'I don't fucking buy it, David!' I simply won't be stopped. 'You don't keep another woman in your life secret without some pretty powerful emotions driving it. Until what . . . did that love dry up? All the emotion finally run its course, leaving you groping for what to do?'

'Amber, you need to be quiet now. It's time for you to listen to—'

'Is that why you killed her?' I finally lay the question out between us in its plain, stark contours. David's face whitens, and his features become even more unreadable.

Deny that, you bastard. Deny it to my face.

'What justified doing that, David? To kill the woman? Couldn't keep your emotional high at a strong enough level with me? Had the need for some passion I couldn't provide?' My accusations flow so fast I can barely make my lips accommodate them. 'Or maybe all these lies, these ruses, were just getting to be too much to maintain? Christ, you and I have been together for over two years!'

David's face grows harder and harder.

'Amber, I've told you I didn't kill—'

I bang my wrists on the table. I'm simply not prepared to listen to him mock me with denials. With one of its legs shorter than the others, the action sends the whole table rattling, the noise reverberating in the suddenly claustrophobic space.

'What about the man, David?'

My non-husband's Mediterranean skin loses its colour entirely. I laugh, almost maniacal, yet satisfied to have caught him off guard once again with more knowledge than he apparently thought I had.

'Ah, so you didn't know I knew about the second body? Stabbed in the entrance to his house, that one. And you know full well that I found the knife upstairs. You can't just empty out the bag and wipe it down, and pretend that erases what I saw!' I force myself to draw in a long breath. The fire inside is threatening to consume me. 'For God's sake, David, the girl wasn't enough? Who was he? Someone who found out about your affairs?

Your lies? Didn't want some big mouth setting your make-believe little world a tumble?'

David has dropped his head again, and I want to read the motion as a defeated slouch. He reaches out to the chair to stabilize himself, but his shoulders are growing tighter, his chest broader. He seems to be gaining in size, right before my eyes, and I can't help but feel a jolt of fear at the sight. I'm making the gravest accusations I can think of – they should evoke despair, protest. Anything other than calm.

His eyes rest at the surface of the table in front of him. His breathing has slowed.

'You can't even bear to look at me, can you?' But I can hear my own fierceness falter. Still, I can't stop. 'I don't even know if that's the extent of it,' I add. 'Haven't been following the news so much over the past day – enough of my own shit to come to grips with. Maybe there have been others.'

David lifts his head. His eyes silence me. Their hazel irises appear eerily dark, almost black. His jaw is like iron. His nostrils are flared, and he draws long, almost supernaturally slow breaths. I can see all the muscles in his arms flex and turn to rocks.

In this instant, I am as terrified as I have ever been in my life.

'Oh, my God,' I whisper, feeling myself push back in my seat, trying to increase the space between us. I'm certain the room has grown colder. 'There are others. Besides Emma and that man.'

I'm shaking my head, willing him to deny it, *wanting* him to deny it; but the ice in the air has me certain he won't.

His lips part in a strange snarl before sounds follow. His eyes are cold and dead.

'Two,' he finally says, emotionlessly, and his mouth hangs open.

Just like that. An admission in a single word. The end of any hope of innocence.

'Oh, David, my God, I can't—'

'Two men,' he adds, his body ramrod straight, but I can hear the wood of the chair squeak under the intensity of his grip on its back. 'After the first. Three altogether. All of them with a knife.'

Even though I'm seated, I feel I might topple over. The man I've loved is not just a liar. He is a killer to a degree I could never have dreamed. And he announces his acts so calmly, as if they were simple, ordinary facts.

Suddenly, in a heartbeat, all my dread and outrage turn to fear. Reality has been laid bare, and what had captivated me as a mystery now horrifies me as a certainty. The man – I won't call him my husband – standing across the table kills and lies and kills and kills again. He's gripping at the chair with hands that have gutted the life out of four people. He's just admitted it. And his eyes are black and resolute, staring into me with a fierceness that, I suddenly realize, cannot be that different from the resolve his victims would have seen as he cut them down and . . .

Terror spikes inside me. Every cell of my body is overtaken with the need to get as far away from this man as I can.

With all the self-control I can manage, I lower my right hand down to my thigh and wrap it around the hilt of the knife.

'David,' I say, with a forced quiet to my words that takes every ounce of my interior control, 'I don't know who you really are, or why you've done the things you have. But whatever role you've been playing with me, it's over.'

He shakes his head slowly, refusing my pronouncement. The movement is measured, almost practised. 'No, Amber. That is not how things are going to go from here.'

Dread numbs my skin.

'I am going to get up,' I somehow manage to insist, 'and I'm going to walk out the door behind you, David, and you're not going to move as I do. The charade of a life we've had together ends right now.'

Once more, there is a strange instant of cascading emotion that flickers across his eyes. Behind the resolve is a glint of despair, then grief, then some other emotion I can't pinpoint. But their presence is like flash paper, bright for an instant but just as quickly gone. When the flash is over, the blackness in his stare is even darker than before. His whole body is resolute and he stands taller, removing his hands from the chair back and balling them at his sides.

'Amber, I am not going to let you do that.' He moves himself towards the door, blocking my path of escape. 'You are not going to leave this room.' His eyes never leave mine.

But I'm on my feet, and the knife is in front of me, its small blade sparkling in the white light. It's aimed at what would be David's heart, if I still believed he had one.

'Just try to fucking stop me.'

55

Amber

David's eyes are perfect orbs of surprise. Everything about him over the past minutes has been a threat: his words, his stance. There's been a dragon uncoiling within him. Bastard thought he was going to control this moment like he's controlled everything else – but he wasn't expecting this. Wasn't counting on his darling, pliable toy of a woman standing before him with a weapon. Even through the fear that eats away at my bones, I feel a sense of pride in that. With all the wool David's pulled over my eyes through the years, in this moment it's me who's managed to surprise him.

I wave the knife as menacingly as I can, and on instinct he spreads his hands. I wish for a moment I'd gone for a larger blade after all, but even this smaller one is having the right effect. It feels comfortable, solid.

For the first time since all this began, I feel in control.

'Amber, you don't know what you're doing.' David's hands are in front of him now, open-palmed. His voice has dropped in pitch but is still disturbingly solid. 'You need to put that down. This isn't the way to deal with your emotions.'

'An ironic statement, coming from you!' I answer back, real muscle in my voice. 'I'm leaving, David. There's nothing you can do to change that.'

'You're upset, Amber. You have every right to be.' He takes a slow, unnervingly calm, breath. For an instant he looks angry, as if he resents this whole conversation. *Bastard.*

'But you cannot leave, not yet,' he continues. 'You need to know the truth before you walk out of this room.'

'The truth? From you?' I manage a laugh that edges back towards maniacal. 'You've been weaving a fake world around me for as long as I've known you. I don't even know who you really are, David. And you, of all people, want to tell me the *truth*?'

He is stoic. 'Amber, I don't want to hurt you.'

I focus my eyes into his like lasers. 'Is that a threat, David? I have a knife pointed at you, you heartless bastard, and you threaten me?' I tighten my clutch around the wooden handle. 'I never took you for an idiot.'

I won't hesitate. Not now. I won't let him stop me.

'It's not a threat, Amber. You still don't understand.'

'You keep saying that!' I stomp a foot, my rage demanding a physical outlet. 'I don't "understand" why you lied, I don't "understand" why you killed. You're right, David, I don't understand at all. I don't understand how I've been so gullible, how you've made me believe the things I've *believed* over these years.' I stress believed, as it's the word that encapsulates my sense of utter betrayal.

'I really loved you.' The words are out of my mouth without my controlling them. 'I loved you from when we first met. From that day on . . . that day when you . . . when we . . .'

But the words don't come. It happens again, right here, and now, of all moments. That black space charges into my head and eats my words. The thoughts that should power them, the memories – they simply aren't there.

Oh, God. I can feel my skin going cold again. The pit gapes at my toes, an indefinable space in my mind black and incomprehensibly blank. My fear instantly transforms. In this moment, it's not the murderer in front of me that scares me the most, it's the void invading me from inside.

I met David in the springtime. I demand that my thoughts comply, that they behave reasonably. *We were . . . oh help me, I don't remember where we were. It was outside . . .*

'It's okay, Amber.' David's voice is suddenly consoling. Less fierce, less ice. 'Your memory isn't able to cope with all this. There are going to be holes.'

'What the fuck do you know about what's going on

326

in my head!' I shout at him. God, I'm enraged, but I'm also completely terrified. Because this instant is horrible, and yet it shouldn't be horrible *like this*. There shouldn't be holes.

I met David in the springtime . . .

I can still feel all the emotion of our first encounter, all the tingling of anticipation. There was salt in the air. The skies were vividly blue. I see them, I taste them. But I can't remember where it was. Or when. I can only hear the gulls, and I think there were walking sticks. The retractable kind, that look like ski poles but . . .

I can't remember any more. The pit in my consciousness has swallowed one of my most precious memories, right as I stand here, with a knife in my hand.

'Amber, I know more about you than you think,' David says. He hasn't moved from his position in front of the door. 'I know enough to be certain that you can't be let out of here. Not in the condition you're in, now that you've discovered what you have.' His hands, again, are constrained fists at his sides. 'You will stay here with me, and I'll help you understand. I'll tell you everything you need to know.'

I don't believe a word coming out of his mouth.

'It's only ever been lies between you and me, David.' I jab the knife towards him. The blackness in my head hasn't made me forget all he's done. 'That's all it will ever be, and I've had enough of it.'

'No, Amber.' He loosens the fists at his sides, but looks no less intimidating. His body seems to have swollen in size again. 'The lies are done. You haven't left me with any other choice.'

'Me!' I can't believe he would try to pass his guilt on to me. It's too much.

'Get out of my way, David.'

He doesn't budge.

'I'm sorry, Amber. I didn't want it to be like this. I can't protect you any more. It's time we bring this to an end.'

And he's in motion. He plants one foot in front of the other – and it might just be my perception, but the earth seems to shake as his foot hits the ground. My panic explodes inside me.

'Stop!' I shout at full voice. I hold the knife sturdily, leaning forward. I'm fully prepared to do what I have to. *I won't be a victim.* 'Don't move another muscle, David.'

'It's enough, Amber. I can't let this go on any longer.'

He takes another step. Adrenalin courses through my system. I have the strength of a dozen women.

'I said don't move!' And the adrenalin does more than simply charge me up. It floods into my eyes, and my vision starts to go blurry, white biting away at its edges. The world wobbles beneath me, but I cling to the knife with all my strength. I still have the wherewithal to be able to aim it at him, plunge it into his chest, if that's what it takes – and it seems that that's what it will take. Once, twice, into that heartless flesh, again and again and . . .

And there is a voice, blasting its way into the back of my head, singing out of the earth in a voice I don't quite recognize, but in tones so familiar I think I could sing along.

He's lyyyyyyyying . . .

The words eat at me, and then the voice disappears. In the silence it leaves behind, David is a step closer. He's almost in front of me.

I'm out of options. There's only one thing left for me to do.

'I warned you!' I wail. 'I told you not to move!' I raise my arm, and the knife shines in his eyes. It shouldn't have to end like this, but I'm not going to give in.

'I'm not letting you stop me, David.' I wipe away my tears with my free hand. 'Or don't you think I'm strong enough? Strong enough to kill?'

I expect to see only fear in his face: terror at a woman transformed, the murderer suddenly facing someone prepared to kill him instead. *It's right! It's what has to be! It's the only way!*

But David's eyes are filled with as many tears as mine, his features contorted in the purest sorrow I've ever seen.

'No, Amber,' he answers softly, 'I know you can kill.' He takes a slow breath.

'It's just that when you do, you don't do it with that knife.'

56

Amber

I heard once that the future is a deep valley into which we all gaze. That we peer in, and we look at the mass of what's to come – only to find that it's mingled, there in that valley, with what is now and what's already been. So our vision blurs, because it cannot take in so deep a sight, and we simply stand mystified before it.

I wonder, in this moment, as my world falls apart around me in the electric light of my kitchen, whether the same is true of the past. Or the present. Whether the haze that covers life is ever really lifted, or if we ever genuinely grasp the reality through which we're drawn.

'I know you can kill. It's just that when you do, you don't do it with that knife.'

David's words are just fog, dulling reality. They're not even really words, not any more. They're only sounds.

A moment ago I was filled with more rage and fire

than I'd ever known in my life. I was ploughing forward with accusations and suspicions, all of which had become certainties. And then . . .

The amorphous sounds coming from David continue. I'm stuck in place, no longer pushing towards the door. I can't feel my feet. With a single sentence, David has broken me. All the fire inside my chest has turned to shock.

It's an odd thing, to stand numb and silent, and watch the world turn to mist.

David's voice at last cuts through the clouds.

'I'm so sorry, Amber. It was you, you who started this. You, at the beginning. It was you.'

A voice that sounds like mine answers from somewhere down by my lips. 'Me?' It's wobbly, just like everything else has suddenly become, but it's familiar.

'The woman in the water, Amber. Emma Fairfax.'

'No, that woman . . . it was you.' An echo of my former certainty returns. I know the truth. I've learned who the man before me really is.

David shakes his head slowly. In my sight, ripples curl away from the movement, as if space itself is warping at his gesture.

'No, my love,' he says, even softer than before. 'It was you, but it's okay. It's all okay.'

I see him reach forward. There's a knife in my hands but I can't make my muscles move. *Odd, a moment ago, I think I was ready to swing it at him.*

David gently opens my fingers and draws the knife

away. I think he sets it on the counter. God, the Formica countertops in this place are a sin. It must have been a colour-blind designer who thought a sensible balance for egg-yolk yellow is lime green.

David softly takes my shoulders and sits me down in one of the chairs at the table. I think I was sitting there before. I remember there was a blade beneath my thigh and my hands were flat on the tabletop. David goes to the counter and draws a large glass of water from the tap. Back at the table, he slides another chair up to face me and sits, close, almost knee to knee.

'David,' I manage to say, my voice frailer than I would like. 'Don't lie to me anymore. I'm tired.' I think I mean to say 'I'm tired of it,' but my sentence ends where it ends.

For the time being he doesn't speak. He draws a little bottle out of his pocket, and with an eyedropper counts off a few drops of a clear liquid into the water glass, then stirs it with his finger.

'This will make you feel better,' he says, passing me the glass. 'Try to drink it all. Your system needs as much as it can get.'

He seems wise, right now. There's a knowing, sensible tone to his voice. *Didn't I want to kill him a moment ago? Wasn't he trying to kill me?* But my reactions have gone as numb as my limbs.

I drink the water – big, full gulps, down to the last swallow – and David sighs. It looks like relief.

A wind blows through the fog of the valley. For an

instant it parts and a glorious vision takes its place. The sky is bright. There is a strong, salty breeze blowing up from the cliffs, the sea crashing against a rocky shoreline far below. Birds squeak from the hillsides and a few soar in the air. 'We met in the Headlands,' I find I'm muttering, the comment out of place but all that I want to say, 'up above Muir Beach . . .' The memory I couldn't find before – there it is. Beautiful. Comforting. There is sea salt in my nostrils.

'I tried to do everything I could for you,' David says as the breeze passes. 'But you're wrong.'

The fog comes rolling back in.

'Wrong?'

The tears are back in David's eyes.

'We didn't meet by the sea.'

PART SIX

NEW LIVES

57

David

My original plan had been so much simpler. Of course, it hadn't actually been a plan. It was just an impulse. From Emma Fairfax, I'd learned about the abuse that Amber Jackson had suffered, and the grizzly details of how it was accomplished. The rough location. The environment. The men involved. Enough that I could have sorted out who they were – and that had been my first impulse. Find them. Punish them. Bring them to justice. Purge the evil from the world.

It had only been reflection on just what that purging would leave behind that had swayed me to a different path. Sure, they men might be locked away, ripped from society; but Amber would still be in it, still hollow, still scarred. Maybe even more than she was there in the treatment room. If she was forced to go through a trial, the forgetting her mind had so struggled to effect would be ripped from her entirely. She'd have to face it all. Vivid accounts. Testimony. The past, taking on new life.

She would go on suffering. It would never end.

But there was another way.

Amber's past was already fading away. Maybe that could be helped. Manipulated. Made into the emergence of a new life, free of the terror that had marked out the old one.

To restart a life. With a little bit of pondering, it became the most obvious thing in the world. The right path. The only path.

Amber Jackson's world was collapsing. She'd made it as far as she had through repression and forgetting, but those walls were breaking down. She was becoming an amnesiac, periodically catatonic, and increasingly emotionally fragile. Dr Marcello had identified it all, and had said it was only going to get worse.

Hard to save that.

Impossible, in fact. That was precisely the point. It was impossible to save *that woman*. Everyone that had tried – all the doctors, the counsellors, the medics – they'd all failed. Because they'd been after the wrong thing.

To save this woman, she would have to become someone new. Someone without her past. Without any past. Because as I knew too well, all that pain that she carried – it can't be repressed, and it can't be dealt with. It needs to be wiped away.

Forgetting. The thing I'd always aimed for in my

memories of Evelyn. I hadn't been able to accomplish it in myself, but with Amber perhaps I could.

The doctors certainly wouldn't go that route. I'd been working around them long enough to know that what I had in mind wouldn't exactly fit within their paradigms of proper conduct. But I knew the meds. I was absolutely certain it could be done.

The right drugs, the right dosage. Her past could be wiped clean. She could be set free.

But, I knew, that could only be the beginning. Erasing the past wouldn't be enough. She would have to be given a new life. A better life. Happiness. Joy.

And I felt a calling, a true *calling*, for the first time in my life.

Her life could start anew, and so could mine.

58

David

Of course, I had to concoct a way to meet Amber Jackson in person, if the plan was going to work. I certainly couldn't meet her there in the ward. There could be no memories of what she'd known before, including her time at the hospital, or meeting me in those surroundings. If a new reality was to be created, there could be no traces left of the past at all.

What followed the meeting would be easier. Drugs, correctly administered, could wipe the slate of her mind blank and keep it that way. Her episodic states of forgetting could become permanent, which is what she needed more than anything. It would take a cocktail of medications that her doctors would never prescribe; but as long as I could get my hands on them, I knew what she would need. Not just enough to muffle the voices in Amber's head, but enough to reboot a life that had been ripped from her before she'd had the chance to grab hold of it.

Thank God, I'd only encountered her the once, in the facility, and I'd stayed out of her line of sight – though she'd been in such a state that there was little chance she'd have any memory of seeing me, even if she had.

That lack of direct contact gave me some freedom. I followed her, not worried about being recognized, after her release came. Hard to imagine she was ever released at all, given the profound likelihood that her condition would recur; but the state hospital system can't keep people in treatment forever for conditions that come and go. She was retained in-house until she returned to functional, given a few maintenance medications, then sent back out until things inevitably got bad again. A system with a few flaws, to say the least.

This time, though, it worked entirely in my favour. Amber Jackson was discharged, and I was free to take hold of her life thereafter. She was mine.

I had all her details as she departed, gleaned from her files at the hospital. Home, workplace, phone numbers, email address, everything that was in her records. I'd snapped it all onto my camera one afternoon, and had her file back *in situ* within thirty minutes. Later I'd printed them out at home and read through those pages carefully, over and over again, committing them to memory. I combined the knowledge with the information Emma had revealed. The portrait of this woman began to expand and take life in my mind.

Then, after getting to know Amber Jackson on paper, the time came to get to know her in the flesh.

I'm sure some people will think me obsessive for the way I followed her in the weeks after she left, but saving a person requires work. It has to be an obsession, it just has to. So I followed her as regularly as I could, learning her habits and her behaviours. She didn't have a regular job, living instead off funds transferred into a bank account each month for disability assistance. An outpatient observation service from the State Health Department was as close to family as she had, and apparently it had been they that had ensured she had an apartment, and a degree of monitoring – which could hardly be called sufficient —meant to ensure she was getting on day-to-day. Though I only saw them once, represented by a woman who was clearly at the end of her tether, carrying a clipboard with files on at least thirty outpatients she was meant to check in on that day alone. Her visit to Amber lasted fewer than ten minutes.

State care, summed up perfectly.

Yet somehow Amber managed to function. She'd been given a volunteer post at the public library, which meant she could check in to 'work' when she felt up for it, and she seemed content when she was there. Despite her condition, she was functional enough to do what was required of her. Such volunteer posts were offered as a community service in any case – for the elderly who wanted something constructive to do, or for individuals with conditions that might require low-intensity surround-ings – and so deliberately involved a light and lightly-enforced route: re-shelving books returned by patrons, tidying and cleaning the reading areas, and being permitted, when requested, to sit and read. What obvi-ously drove her enjoyment the most were the quiet times when she could sit at the rack of newspapers the library kept in stock, devouring them like food. She soaked in the news. When the papers were exhausted, she browsed the Internet. It seemed to make her happy, or maybe not happy, but at least content. Happiness was too much to expect.

But the pattern of her days was useful. Seeing what she enjoyed, what calmed her. A plan of action began to take shape in my head.

In all the weeks I followed her, I didn't see Amber make contact with a single person that might be called a friend. A few people in the library knew her, obviously, but their relationships were professional and distant, and in most cases unspoken. Amber Jackson was a loner. For my purposes, it was ideal.

After a couple of weeks I approached a teenager in a local café – the obvious neo-Goth hacker type with a laptop perpetually bound to his fingertips – and paid him off to hack into Amber's email. The address from her medical files pointed to an obvious public mail system, and if I weren't so eager for it to work I would have been disturbed by how quickly the young man was able to break through her password. He muttered something about how stupid people were with their privacy, and glared at me to make it clear that I was no exception; but he took the cash I offered him anyway, and disappeared back into his own world.

Once I was in to her account, I could track Amber's thoughts as well as her movements. She received a few emails each week from predictable sources: a bit of spam, a few subscription notices, sale announcements from Macy's – but her social life was as non-existent online as in the real world. She corresponded with no one. No one, that is, but herself. Amber used her email account more as a journal than a communications tool, and the vast majority of the messages in her inbox were addressed to herself. Little notes, thoughts, plans. Nothing deep, nothing overly revealing.

Except that she wrote about her love of the coast. Of the Marin Headlands in particular. Then, one day, she began to plan for an outing. A weekend walking trip north of San Francisco. First there were just brief mentions in her journal entries, little notes toying with the idea; but then came more concrete preparations – lists of paths through the Headlands, restaurants, hotels. Her dream started to take the shape of an actual plan.

And I knew I had my way in.

The details formed quickly in my mind. The coast would be our starting point, hers and mine. She would be alone, away, in a situation she loved. The perfect locale for creating a fairytale encounter to begin it all.

Let her old life end and her new life begin in a setting that brought her peace.

I took note of all her preparations: dates of travel, her online booking reference for the old-world-style accommodation she finally settled upon: the Pelican Inn, just off Muir Beach. Her shopping list. And I shopped, myself. I'd never been one for hiking or for the Headlands themselves, but an afternoon out with the credit card had me geared up with the right sort of shoes, a puffed red jacket that I was assured was 'just the sort of thing hikers like,' though it felt a size too small for me; gloves, even a suitable shade of sunglasses. A day's shopping and I looked like such outings were a part of my blood.

On the day she was set to depart, I did too. Not just from my little home, but from everything. If her life was to start over, then mine was going to have to change radically as well. I'd already listed my apartment and found a suitable couple's home north of San Francisco, in a town called Windsor, outside of Santa Rosa – far from my past in LA County and Amber's on the northern shores of Monterey Bay. I'd handed in my notice at the state hospital the same week I'd applied for a change of name. If you're going to go, go all the way. A new name was just the extra step that seemed necessary to ensure there weren't accidental overlaps with my past, or Amber's, once we were together. I wasn't ready to give up David – mostly out of fear that I'd forget, or slip up, and that would get her curiosity peaked. So I kept the first name I've always had, and just changed the remainder. My surname was linked to my parents, anyway, and there was certainly no romantic attachment there. So David Penske became David Joseph Howell. Joseph because I'd once had a friend of that name; and Howell because . . . well, I just liked the sound of it.

The Howells. A sweet sound, ready for a sweet life.

I managed to land an assistant's position at one of the dozens of CVS Pharmacy branches in the Bay Area, which took a little doing. God knows I was qualified, but all my records were under my old name. Nothing, though, that a little forgery and document manipulation couldn't alter – and that was part of the rationale of aiming low: an entry-level role at a massive chain. Background checks were not going to be as intense as they might be elsewhere. As long as the credentials looked right, the paper was thick and the seals convincing – all of which, I ensured, they were.

I couldn't let Amber know where I worked, of course. My new job was another layer of buffering, but I didn't want her provoked with any opportunity to draw out memories from the past. That one encounter in the ward was distant, but seeing me in a white lab coat, clipboard in hand . . . there was always the chance that memories could push through. But I also couldn't play too multi-faceted a false life forever. So I settled on the idea of simply giving her a different pharmacy name for my employment. Something in the Sunset District of SF proper. Not like she'd ever have need to check. I could be honest about my work, without running the chance she'd stop by one day and see me *in situ*.

Then came finding a job for Amber herself. Something she'd be able to do once our new life began. Recognizing how much she'd enjoyed browsing newspapers and searching the Internet at her volunteer role in the library, and having made a few incognito trips inside to learn from the head librarian there that, despite everything, she was capable at the minor tasks put before her, I decided to build off that. A little local bookshop in Santa Rosa, not far from Windsor, had a 'Help Wanted' sign in the window, and the ethos seemed a perfect fit. Quiet, low-stress, surrounded by books and papers. Of course, the place had to be prepped. We'd be married by the time she applied, so I found the owner, a pudgy, friendly little man called Mitch, and simply lay a scenario out before him. My poor wife, who had gone through childhood trauma that had left her severely mentally disturbed, but who was now being treated and was able to work in society, wanted some little role in the workplace. She couldn't hold down a normal job, of course; she needed something quieter, permitting her to withdraw into herself now and then. Her emotional state, I insisted with great personal sentiment, was as fragile as a butterfly. She could be sent back into her traumatized state by even slight mentions of her background, her past; yet she was making a new start, and all her doctors agreed she was perfectly capable of the kind of work the bookshop might offer, as long as they were willing to let her be a little . . . different, and keep her in the present, not the past.

I'd had the doctors' notes to prove all this, of course. I'd already had to step into the realm of forgery for myself. It wasn't hard to carry it further.

The man called Mitch had listened to the story with real compassion on his face. My poor, sweet wife, whom her doting new husband was trying to provide for as best he could – she was someone he said he felt his little shop could help. He was more than willing: he was eager to offer her a hand. His staff, he assured me, were like a family, and they would all be ready to agree never to ask her about her past, never to question her emotional state. To let her have her space when and if she needed it. She would be their special case, and they would all feel noble and enlightened for taking her on.

So everything was organized. All was in hand.

It was time to start over.

The afternoon our new life began will be etched in my mind forever. Amber was hiking north, and from a distance I could see she was making good speed. A woman who did this often, who was accustomed to walking at a firm clip. She had walking sticks in her hands, the retractible kind that look like ski poles and which I've never been able to figure out the purpose of. She seemed more interested in the walk itself than in the scenery or wildlife along the path.

I opted to walk near a group of three others who were out together. Looked like a men's weekend, off away from the wives, and though I wasn't part of their ensemble, by walking just a few paces in front of them I figured I could easily be mistaken for a group member. It struck me this might be less intimidating than an encounter with a lone man out on his own.

I watched her approach as we moved – that face, that beauty, that haunting emptiness, all drawing towards me; until, at last, the distance between us was just a few paces.

By a stroke of luck, it was at a narrow section of the path.

'Excuse us,' I said with careful, casual politeness. The wind was blowing, so I added volume to my words.

She offered the edges of a smile and started to step to the side. This was the moment: the opportunity for a gracious, kiddish flirtation to set things in motion.

I watched her feet, and when I was sure which direction she was stepping, I matched it. An instant later our heads collided (knowing it was coming, I made sure it wasn't too severely), and the motion of our bodies meant that they followed: chests and arms into the action, grasping hands at each other to keep from falling.

That's how it all began. The perfect life. Salvation.

'Oh hell, I'm so sorry,' I muttered. I reached out to stabilize her, my script engaged. 'That was entirely my fault.'

As was only predictable, she politely claimed the fault

was hers, rubbing the soreness from her head. And then she looked up and our eyes met. They locked.

God, her eyes are mesmerizing. Like twin pools of the sea . . .

I let that moment linger, not too long, then looked away with rehearsed embarrassment. She apologized, and I assured her there was no need.

'These surroundings . . . they can take you in.' I smiled at her, and I could see in that instant that my plan had worked. She was caught. Her eyes clung to mine; there was something magnetic in her energy.

'I'm David,' I offered. With an extended hand she answered. 'Amber. It's lovely to meet you.'

I didn't leave that encounter before Amber had shared the name of her lodgings with me – the little English-styled pub and inn up the way, whose address I knew full well from the research I'd done beforehand. She'd invited me, though – an important step. She was hesitant, unfamiliar with talking to people in this way. But I had practised being as right a fit for her emotional condition as I could manage, and humour seemed to play exceptionally well. We laughed, took in the scenery, and eventually she found the will to suggest I might want to 'bump into her' again.

It might have been a casual comment or merely a joke, but it was all the summons I needed.

I went the same evening. I could have waited another, even two. She was planning to be in the area for an extended weekend, and the option to let the expectation grow was entirely reasonable. But I didn't know how long her boldness might last, and I didn't want to wait. So I walked to the little Pelican Inn, pushed open its squat wooden door, and took Amber up on her offer.

We sat by a fire near the bar for a few hours, she on the red wine and me nursing a series of beers, talking through the delightful catalogue of nothings that two people peruse on a first evening together. A few hours in and I knew her favourite kind of music and which type of pasta sauce she preferred, and she knew I liked dogs more than cats and never missed an episode of *Top Gear*, despite the fact that I have otherwise no interest in cars. By the time closing rolled around it was conveniently too late for me to make my way elsewhere, and though Amber seemed entirely unsure of how the conversation should go from there, or what the right moves were to make, it was clear she didn't want me to leave. It took her multiple attempts and a flurry of roundabout sidestepping, but eventually she invited me to her room.

I wanted everything, just then. All of her, the whole moment. But I couldn't bring myself to do more than sit beside her on the bed, continuing our conversation. Listening to her laugh. Feeling the yawns grow until we were lying side-by-side, staring at the ceiling together, talking of beautiful trivialities in softer and slower voices until she gently fell asleep.

In that moment, lying there beside her, I felt the purest

contentment I'd known in years. Maybe ever. My plan, my hope, was coming true.

The final step was the only one left. I had to make this bliss permanent.

I rose from the bed, moving as softly as I could, and went to my coat. In the pocket was a small plastic box in which I'd prepared the syringe. The needle was so thin the chances of it waking her were slight, but I was still set to be tender. I'd already prepped the drug. All the doses would have to be large, but the first one especially so. I'd calculated it against her body weight, her age, and the effects I needed it to have.

Amber's lips were slightly parted as I knelt down beside her, her breath gently flowing between them. I leaned forward and kissed them softly, a buzz surging through my flesh at the first contact of our skin against skin. I slid the needle tenderly into her shoulder, keeping my eyes on her closed eyelids. I could almost visualize the last clouds of her past being eaten away by the medicine. Her old world, with all its torments, evaporating at last.

From that moment, there would be a new reality for a new woman. Amber Jackson, the girl who had suffered at the hands of abusers in her neighbourhood, who'd been coaxed by a wretched, pretend-friend to a torture no child should have to undergo, and who had been mentally destroyed by the act – that woman was gone. When morning came, out of this bed would rise Amber Howell, a woman with a good life . . . that's what I would give her. A new home. Maybe a pet. A life without the memories of pain.

The drugs would have to come every day, forever. That was a cost, but it was manageable. There would be ways to get it into her system. I'd have the rest of our lives to ensure it was done well, without her ever knowing.

Who knows, perhaps I'd find she liked smoothies.

59

David

Now she sits opposite me, as broken as I've ever known her. All the pain I wanted to take away is back. The hollowness has gutted her again, and I'm not sure I can handle seeing her in this torment.

I'm angry, too. Furious that the hope of redemption has been stolen away from me, and from her. It had been such a noble idea. A truly worthy project. Yet it had come to nought. I had been correct at the beginning, in those first impulses after our meeting. The people who had done this needed to be punished, because, as I now know with certainty, they had done something irreversible. I couldn't save Amber. They had made that impossible.

Now, the woman I love is a shell again, echoing what I've had to tell her.

'I killed that girl.' Amber repeats, but her face is

impassive. She is overwhelmed by the information she's being forced to absorb. There don't seem to be any emotions left. 'That's not possible. I don't even know her.'

'No, you don't,' I answer. The tenderness in my voice is entirely unforced. 'But the woman you were before, she does.'

'I'm Amber Howell.' She wags her head. 'I've always been Amber Howell.'

I clutch her hands more tightly.

'The woman in the water – you knew her when she was just a girl, when you were too.'

'The woman in the water.' Amber says the words robotically.

I can't bring myself to say more, and I don't know what I expect her reaction to be. Tears? A sob of memory, of all the vile pain she's undergone? Anger?

Instead, Amber pulls her face into a smile. It's compassionate, as if I'm the one who needs to be consoled.

'Oh David, you don't need to lie to me any more. This story, it isn't necessary. Reality is enough. You, that girl . . . just let it be.'

She holds out a hand and wipes a tear away from my cheek, and I know she will never understand.

60

Emma Fairfax

THREE DAYS AGO

I'm not sure how I convinced myself to stay away this long. I've done so much evil in my life. I thought I was done with it. There in the hospital, two-and-a-half years ago, I was ready to make amends, or at least come to grips with things. Told everything to that doctor. Confessed. Opened up about the girls, and what those assholes did to them.

What I helped do to them.

That's still hard to accept. I don't know how I've lived with it all this long. And I don't fucking get why the docs in the ward chose to let me. Just to walk away, after all I told 'em. Hell if that ain't as criminal as what I did.

No, it isn't. Shit. But it still wasn't right.

But, fuck. I don't have to let someone else torture a person I already screwed over.

I knew something was wrong with that second doc at the hospital. Not the main one, but the meds guy who was always with him. The way he looked at me, the way he talked to me when his boss wasn't in the room. Creepy. No other word for it. Way too fucking intense, and too many damned questions.

Then, to take everything I told him, and just keep it to himself? No, something definitely wrong with that.

I couldn't just sit on it.

I tried. God, they let me go, and I wasn't going to slap back at that. Wasn't sure I'd ever see the outside of a mental hospital or prison again during those days; but when they let me walk, hell, I was going to take freedom.

Guilt follows you around, though. I guess I've known that most of my life, but it's taken the whole of life to sink in.

I wasn't ready to be a part of more evil.

So I started to explore. Two years after I was out, I got to work. Got the name of the doc who'd handled the meds and I started a little . . . I guess on TV they'd call it an investigation. My little spy game. And what's a girl supposed to think when you discover a man's left his job and changed his name? Does he not know there are records of such things, if someone's really looking?

Is there a *good* reason for a person to do something like that?

It's how I knew he was up to no good. From there, I

had to track him down. Took some doing, but I found the CVS Pharmacy in San Francisco where he works, and snuck in one day to have a peak. 'David Howell' was there, white lab coat just like in the hospital. Living a new life. Fucker.

I didn't let him see me, but that was all the proof I needed that something was wrong. So I kept up my search. Found out he lived in Windsor, up past Santa Rosa, and was . . . married.

Can't really describe how it made me feel to learn that piece of information. Because I knew, I just *knew*, right from the first second, that the woman, the 'wife', was going to be Amber Jackson. The look on his face when I'd talked about her, it was . . . obsessive. Possessive. And then he vanishes from his job, his name, and reappears up north with a new wife?

Amber Jackson was being abused again. I could feel it in my bones. And I'd led her to him. Fuck! Just like when we were kids, only this time I hadn't known what I was doing.

She's haunted me my whole life, that bitch. But then I've gone and sent her into hell another time.

So there was really only one thing to do. I had to go to Windsor, find Amber, and tell her what was happening. Tell her who her 'husband' really is. And set her free. One good, decent, act to maybe redeem some corner of my life.

And so I'm here. Sun's nearing the middle of the sky, nice and warm after a night spent alongside the river, just out of town, for lack of any better option. Stars ain't a bad roof if the weather's okay, I gotta admit. I've been here almost a week, watching Amber's movements, getting a sense of the patterns of her days. I want to approach her when David isn't there, when I can talk to her openly about everything, without his influence. I think I've got their routine worked out.

So I spend one last night of calm under the stars before I meet with her. Because it has to be today. No more delaying. I've learned all I'm gonna learn. Gotta act before I lose my resolve.

Then maybe, maybe, I can bring some good to the woman I ruined all those years ago.

61

Amber

Every morning, my eyes look back from our bathroom mirror and they taunt me. They seem to know they do, and they sit so prominently on my face purely as a way to rub it in.

I'm ignoring them today. I'm ignoring them because I'm not one to get obsessed with the what-ifs of how life could have been if my parents had matched me up – had given me a name to pair with the blue between my lids, or had passed along genes that gave me the amber I so wish matched my name. I'm not that sort of lady. Life gives you what it gives you, and you learn to love the story that's been placed in your hands.

I'm out the door at a little past one thirty, having spent the whole morning lolling about the apartment, playing a bit with Sadie in the back garden and then pottering about the place in the way one does. Even made myself brunch, consumed almost at lunchtime. We've been given a day off from the bookshop on account of the air filtration system in the building, which county health and safety has demanded the store upgrade before we're let back in among the volumes, and I'm determined to make the most of the day. There are trails and paths on the outskirts of Windsor that I've only rarely walked. Some I've never even set foot on. David and I have lived a stone's throw from the deep inland curves of Russian River for years, and I've yet to stroll its banks. Seems irresponsible, if nothing else. And I don't know if David's ever taken Sadie there either, and that seems almost sinful. Dogs and nature are pure-bred partners. So today's the day to explore, for both of us.

The sun is out, the sky a bright afternoon blue dotted with cotton-white clouds. A more or less perfect day. It only takes fifteen minutes to abscond from the town proper, walking east on River Road into the hedgerows that lead to the water, and by the time I reach the river the boughs of greens and browns are playing delightfully with sunlight and shadow. The breeze is gentle and warm, and the shade occasionally cool.

The water of Russian River is green, flowing slowly. At times it is wide, and I know it only gets wider and deeper as it flows towards the coast; but I prefer its narrower stretches, where a good throw could skip a rock from one side to the other. I stop for a moment along one of these stretches, stand at the water's edge and watch the little flurries of life there. The growth of algae, insects slogging along its gelatinous surface. Birds wandering through the reeds looking for breakfast. A frog, eyeing the whole scene with seeming disinterest. In the background, somewhere out of sight, the sweet song of water thrushes, texturing the air.

I should come here more often. I live next to an entire universe that only reveals itself to a slow stroll and a sympathetic eye. To a world racing by at breakneck pace it's like Clark Kent with his glasses on – a mystery masked so gently, yet so fully.

I follow the path further away from town, along the river's edge. It might not be a mighty ocean, no, but any water soothes me. I think of the sea, with its great waves and tides. The lakes further north, tucked like little jewels into the texture of the earth; and here, this gentle flow, ebbing and flowing like life itself.

The tree cover grows thicker as I walk, the path less well tended and more given to the potted texture of nature. It's obviously been used before, though it's starting to feel like it's not a maintained footpath. Just a route people like to follow. There are footprints in damp soil – fresh, most of them – and there's a sound, too, up ahead. Not nature's voice, but man's.

Or rather, a woman's.

She is singing gently to herself, whoever she is, the way I sometimes do when I walk alone. Half a known tune, half improvisation, notes spontaneously matched to whatever words might fit them. I'm already smiling. We don't normally witness these little intimacies in other people. The moment someone enters our line of sight, we tend to go silent.

A few steps later I round a bend, and the woman with the singsong voice becomes visible. She's a few yards off, her back to me, and there's no sign she's sensed my approach. Her singing continues, uninterrupted.

I'm in a good mood, and it seems only polite to let her know I'm here. I don't want to startle the woman, much less embarrass her. So I draw Sadie closer to myself and let out a noticeable cough, an 'accidental' clearing of my throat, and the woman stops her singing. She turns, a shadow hiding her face from view. And then the breeze blows, and I can see her.

EMMA

Oh Christ, she's not supposed to be here. She's not supposed to be the one who finds me, it's meant to be the other way around! I walk into her neighbourhood. I approach her apartment. I ring the bell. That's the plan. Fuck, that's the goddamned plan! I've worked it out, got my remarks all lined up in my head.

She doesn't take walks along the river. She doesn't walk the dog. That's her 'husband's' job.

This isn't how this goes!

I'm frozen. I cannot move. I have no pulse, no breath. Everything in me vanishes, and all in an instant.

As the woman turns and faces me, something happens inside my heart. I'll never be able to explain it, but the whole world ceases to connect to me. It carries on existing, it doesn't just evaporate – I can see the water, and the woman, still moving. But I'm no longer here, and no longer me. Another woman is standing at the shoreline, gazing at this stranger.

'You!' The word comes out of the throat attached to the body I'm in, first as a whisper, but then as a roar. 'YOU!' My vision has gone a glaring, phosphorescent white, and she's the only thing in it.

The woman somehow recognizes the me I've become, a stranger even I can't identify. Her face contorts in what looks like horror.

'What the fuck are you doin' out here!' she shouts, but it isn't really a question. She's shocked, not confused. 'I didn't want you to see me yet. Not like this. You never take walks out here! I've been watching!'

Something is familiar as she speaks. I've never heard her voice before, but this other woman, this new woman inside me, has.

Long ago.

A forgotten span of years.

Pain rips through this body.

'Who the fuck are you?' I shout. I find myself adding

'Bitch!' even without knowing why. I hate this woman I've never seen before. *I hate her*. The very sight of her sets my bones on fire.

'Don't ask me that. Oh God, you don't remember at all, do you? Look what he's done to you! No, don't even look at me.' Her words are panicked now and she's moving about as if she wishes she could simply vanish. She has a pack of cigarettes set out on a tree stump and she quickly sweeps it up, shoving it into her pocket and trying to leave. But I'm standing in the only exit from this particular cul-de-sac off the path. Sadie is tense at my ankles, and lets out a sharp bark that bites through the air.

'I'm . . . I'm so goddamned sorry about before,' she stutters as she moves. 'I know I don't have no fucking right to be here, but I . . . I can't let him do this to you. You don't know who he is. There are secrets he's keeping from you. From everyone. I mean, oh Christ, I don't even know what he's done to you. Maybe he's like . . . like them. Fuck!' She's frantic, like she's trying to remember words from a script she's been shocked into forgetting. She keeps trying to push past me, but I stand firm. 'I didn't do what they did, you know, back then!' she continues. 'Those fuckers. You do know it, I know you do! You can't have forgot that. I was just their bait, for Christ sakes!' She seems to want me to understand her. 'I wasn't like Gerald or Ross, or that bastard Ralph. I never laid a finger on you! And I just had to make sure, to see for myself, that he wasn't doing the same thing to you. Help you get outta here.'

She goes on, struggling, but her words hold no meaning for me. She's just a babbling woman by the babbling water. Yet my hatred is exploding within me.

Sadie barks again, fully aware of the tension hovering over her. She pulls to break free.

'I tracked you down to this little – fuck, I don't know whether it's a town or a suburb, or what.' The woman speaks breathlessly, urgently. 'Had to figure out how to approach you. How to avoid *him*, because he just ain't what you think he is.' She looks like she might cry. Her face is turning a deep red.

But my muscles convulse. Everything is going hot around me, like the trees have burst into flames. The new woman in my belly grabs my voice and screams out into the universe by the river.

'Bitch! You had no *right*! You have no idea how you hurt me! What you *did* to me!'

And the words seem sensible to me, as if I know what they mean.

The woman is frantic. She's embarrassed. She's horrified. She looks sad, like a little girl. But she also seems practised at defiance and bunches up her features. A beautiful creature, despite her glower. Cropped black hair, short and fine. Soft cheeks. Rose-painted lips.

A monster.

'Just forget you saw me,' she finally says, 'forget about all this, like you've forgotten about everything else.

Coming up here was wrong. I shouldn't'a done it. There's nothing I can do to help. Just . . . shit, just put me out of your mind, if you can.' And now she's walking towards me, intent on sidestepping my position. 'Try to forget.' And there's a tear in her eye. I can just see it in the slanted light.

Sadie's barking is now incessant, and she pulls so hard that she snaps the clasp of her leash and lurches forward to dance around the feet of the other woman, snarling at the stranger with all the intimidation her ancient frame can muster.

The leash dangles limp in my hand. I don't know what this woman means for me to forget, but I'm suddenly in motion to match hers. Not thinking, just acting. My hands are trembling, yet even so they reach out, grab this woman by the shoulders and violently wrench her off her course. They throw her towards the water.

'What the fuck are you—'

But the woman inside me doesn't let her finish. I fling myself after her and knock her onto her back in the shallow flat at the river's edge.

'You ruined me!' I'm shouting. The cry bursts out of me like an eruption. 'You told me it would just be to meet some new people! A bit of fun! And you tore my life away!'

And I sense there are three of us here, now. There's this woman I've knocked into the water, and me, and the third woman, harboured within me. I don't know who she is or what she's saying, but I don't really feel I need to understand her words. It's enough just to let her have her voice. So I let it tear through me, and it cuts like razor wire, shredding my heart.

'Amber!' the woman in the water cries. She knows my name. 'Amber! I'm sorry, I didn't mean—'

Her eyes are pleading, terrified, but we don't let her finish the cry. Neither myself nor I care what she has to say. We don't want her explanations or excuses.

I leap on top of her, straddling her stomach, and in a swift motion coil Sadie's red leash around her neck. I pull on its ends, and as she writhes and tries to fend me off, I pull harder. Through the rough fibres I can feel the vibrations of tissue and bone collapsing as I cinch tighter.

Our struggle lasts a few seconds, though I don't know precisely how long. When it's over, the woman in the water is still. Her eyes remain open wide, but her breath is gone. And I feel as if a great chorus of joy is bursting out of the heavens.

I stand as the song radiates through me, a grief that I didn't know I possessed passing within and then out of me.

But as I right myself and gaze at the scene, something is wrong. Parts of the chorus of this moment don't join in proper harmony. The shoreline, I realize, is muddy and unpleasant. It isn't inviting, as I feel it should be. The earth should *invite* this moment. I'm not sure why, but I'm certain of it. This moment of righteousness. And the birds I know are in the nearby trees have gone silent, like Sadie herself. The world is mute when it should be singing.

I kneel down at the woman's side and stare into her lifeless face. For all the rage I felt a moment ago, I now feel only a quiet recognition.

'Emma,' I whisper, taking in her features. Her name comes with faded memories of a street corner, and a house, and being led to a door in a basement room with a fold-out bed and . . .

'Emma.'

Her name, spoken a final time. Enough to let her go.

I get up, step back onto the almost-path, and wipe the wet and grime from my trousers. It's all over me, saturating my clothes. 'I'll need a shower when I get back,' I announce to Sadie. David won't like to see all this. He'll worry I wandered into unsafe terrain, that I've hurt myself. A man who loves so intently shouldn't be made to worry.

So a shower it will be – and with that thought, things seem to return to normal. A switch, flipped. The scenery is once again in colour, and there is birdsong back in the air. I hear the little burbles of life by the water. My voice is once more solitary, and my thoughts content.

There is pine and earth in my nostrils. Sadie rushes up to my ankles.

I glance back at the river. Something is floating in it, off to my left, awkward and abnormal. Its colours don't resonate with the palette of nature, but I don't dwell on it for long. It's the edge of the shore that draws me, so much more powerfully. There are tadpoles swimming in the algae, fluttering in the anticipation of life. They're ready, anxious to become something new.

It's such a beautiful thing, this little world that exists a jaunt away from home. So much life. So much strength. So much peace.

62

David

When I return home from work, Amber is not in her usual frame of mind. There is a smile on her face and she's stirring a pot of something that fills the kitchen with a rich scent. But there's something unusual about her, and in the circumstances I've crafted for our life, unusual is never good.

I try to counterbalance it with as normal a dose of behaviour as possible.

'How was your day off, hon?' I walk over and embrace her from behind, wrapping my arms around her stomach. I plant a long kiss on her neck. The lime scent of our favourite shower gel, fresh on her skin, mixes with that of the organic garlic and onions on the stove. I can feel her smile.

'Just lovely,' she answers, turning around far enough to brush a kiss across my lips before returning to her stirring. 'Refreshing.'

I glance over at the countertop. The coffee pot is empty, which means she had her dose this morning; and one of the wine bottles I'd prepped is also open-necked by the microwave, a large glass poured next to her cooking. Her medication isn't an issue.

But the moment doesn't feel right. I sense it, and I've learned to trust my feelings about things like this.

'I'm going to go change out of these shoes,' I announce, releasing my grip from her waist and walking towards the stairs. I can't allow myself to behave abnormally, despite my foreboding sense of concern. It would only compound things. 'Been a long day at the pharmacy. I'd kill for a few minutes with a cold beer.'

Sadie's leash isn't hanging by the door.

Inconsequential, but unusual.

'Supper won't be ready for another half-hour,' Amber says, 'so you have plenty of time for your mannish end-of-day collapse.' She glances my way and smiles, then is back at her labours.

No, something is definitely different.

I ascend the stairs to our bedroom and go to the closet to kick off my wingtips, trying to put my finger on why I just feel – wrong. My feet genuinely are sore, though it's more from a poor choice of shoe than anything truly trying at work. Anyone working at a pharmacy gets used to spending time on his feet.

I crouch down to undo my laces, when I spot something peculiar in the corner. The wicker lid of our clothes hamper is askew. Amber's normally tidy about such things, but even so, if I weren't already in a suspicious mood I probably wouldn't think any more about it. But something isn't right, and until I know what that something is, any change of habit might be revealing.

I right myself and walk over to examine the hamper lid. A trouser leg dangles over the edge at its rear. It's covered in something, and I remove the lid entirely to have a better look.

An entire outfit is crumpled inside, all of it wet, smelling of earth and moisture, caked in mud.

My stomach tightens.

The clothes, in and of themselves, mean nothing; but it feels like they're screaming out at me. *This is it! Something has happened! Something has gone terribly wrong!* My suspicion becomes overpowering.

I take the muddy clothes in hand and descend the stairs.

'Amber,' I ask, rounding the corner into the kitchen, 'where did you go today, with all your free time?' I demand that my voice stay light, though my anxiety is monumental. Amber's back is still to me.

'Took a walk by the river,' she answers. 'You know, just up the way? Never gone walking there before. It's such a beautiful spot.'

'Is that where this happened?' I hold up the dirty clothes as she turns around, and in the instant that her eyes make contact with them, a flash of uncontrolled blankness crosses her features. She stops moving, her pupils dilate, and her whole body goes rigid. For an instant, she is a woman made entirely of stone.

Then, almost imperceptibly swiftly, she returns to life. 'Oh, that,' she answers nonchalantly. 'I must have fallen in, I guess. Don't quite remember. One of my clumsy moments, I suppose.' She gives me a loving smile, and turns back to the soup. But I saw the split-second change, and I've never been more terrified in my life.

I'm out of the apartment before another five minutes pass. I came up with a quick excuse – I need a little air after a hard day, just a quick stroll and I'll be back for the meal – and as I go through the door, I try not to let Amber spot me racing as quickly as I am.

Her reaction to the muddy clothes has me petrified. That expression: I've seen it before. It's the hollow look and the blank eyes of the tormented creature I'd saved – and they've burst through into the present. I'd prayed so hard that I'd never see them again.

I'm trying to formulate a plan as I walk. I need to retrace Amber's steps. Something happened on her walk, and I'll be damned if I believe it was just a clumsy slip into the water. An accident doesn't cause hollowness. When she saw the clothes, it triggered a memory, and one she's already repressed.

What kind of memory can carve through her consciousness, through all those drugs, and then be pushed down so quickly?

My pace along the path is becoming a jog. The light is failing as dusk takes over from daytime, and I feel the desperate need to cover as much ground as I can. Out here, somewhere, is something that . . .

The answer to my puzzle comes a few minutes later, around a bend at the water's edge. Beyond the kept-up areas, into the forested cover of the river's wilder shores. I'm following muddier paths now, twisting in turns that weave through weeds and overgrowth. And then a few steps, onto a little cul-de-sac in the path, and with shattering certitude I know what's broken Amber's peace.

There is a woman lying in the water. In the surroundings, in her attire, she looks barely more than a girl, though she's clearly around the same age as Amber herself, maybe a little older.

No. I can't pretend.

I know exactly how much older.

With everything in me I wish I didn't know who this woman was, because with that knowledge comes an awareness of what has actually taken place here, and just how disastrous it really is.

I step to the edge of the water, and Emma Fairfax's lifeless face gazes back at me. Her eyes are fixed open. Despite a red stretch of rope wrapped around her neck, which a moment later I recognize as Sadie's leash, she looks almost peaceful.

Like she did when I met her two-and-a-half years ago, back in the psych ward. Beautiful, but haunting. Wretched.

All at once, I understand. She and Amber met, right on this spot. Today.

Why in Christ's name did you come here?

Emma's eyes look through me. Had she wanted to confront Amber? Try to make some kind of – I can't even fathom it – peace, after all these years? The thought brings the taste of vomit into my throat. *Peace.* Or maybe she had wanted to check on me. Some humane act. But her eyes are hollow and inhuman.

Amber will have seen these eyes, too. God. It causes me physical pain to think what that encounter must have felt like for her. Two worlds, one she doesn't remember she was ever in, colliding. Would she have recognized Emma's face? The memories have been so disassociated by now, it's possible she wouldn't actually know what was happening inside her. But something obviously clicked. Emma's body bears witness to a pain that hasn't subsided.

To come face to face with the woman who had turned you over to the men who abused you as a child. Who could bear that?

And who could blame anyone for reacting to it?

That's the thought that overtakes me, gazing down at Emma Fairfax's lifeless body. This monster I so hated as she told me of her crimes. She's finally received justice for her life, and at the hands of one of her victims, whose mind might no longer remember her torments but whose soul hasn't forgotten. It strikes me as, in the strangest of ways, entirely just. Righteous.

But with a flash of certainty, I know that no one else will see it this way. And a swirl of thoughts starts to bend through my head, new ideas, new plans.

The sure knowledge that the plan I'd abandoned all those years ago, was the one I had to enact now.

PART SEVEN

FINALE

63

Amber

I'm in bed. David brought me here a few minutes ago.
I couldn't walk, my feet too heavy to lift, and he carried
me up the stairs like we were newly-weds. The killer, the
man I thought was a killer, who calls me a killer instead.
Holding me in his arms.

'You drugged me.' I mutter as he adjusts my position
on our mattress, propping a pillow beneath my head. I
remember watching him drop the clear substance into
my water as I sat collapsed at the table. 'You bastard.'
But the word has so little power behind it. I don't have
the venom inside me that I had before.

'Medicated,' he says, as if the alternative vocabulary

385

explained everything. 'You feel it now, right? Coming back into your system?'

My toes are tingling, but I don't think this is what he's referring to. The abyss I'd been falling into is closing up, and the light above me has become more inviting. A sense of hope I'd thought I'd lost – I can almost grasp it. I suspect it's this his 'medicine' is bringing about. The gaps in my soul are starting to fill and solidity is slowly returning to my mind, though there's a headache forming at my temples, squeezing at me without mercy.

'It's been the only way to keep your childhood away from your present,' he adds, pulling a blanket over my legs. 'To let you be free to be someone new in the here and now.'

Whatever.

I decide to give in to the drug. I can feel its effects circulating through my system, each beat of my heart driving it to the extremities of my members. It is taking me over again.

Taking me over.

'What gives you the right?' I ask, drowsiness pulling me away. For the moment, though, the will to protest is still stronger. 'What gives you the right to steal my past from me?'

'Oh, Amber,' David answers. 'I'm so sorry you were brought to this. Your past, your childhood . . . it's not something you need to remember. I promise you. It was truly terrible. Just let it go.'

There's a look about David, like he's unwilling to tell

me more. This new, sudden spirit of openness, and he still wants to hide things from me.

'That can't be right,' my voice trails off. 'It was mine, however bad it may have been. Who did you think I would be, if you took it all away from me?'

Then my voice is just an echo, bouncing against the bone of my skull, fading into nothing.

64

David

Christ, everything in me is on fire. I feel I've betrayed everyone. Amber. My sister. Even myself.

But it's Evelyn's voice that is strongest in my head. She'd shouted at me there at the river, when I'd seen Emma's body floating in the water and realized what Amber had done. She had started, right then, to scream in my chest, pounding, clawing her way at my insides. A beast caged far too long, yearning to be let loose.

In her cries, I could just make out her will. She pushed me away from the water, away from the false world in which I've lived since I took Amber into my arms.

'You know their names,' she whispered into my head. 'The names of the men who did this to her. The men you should have punished from the beginning. You know who they are.'

And her instruction is clear. My own voice, hers, it doesn't matter.

Go, now. Go, and find them.

Things were never going to be right again. That was something that simply had to be accepted as fact. My gut instinct told me everything I needed to know. The encounter with Emma Fairfax had started something in Amber that wasn't going to stop. A cascade into the past. She might have repressed it for the moment, but it wouldn't stay buried forever.

That encounter had started something in me, too. The change inside was palpable, and I left the river racing through my new reality. Emma had come here. The old world was forcing its way into the new. Like I'd once thought it would. Sometimes, the worst of life's sorrows is to learn you're right. She'd come here, and that meant at least one person had found out what I'd done. What our life here had become. And if one, then more could easily be possible – and then the past in all its horror, cascading into the present. Amber, forced to confront the bastards who'd hurt her. The pain they'd caused, rekindled.

Amber is all that matters. Emma is a corpse, like she's long deserved to be. The only question was whether now Amber could be saved from becoming one, too.

During the first day that followed, there were signs that she was doing better than I'd have anticipated. Apart from the brief flash of recognition when I'd shown her the dirty clothes she'd worn at the river, there were no further indications that the trauma had broken through into the rest of her life. When I came back from the water, careful to keep all the horror and sorrow from my face, she appeared to be functioning as normal. Calm. She had her humour about her.

I increased her dosage anyway. Christ, I halfway wanted to take a dose myself.

Then, the next night, as I'd taken her warm body on to mine and we'd intertwined ourselves in the kind of passion I've always thought helped free her from her memories, she'd said it.

'Emma.'

That was it, just her name. But with that single, whispered word I realized that Amber hadn't escaped the experience at all. What she'd done to Emma had dislodged something within her, and she'd made it barely more than twenty-four hours before it was breaking into her thoughts, despite the drugs. Even her words, and even in such an intimate moment.

Measures were going to have to be taken, and quickly.

My first thought was that we needed another re-start. I wasn't sure if it could be done a second time, but the massive dose of the drug cocktail I'd given Amber at our encounter in the Headlands had effectively knocked her memory clear the once. It at least held the potential of being able to do it a second time.

But I didn't have enough. The dosage has become a science over these past years, and the only way to keep off the radar of suppliers, who are always looking out for junkies or dealers, has been to source the various compounds in small doses. I get some from my own counter at CVS, others from little independent pharmacies around the Bay. A few from online retailers in various parts of the country, delivered in increments over lengthy spans of time. Inconspicuous. Hard to trace.

Not good, though, when I need a lot, and need it fast.

At the pharmacy the next morning, I powered up my computer intent on placing orders. Some things I could buy in person later in the day from a nearby shop, but I needed to set the shipments in motion immediately. I could rush the postage, get them here within twenty-four hours.

It was all in hand. I stepped away from the counter at lunch, ready to run the necessary errand.

But it wasn't fated to happen. Life sometimes forges its own turns, and they take you where they will.

Or where you won't.

65

Amber

I think this is a dream. I'm out for a walk and the earth bounces a little beneath my feet in the way that non-dream earth never does. Trees bend to meet me. The songbirds don't just sing: they follow me around as they do, dancing in the air just above my shoulders.

The whole world moves in creative ways, all to help that other woman, the one inside me, whom I met at the water's edge. She's on a march. She was in my belly, she says, buried and abandoned but filled with pain. The world bends to help her, now, cooperating in the desire to unbind the next links in a chain I didn't realize was shackling my own feet.

I remember all this. I remember her, though I don't know from where. A familiar voice. It makes me strangely happy to hear it.

And we ring the neck of that monster together,

tightening the red rope around it. Who is she? She has such a pretty face. But it feels good to use my own hands to force the breath from her throat.

Our hands. We are doing this together.

I blink, and it all goes away, the way it does in dreams. The river is gone, and the bouncy earth beneath my feet has become carpeting. A strange room, with musty smells. All the good feelings the other woman within me had brought on a moment ago are gone. Inside I feel a horrible replacement: Terror. Anger. Fear. All of them stirred together like some vile soup.

Inside, I am completely alone.

My vision is slanted. The walls are a strange colour. I hate this place.

I see the first man's face. He's middle aged. Overweight. Silver hair flops on a sweaty head. Then another man, fatter than the first, a beer belly protruding over tight trousers. And a third, slender, almost sickly, with a gaunt face.

Then violence, just like at the river. My hands touching their flesh. Clawing. Rage.

Attack.

And I hear my voice cry out, a bestial roar like the one I'd emitted at the river. 'You'll pay for this! You'll pay!'

Only it's not my voice. Not the voice I hear today. It's the voice of a little girl. The voice I'd had when I was a child.

I don't know why I hear it. But that's the way things go in dreams.

66

Amber

Morning comes. Sight of our hideous bedroom ceiling assaults me as I blink away the blur of night-time – and then the thrashing in my head, worse than I can ever remember it, begins. And memories, hurting me worse than the pain.

I lie still for a few moments, listening for sounds that might tell me what kind of events are going to arrive next. Sounds of normalcy. But I sense normalcy is a thing only of the past. I won't see it again.

I remember my dream.

I start to weep.

The woman in the water. I see my hands on the rope around her throat. I can feel it, so vivid that I know it can't just be imagination. I can feel the cord pull against the meat of my palms, the squirm of her flesh beneath my legs.

I'm sweating through my sheets. *David was right. I killed her.* His words last night were impossible. Only this morning, I have the awfullest sense that they are true.

I can feel her flesh.

And the men. That part of the dream snaps into my mind. What makes the tears stream down my face isn't just the memory. It's that the memory matches what I had learned about the other killings by the river, scanning through the Internet in the bookshop over the past two days. The man with the silver hair. His build.

Middle aged. Overweight.

The police report said he had silver hair.

It flops sweaty on his head . . .

And then there are other men, and I remember David telling me three had been killed in the past days. I can feel their flesh in my hands. I can still feel the jostling bodies.

I can hear the scream in my voice.

And I know David didn't do this at all.

I kick the blankets off my body and grab a robe to cover myself up. I can feel the puffiness at my eyes, and with the tears from my exchange with David last night I probably have brown mascara streaks running down my cheeks, but I don't care. It doesn't matter any more.

I step up the stairs quietly, but without trying to hide the fact that I'm up. I want David to know. I've had my fill of hiding.

A few seconds later, I round the open door into his study. The scene of the things that set this all off. He's at his desk, where the photographs once had been, his briefcase open and his laptop lit up in front of him.

At the sound of my entrance, he turns. His face is cautious. Plain.

'Good morning, Amber.'

The words, the sheer, absurd normalcy of the words, jolt me. Any equilibrium I had evaporates instantly at the sound of his greeting.

'What did you make me do?'

No 'good morning' for him, no pleasantries. I'm not in a fit state for any of that. It's only by a minor miracle that somehow I'm thinking clearly enough to ask the one question I need to know the answer to.

David has tried to control my life. He's hid my past from me. *He* is the cause of my pain and my unrest. But I now know, I know, that I'm the cause of something worse.

'What did you make me do?' I ask again, keeping our eyes locked.

His face has grown dark. 'Amber, I haven't made you do anything.'

'I'm not a killer,' I protest. 'I feel guilty swatting a fly. I don't step on bugs. I . . .'

But I can't finish. I try to avoid visions that feel uncomfortably close to memories. I know that I've become something else.

David swivels his chair to face me more fully. There's

a large glass of water next to him on the desk, and I remember last night and the glass he offered me. I doubt his is laced with the same quantity of 'medications'.

'Amber, you're not a bad person,' he says, incongruously.

'God knows what you've been giving me,' I say, nodding towards the water, 'What its effects are. You ever think it might do real harm, despite calling it medicine?'

His head shakes slowly. 'Amber, maybe you should sit down.'

'I don't want to sit, David! I want you to answer me!'

A sigh. A moment for thought. 'As you wish.' He taps his fingers at his knees. 'The drugs don't make you aggressive, Amber. They do the opposite. They calm you down.'

'Calm! Do I look calm to you?'

'They let you be yourself, that's what I'm trying to say. To a degree. They numb out the past.'

Myself, to a degree! Fuck him and his obsession with my past. I haven't thought about my past half as much as David apparently has.

'The past is gone, David. Behind us. Before I met you, my life was . . .' I search for the right words.

And I trip.

In this moment, right now, I'm aware that I have only a few memories of life before David. I'm sure there must be more, but it's just him, our meeting, and . . .

There are no other memories to fill the words.

'You can't remember, can you?' David finally asks,

witnessing my state. I gape back at him. I can't even muster the clarity to be indignant.

'You don't have those memories because they're too painful, Amber.' He's speaking now in the voice of a counsellor, like he's practised this. I find it condescending, and it makes me squirm. 'Your consciousness tried to get rid of those memories years ago,' he continues. 'It just needed a little help.'

'There's nothing painful in my past,' I spit out. 'My "consciousness" can cope with things just fine,' *you condescending prick*. 'Before you I was just, just . . . I don't know. It isn't important.'

'It's all that's important. It's everything.'

'Stop with the bullshit, David! My past means nothing! An ordinary childhood, with an overbearing father and mother who—'

But the sentence stops mid-syllable. As I desperately push my memory towards my childhood, a great white light explodes within my head. I feel as if I've been struck with a bat, my ankles starting to give.

'Amber, don't.' I can just make out David starting to rise from his seat, but I don't want that. I grab the door frame for balance.

'Don't get up!' My own words thunder in my head. 'I'm fine.' I repeat the phrase again mentally. *I'm fine. I'm fine. I'm fine.* I will it to be true.

Gradually, the room slows its spinning. My feet recover some of their strength.

I won't give in to this.

'I was a normal child with—'

'Amber, please stop,' David interrupts. There is raw concern on his face, but I'll be damned if I'm going to take orders from him.

'I was a normal child with a mother who always knew what was best and who—'

The whiteness erupts within me. The struggle for memory sets it off again, and this time the vertigo is overwhelming. Even with my hand locked onto the door I feel my balance going. Blinking does nothing to control my sight, and I sense the floor coming up to meet me.

'Amber!' David's voice is suddenly at my ear, and I feel his muscular arms wrap around me as my legs give out entirely. The room is a blur. I can feel him guiding me towards his desk chair, sitting me down and stroking my shoulder with a warm hand as my body calms down.

'Enough,' he says. 'Please, don't do this to yourself.'

I begin to come out of the strange collapse, regaining the trappings of equilibrium, and I notice the water in my eyes.

'I have to, David,' I hear myself saying. 'I have to remember. I can't go on like this, being myself and not myself.'

He raises his hand from my shoulder to my cheek and runs it tenderly along my moist skin.

'You're right,' he finally says. 'You can't go on like this any more.'

I feel so completely helpless.

'What am I supposed to do?'

'If you'll let me,' he answers, 'I'll tell you a story.'

67

Amber

David has been speaking for at least forty minutes, and his story is worse than any I could have dreamed up. He's talked of children and basement dens, of abusers and rape and plots. He's spoken about a psychiatric ward and a woman so broken by her past that she was little more than a shell. He's told me of her salvation – attempted, if nothing else – of her new life with her new man.

I've listened to this all in silence, numb from the words. How else is one supposed to listen to the impossible?

But eventually, words have to come.

'David, why did you do this? Why couldn't you have just let me be me?'

'Don't you understand, Amber, you needed help. I had to save you.'

'I was thirty-six when we met,' I say. 'Thirty-six. If any

of what you say is true, that was more than twenty years after whatever had happened to . . . me.' It feels strange to speak about a past I cannot remember. 'Can I really have been so bad, if I'd made it that long on my own?'

'You were getting worse, Amber.'

'How do you know?'

'Because the doctors told me that you were—'

'You said the doctors had been giving dire diagnoses for years,' I interrupt. 'And yet still I lived my life.'

'It was falling apart. You weren't able to—'

'You said I worked in a library, before you . . . did this. Read papers. Was content.'

He sighs. 'Yes.'

'So I was able to have a reasonable life. Even to enjoy myself.'

'Amber, it wasn't so simple as that,' David protests. He has a pleading look in his eyes. 'You were slipping away. More and more distant. More and more lost. If I hadn't stepped in, it would have been the end of you.'

I pause, trying to absorb all he's revealed to me.

Then, a single word. 'Maybe.'

David peers up. 'What?'

'Maybe, David.' I straighten myself. '*Maybe* I would have faded away. *Maybe* I was going the route you thought. But I had a life. I had a job. Maybe I'd even thought of a family. Can you really say you know? How could you? And now, how can I? You took all that from me.'

His eyes glass over. When he speaks, his voice trembles with emotion.

402

'I've given you everything I could,' he says. 'Love, a home, a full life without all that pain.'

And I don't know what to say, because despite everything else, he actually has. He has given me a life, together with him, that in almost every way was perfect. Our beautiful home. Our dog. Our trips. Our romance.

But he made me into someone new in order to do it. And I can feel the contours of another woman's neck in my grasp, and the flesh of those men, and I know that David created more than he had bargained for. He had created a monster. A killer.

He had created me.

In the end, David's stories are too much for me. What he's revealed is beyond my comprehension. They are the ravings of a story too horrible to be true, yet too personal to be anything else.

I want to believe it's all a lie, simply tagged on to the litany of others David has told me. I'm actually praying I'm being deceived – something that even in the moment feels horribly wrong. I *want* to believe I'm being taken for a fool. And I would, if it weren't for the fact that I've gradually gone numb as David's spoken – a numbness that isn't nerves, or shock, or even horror. It's the numbness of something inside me, fading away. Something new emerging. Parts of me that I've never realized were there, making themselves present. A whole life, a woman, I've never known.

And the reality of what she's done.

The feel of the woman's neck. The rope. The flesh of those men. The feel of the woman's neck. The rope. The flesh of . . .

I look at David, unsure what I am meant to think of him. I want to hate him, but I still love him. I really do. I'd convinced myself he was a killer, but the killer was me. And yes, he made me into that, and I don't know if that's better or worse.

But I know it's something I can't live with.

My strength surprises me when I put it into action. In a single motion I'm up from the chair, and I push David back onto his ass on the floor as if he were a toy. He stares up, shocked, as I loom over him. For a moment our eyes lock, like they've done so many times.

'I'm sorry David. This is over,' I say flatly. 'But it's not finished yet.'

And without another breath, I storm out of the room. I sweep through our bedroom a floor below, grab what I need, and then race down the remaining stairs.

I'm out the door before David has regained his footing.

68

Amber

I'm ankle deep in the gentle waters of Russian River. I've heard the incomprehensible story of my life, learned that it has come to its final chapter, and I've come here.

I never thought the last chapter of my life would look like this. I can't truly remember the first chapters, but I'd never have thought the story concluded with me bringing death, and to so many. But maybe my story was always going to end like this. Like most, the final page was presumably written long before the first, the conclusion the one sturdy fixture towards which everything before it was always going to lead. God knows there have been enough authors involved with mine. I'm not sure if it's really even mine at all, any more. But however they begin, and whoever writes them, there's no story that doesn't finish with the end.

I don't go back to the place I'd left Emma's body.

There might still be detectives or police there. It's probably roped off. Nothing I wish to face at this particular moment. Not because I want to avoid responsibility, for this or my other actions. It's just that I don't want anything to throw me off track.

I know what justice needs to look like, now, more than anyone else.

I approach the water along another path, in a different direction, and walk until I come upon a suitable bend. It's framed in by tall trees that form cathedral walls beneath the bright sky high above.

The last body in the water, I think I've always known, has to be mine. There has been a pattern, hidden away in the recesses of my life, acting itself out in measured rhythm. Like my feet, one step automatically following another, whether I ponder their motion or not. Like they've lives of their own. Now their last steps are here. The river needs to receive one more offering. The final step. Then the journey can end.

I've got so much wrong in my life, and in these past days in particular. This, though, I will get right. Whatever the story of my childhood was, whatever David has done to me in these latter years, it doesn't warrant what I've done. Others have brought me abuse, lies; but I've brought death. And death always cries out for death, and blood for blood.

I'd grabbed my trousers and a loose blouse off the back of the door as I'd stormed out of the apartment, and my handbag as I'd marched through the kitchen to the door. The river's not far from our western edge of Windsor, only a ten-minute walk from our door at the pace I was keeping. And nature became my changing room once I arrived here – the first time I can remember ever being so exposed beneath the cover only of trees.

My bathrobe is now on the soil of the shore just behind me. It doesn't seem right to have things end in a state of undress.

I took my little compact out of my purse once I'd dressed myself. A touch of foundation on my cheeks, a bit of mascara on the lashes. Nothing too fancy. A face just polished up enough to shine. I kicked off my shoes.

Nothing to do about the hair, still frizzled and waspish from sleep. But the water beneath me has an undulating flow, the way the current always does near the shore, ebbing and flowing like life itself. I imagine my hair will sway nicely in that motion, catching the sunlight.

There's a natural, earthen music around me. A sweet song. I think the thrushes are singing. I take a few deep breaths, calming my soul. A few final moments to ponder.

I can't decide, in the end, whether David is a beast or a blessing. How much of what's happened over the past few days might not have happened if he hadn't fabricated a world of lies from which I had, eventually, to break free? Maybe the story wouldn't have had to end this way. Maybe there could have been a few chapters of comfort, or peace, or a conclusion more like those of storybooks and fairytales.

But then, maybe there wouldn't have been a story at

all. Maybe I would have simply faded out of existence years ago, like he said, slipping into nothingness. David may have destroyed me in the end, but he gave me life along the way.

And really, my destruction was my own doing, not his. Whatever else he might have done, David's never wrung the life out of a woman, or stabbed a man – or three – out of vengeance. He's too loving for that. Until now, I'd have thought I was too.

A story gone wrong, but David has provided me with the right way to bring it to a close. Knowledge of reality, and of my acts within it, gives me a script for the ending. A string of bodies, starting with the woman found in the water . . . I can simply be the next. The next, and the last.

I have the knife in my hand already. It feels familiar there. I remember holding it in the kitchen, aiming it at David. The same way I must have aimed it at those men, only going so much further . . .

This time, it will be pointed in a different direction.

It's an odd thing, to play the observer at one's own death. I can see the whole thing in my vision, unfolded in front of me as a *fait accompli*. My body, eyes towards the heavens, back resting in the soft mud of this shore, a crimson stream flowing from my side and mingling with the water. The clouds dancing high above.

Part of me is ashamed, certain that I should feel more emotion. There's a universal wisdom that suggests dispassion isn't the right response to death, especially one's own. There should be anger. Grief. The stars should droop down from heaven and mourn. And it's not that I don't feel anything at all – of course I do, given everything that's brought me here. It's unfair. It's unjust. It's the stain of evil, the kind that marks the universe itself, that can't be rubbed away. And I should be furious, and embarrassed, and ashamed and guilty at the thought of David realizing what I've become.

But all that emotion is a step removed. It's not going to overtake me now, the way it has so many times before. I'm observing my feelings, as much as I'm observing what's to come of my body, floating in this stream.

For just a moment, though, sorrow bursts through. I'm not sure, but I have the feeling that life is meant to culminate in something more than this. Something meaningful. Life, in all its complexity, shouldn't come to its conclusion in a river, with sand in my hair and reflected sunlight the only thing left in my eyes.

But then the sadness departs. *No, this is right.* This is how it's supposed to be. Of course the shore is the end; of course the water and the silence. *My story . . . my conclusion.* David may have tried to rewrite it, but stories go where they go.

The knife is drawn. I've lifted the edge of my blouse, pointed the blade towards my exposed flesh. It won't be difficult. And for a moment, I believe it won't hurt. Just a quick motion, and then release.

However they begin, there's no story that doesn't finish with the end.

69

Amber

'Amber, stop.'

The voice cuts into the moment. It's not right. It's David's voice, but David isn't supposed to be here. I've left him behind. The end comes alone, no more ties to anyone – their truths, or their lies.

But his voice sounds again. He's not yelling, but pleading with more emotion than I've ever heard in his words.

'You don't have to do this. It doesn't have to end this way.'

I turn to face him. I can't help myself. Resolve or no resolve, it's David. The man by the seaside in that ridiculous red jacket. The man of a thousand bad breakfast drinks. The only man I've ever called my own, and who's always called me his.

'It's the only way,' I answer. I try to smile, to reassure

him it's okay. The tip of my knife rests at my skin, where it belongs.

'No, Amber, it isn't.' He steps forward, into the water. I look down as it laps up over his shoes and reaches his ankles. 'Despite everything that's happened, Amber, this doesn't have to be the way your story goes.'

The words are sweet, but not believable.

'I'm sorry, David. You can't wash away a life, however terrible it may have been. Sorrow is real, awful as it is. It has a right to exist. You can't just get rid of it on a whim.'

His eyes are orbs, radiating sadness and regret.

'Amber, I—'

'But don't worry,' I say. 'I know . . . I think, at least, that you were trying to help.'

I continue to stare at him. David really is the very sweetest of men. Sweet and a fool. Sweet and so very, very wrong. But his face is as beautiful as it's ever been. God, I love that stubble around his chin.

Tears form in his eyes.

'Thank God,' he sobs, trying to keep his composure. 'I needed to hear you say that. That you realize I never wanted to hurt you. I've tried to save you. Everything I've done . . . I love you, Amber Howell. I tried so hard to rescue you. To help you not repeat my sister's story. Not to be . . . to become, Evelyn.'

The tears in his eyes tremble, and burst over their lids. I reach out the hand that isn't clutching the knife and wipe them away from the sides of his face.

And I am confused, because David's story is falling apart again. 'Evelyn?' I ask. The name is unfamiliar, and so is the context. 'You don't have a sister.' And I almost pity him, now, though I don't know why. A liar, who can't stop.

'I did,' he answers. A sob. 'When I was a child. Just a little boy. The most beautiful sister in the world.'

'Please,' I take my hand from his face and hold it up between us, 'no more stories. No more inventions. Just let me deal with the reality of what I've done, David.'

'Amber, you haven't—'

'I have to take responsibility,' I insist. I want him to acknowledge that this is something I must do. 'I can't let you be dragged into what I've ended up doing.'

'Amber, you didn't.'

'I did!' The words fly out of my lips. 'You told me I did!'

A pause, and then . . .

'Just the woman, Amber.' David's face is strained. He is trying to sound reassuring. 'Only her. Only Emma. Because she was the one who led you to them. Led you to your pain. You remembered, and you reacted.'

I really don't want to think about these things any further. It's too much as it is. But now the story is being tugged at again. The pages are changing, as they seem to do every time David opens his mouth. I struggle to make the pieces fit together.

'No, David,' I answer, 'that's not what happened. There

412

were men. Silver hair. Fat. Older.' I feel their flesh. Smell their horrible scent.

'You didn't—'

'Stop it!' I cry at him. 'Don't lie to me now. I can feel them on my breath, David. Their sweat on my skin. It's real. These aren't visions! You can't hide me from what I did.'

'But you didn't,' he persists. 'You didn't kill them, Amber. I did.'

David's words have shut out the singing that nature had provided for the serenity of this final moment. It had come to grips with things. Accepted fate. Been ready to embrace the end that my beginnings demanded.

And then . . . this.

'You?' I can feel my eyes wide, round, radiating the surprise and disbelief that's swelling up inside me. 'That's absurd, David. Damn it, don't try to trick me! Let me at least acknowledge who and what I really am!

'I killed them, Amber,' he repeats. 'This isn't a lie. I'm not trying to deceive you. It was me.'

I shake my head. 'That can't be right, David. You can say what you want, but I *remember* it. Them. In my dreams, when I'm awake. Right now, in this moment. Their flesh. The struggles. The pain. My screaming voice.'

The tears flow over my eyes again. There are tears in David's too.

'You aren't remembering killing them, Amber,' he says.

'You aren't remembering anything you did to them at all. You are remembering what they did to you.'

I see their bodies, feel their flesh. The men reek of cigarette smoke and sweat. There is violence in the air, locked into a room that is too small to contain such horror.

'Stop!' I cry out, rage and pain in my voice. But it isn't my voice. It's the voice of a child. Of the girl I once had been.

'Get the fuck off me!'

But the men don't get off. One pins me down while another rips at my clothes. I feel them tearing away from my body. I can barely breathe, something having taken the wind from me.

'Keep it down, you little brat!' one of the men shouts. And he leans forward, and I feel his skin, and the sweat of his flesh, and . . .

And the little girl's voice, my voice, weeping as the world breaks apart.

70

David

I don't know if she'll be able to accept what I'm saying, here in this moment. How can she take another implosion to her world, even if it's the truth?

But I can't let her think she's done all this. She killed Emma, that's the truth, and her coming to grips with that is going to be a project for the rest of her life. But it was explicable. Understandable. I think that even in a court, the circumstances would be compellingly mitigating. A horrible, painful, emotional reaction to abuse no human should ever have had to endure.

But Amber did not kill her abusers.

That was me, and it's time I'm as honest with her about that as I've been forced to be about the rest.

Three days ago I'd begun fulfilling what fate had been demanding of me since I'd first met Amber in the ward.

The plan I'd abandoned for the sake of mercy, really was the merciful one; and it was time to enact it.

It took several hours of driving, but Felton, California was where Emma, all those years ago, had said the first man lived. I remembered my conversation with her vividly – I still do. Felton, and a man called Gerald McEwan.

I knew where I had to go.

The town is about three quarters of the way between San Francisco and Monterey Bay, nestled between steep, forested hill rises. It's hardly more than a little sprawl of residential neighbourhoods, without much else. The address I'd been able to locate for Gerald McEwan was 9160 Plateau Drive, which the satellite view in Google Maps told me was a slate-roofed house on the right hand of a bend in the street as I drove south. I scanned the house numbers, driving slowly so I could survey everything I saw.

I pulled alongside the kerb opposite the house, once I'd found it, and switched off the engine. Time to finalize just what exactly was coming next – there couldn't be any delaying.

It was time to bring things to an end.

When I was finished, I opened the front door and crossed the street back to the car. The wooden door behind me was painted red, which seemed fitting.

I don't remember precisely how the confrontation went. Only that I rang the bell and waited until the man opened the door, and then, a few minutes later, I was inside, standing at the base of a staircase. His body lay in a pool of blood that spread over the tiled landing, its silver hair still beautifully coiffed against his head.

He was motionless, lifeless, and my heart was filled with satisfaction. The ending had begun. Progress that couldn't be undone.

Bringing it to completion meant there would need to be two more bodies. The two remaining men who had wrought such evil.

They still lived in the same neighbourhood as they had decades ago. Ross Michaels. Ralph Andrews. Such innocuous names for beasts. Emma's voice rang in my ears as I recalled her giving me all the information she had on the abusers, striving to void herself of the guilt she had carried since her childhood.

The fact that theirs was the same neighbourhood as when she'd known them was something I didn't realize until I'd tracked them down on the computer, as I had with McEwan, and gone there myself. It was then I realized that the neighbourhood, and the house, matched the description Emma had given of where the abuse actually took place. As I'd driven through the residential streets of the Circle district in Santa Cruz, leading to the corner house my computer had revealed as Andrews' address, the scenes all around me were strangely, terribly familiar. Emma's words had been so vivid.

This is where it happened. Where so many lives had been destroyed.

I got out of the car before I reached the address itself

and took to my feet. It wasn't a predetermined plan. Part of me just wanted to empathize – to walk the streets those girls had walked while they were being led to . . .

Fuck.

I recognized sights Emma had described. The distinctive, circular curvature of the roads in that part of town, the little wrought-iron gate that led through a brickwork fence to the front yard of one of its houses. I ran my fingers along the brick and moss of its surface and thought of the innocent children who had done this before, and what had become of them.

I recognized the house itself, too. I had the address in my pocket, but it wasn't required. I remembered its description. Its little patch of green out front, and a tree with drooping branches covering almost the whole of the corner patch of yard.

The tree's trunk was damaged. Scars ran across the bark and wood, remnants of the head-on collision of Emma's car several years ago. The collision that brought her into the system, that brought her to me, and has ultimately brought me here.

God bless that tree.

Beyond it, the house. Unassuming, like so many others on the street. The greenery in the garden was tended moderately well, nothing bordering on obsessive or fancy, and a mini satellite dish hung out one of the second-storey windows.

The front door was a mirror copy of those all down the street, but I knew there was also a side door, just round the corner, and that this was the real entrance to the house. The one that was actually used.

In the moment, I simply walked up to that little door and knocked. As if it was the most ordinary thing in the world. Knocked, right at the gate of hell.

The man who answered looked like I expected. The way a man like that ought to look: the portrait all of humanity carries of a beast. He was fat, with a beer belly protruding over trousers he'd belted up far too tightly around his midriff. The comb-over atop his head was appalling.

'Are you Andrews?' I asked without any introduction. The man's brow lifted. His forehead didn't require the motion to be wrinkled, his age giving him permanent creases along its surface.

'I'm Ralph Andrews,' he answered hesitantly. 'Who the hell are you?'

I didn't reply. Rage made it impossible to speak. Instead I simply pushed past him. The door led into the kitchen, and I walked around Ralph Andrews into its bright light.

Another man was sat at the table. Scrawny. Like a wire doll decked out in the thinnest layer of flesh. His skin was pallid, too yellow and too grey at the same time. Bags drooped under both eyes and his face bore the recesses and hollows of chronic illness.

'Who are you?' I asked boldly. My demeanour seemed to have them both in shock, but the seated man, clearly uncomfortable, answered.

'Ross. Ross Michaels.'

And I think I felt pleasure, if that's the right word. Pleasure that I had both of them in front of me at once. The two remaining links in that horrible chain of suffering, still connected to each other after all this time.

All at once my pleasure was accusation and rage.

'So the two of you are still fucking friends in arms. Partners in evil, after all these years.'

'Evil?' Andrews asked. 'Listen here, mate, I don't know who you are or what the holy fuck you think you're doing here, but this is my house. I could call the cops, you know. I didn't invite you in.'

'No, you don't know who I am.' I telegraphed all my anger and bitterness at the fat man. 'But you've known someone I love for a long, long time.'

He passed an uncomprehending glance at Michaels, who shrugged his spindly shoulders.

'You knew my wife.'

More stares.

'Her name is Amber,' I continued, 'and you . . . brought her here.'

The words had a radical effect on both men. Michaels sat abruptly forward. Andrews took a step back, away from me, and both men's faces paled, turned towards each other.

'Ah, so you do remember the past,' I sneered at them, holding my position. 'You haven't completely forgotten.'

'Please, I'd like it if you would leave my home.' Ralph Andrews was a ghost, but he motioned me towards the door.

'I'll bet you fucking would,' I answered. 'Just disappear, like all your little houseguests have done over the years. After you'd finished with them. When your fun was over and you'd beaten and threatened them into silence.'

Neither man answered. I'd thrown their world off balance.

'Tell me, do you still have your den downstairs? The one with the extra lock on the door? The one you forced them into, when you had them brought here?'

I could smell these men's fear, like acid wafting in the air, poking at my nostrils. They couldn't pretend with me. I knew what they'd done.

'We . . . we don't do that any more.'

The abrupt confession came from Michaels' scrawny form in the chair. He was balding, retirement age like his associate, and nervous sweat balled up on his splotchy scalp.

'Shut the fuck up, Ross!' the other man snapped at him. It sounded odd to hear such an old man, who looked like he ought to speak in grandfatherly platitudes, utter profanities like a teenager. 'Don't say another goddamned word.'

'Oh, you don't have to hide anything from me, Mr Michaels,' I said. 'It's not as if I don't know perfectly well what went on down there.'

'You don't know shit.'

'I met Emma,' I said, and he froze. 'That's right, I met your bait. I know exactly what you fucking did to my wife.'

'It's over!' Ross Michaels blurted out. 'We finished all that, years ago.'

'I said shut up!' Andrews repeated.

There was something satisfying in seeing them grate at each other this way. I wondered, for a fraction of an instant, what their lives had been like since Amber was last here. I didn't believe for a second that they'd given up their abuse. Monsters stay monsters. But they'd also grown older. Had they tried for normalcy? Retirement parties and lecture cruises with their wives? Cups of coffee in the kitchen that was the gateway to all their evil, like none of it had never taken place at all?

Then I appear, and they're biting at each other, all that charade vanished, and all at once.

I might have been smiling.

I turned to face Michaels in the chair. 'I don't give a fuck what you've stopped. A killer might stop killing, but that doesn't give him a pass for what he's done.'

'We never killed anyone!' Andrews answered for his collaborator, seemingly appalled by the accusation. 'We were never even violent.'

'Never violent?' My smile vanished. Rage took its place. 'That's all you were! You beat those kids before you fucked them!'

'We only did what we had to do to keep them quiet. Our aim was never to hurt them. Not really.'

I couldn't believe I was hearing the words. The self-justifying, reality-denying nonsense of a monster trying

422

to downplay his monstrosities. My vision started to wobble, and my peripheral sight was fading.

'What you did . . . it was worse than violence!'

'We never—'

'It was worse than killing! Do you know what those girls became? The lives you condemned them to, of emptiness, shells of themselves? Do you know the agony you drove into their souls?'

The tears in my eyes were hot.

'Look man, I don't know who you are but—'

'My name is David.' I spat at the two men. 'My wife was Amber Jackson, when you knew her. And she was the most beautiful creature I have ever known.' I had no intention of letting them know I'd worked to rescue her. Let them feel guilt and shame and nothing else.

There was nothing more to say. Michaels was faint, weak in his seat. Andrews breathed heavily. The knuckles of my clenched fists were pure white.

'I'm, I'm sorry . . .' The words fell out of Andrews' mouth, and they were the final straw.

Sorry would never be good enough.

I was no longer filled with the explosive fire of rage. It disappeared instantaneously, as he offered that final, unjustifiable, unearthly statement. It was replaced by a stolid, sturdy sense of inevitability. Of course men like this are as sinister in their old age as they were in their middling years. Of course evil doesn't fade. It just takes on a new face and pretends the past is a slate that can be wiped clean and forgotten.

There was only one way to deal with it.

My eyes didn't have to scan the room long before I saw what I needed. They'd made it easy for me, really, having a collection of matching kitchen knives hanging from metal strips on the wall above the counter. They were barely more than a foot or two from my position. Like this had always been meant to be.

It seemed, at that moment, as if Andrews was speaking again; like there were words coming from his direction. Probably more denials. More self-justifying crap. But I didn't really hear it. Instead, I turned towards the door, a knife in each hand, and lunged towards the monsters as the whole earth sang out for redemption.

71

Amber

Reality is slipping away, here with my ankles in the water.
David's words are meant to comfort me, I think, but I
am beyond comfort. And yet, though they're void of
comfort, somehow I sense these words are true. Perhaps
the first true words he's ever said to me.

*'You aren't remembering killing them, Amber. You are
remembering what they did to you.'*

Me, the monster. Him, the monster. So much was
collapsing around me. Explanations, stories, all colliding.
But visions appearing, too. Reappearing. Of those men,
and my childhood, and . . .

Oh, God.

'David,' I say, 'I can't, I can't remember . . .'

'I know you can't,' he answers tenderly, 'but I think
you will. As much as I wanted you not to, I think you
will.'

'They hurt me.' It seems a complete statement. I don't know how to expand on it.

'Yes, Amber. They hurt you, and a lot of other girls.'

'And I killed them,' I repeat. But now, even I don't fully believe the words.

'You didn't,' he insists. 'I promise you, you didn't.' He tries to step closer, but his feet are stuck in the mud beneath the water. 'I was trying to protect you.'

'Protect?'

'At least, in part.' His face contorts. He's frustrated with himself. 'But I have to be honest with you, now. It wasn't just for you. I was acting for my sister, too. For her memory. For the justice she deserved, a long time ago.'

His sister. This new story, again. I don't know why he keeps repeating it.

He attempts a consoling expression.

'My life with you has been a lie,' he says, simply. 'I'm sorry about that. There's a lot about me you don't know. A lot I've tried to repress.'

'We lived a good life,' I whisper.

'We did,' he answers, and he seems grateful to hear me say it. 'But it wasn't your life. I understand that now. And it wasn't mine. You've never really been my Amber, and I've never really been your David.'

His face looks different. I see honesty there. I'm not sure I've ever seen it before.

'All I wanted,' he says through tears that start to flow more freely, 'was to love you, and to save you. And the love, Amber . . . that was only ever real.'

For some reason, I want to agree.

'I know, David. I love you, too.' I genuinely, actually do. 'And I'm sure your sister loved you.' I hesitate. For a moment I wonder who his sister was. I wonder who he is. There are so many new questions.

'And I think,' I finally add, 'that you really did want to save me. But in the end,' I lower my hand from his face, where it had automatically drifted, 'that wasn't possible. Some people are beyond saving.'

'I don't believe that,' he answers. His voice implores. 'There's always hope.'

'Not here, David. Not in the river, with a string of bodies behind me. You've tried your best for years, and in these past days – I guess you did everything you could. I could wish you hadn't. That you'd been willing just to love me instead of trying to save me, or create me. But it is what it is. And at the end of the day, I've become a killer, David. That woman . . . those were my hands that pulled our dog's leash around her neck, whether it was you who killed the others or not. I've become a, a . . .'

I'm strangely calm as I speak. This is simple reality. It can't be denied. Like distinguishing up from down. You don't get emotional about it, you just identify it for what it is.

'There's no way to rescue this situation,' I say. 'They'll figure out I did this, eventually. Of course they will. And I can't face what will come.' My voice wanders. Then, 'It just needs to be finished.'

'But there is,' David answers, suddenly resolved. I keep

my eyes on his face, which has grown serious and resigned.

Peaceful.

'There is a way out everything that's happened. A way to save you, like I've always wanted.'

I am ready to protest again. David is a man who doesn't want to admit failure, who needs to realize that reality doesn't always bend to our wishes, however well intentioned.

But he's speaking again before I have a chance to say anything.

'This way, Amber, I've already set it in motion.' His eyes sparkle as a branch moves high above and the sun hits them. Shining bright and bold in the unique hazel that's wholly his. All the intimidating darkness I'd seen in them in the kitchen is gone.

'What are you talking about, David?'

'No one is going to come after you.' He lifts an arm and wraps a comforting hand around my shoulder. 'I've made sure of that. You'll be safe, Amber. Above suspicion.'

'That's impossible.'

'You'll be able to go on with your life. To make something of it. Something better than all this.'

There's a certainty to his words that throws me. What he is saying simply isn't feasible.

His hand is at my cheek again.

'I want you to know, I really tried.' His fingers dance at my ears. 'I did everything I could, from the moment

I found you till now. I'm just sorry it wasn't more. I'm sorry I couldn't escape my past, or yours. I'd tried for so long, but . . .'

His face suddenly grows serious.

'I've left a note on the kitchen table, Amber. I wrote it last night, just in case. When you stormed out now, I knew it was time. You'll find it there, when you get back.'

'A note?'

'Guard it, Amber,' he continues. 'It's your ticket out.'

'David, I don't understand what you're—'

'It'll make sense when you read it. And you'll have to show it to the police, when they eventually come. I admit everything. I use terms clear enough to satisfy any investigator. I promise.'

I'm not hearing him correctly. 'David, you admit what?'

'The whole of it,' he answers. 'That I killed each of those men, that I murdered them in rage. It's not a lie, Amber. I'm only confessing the truth. That I was never able to get past what my sister had been through. That it filled me with fury at men who would do that to anyone, and that I decided to bring justice about myself.'

'David, that's not going to end this.'

'And,' he adds, squeezing my shoulder, 'that I killed Emma Fairfax.'

I freeze. I can feel the earth tremble beneath the waters.

'David, you didn't.'

'It's all in the letter, Amber. It's done. It's what the

police need to hear, if you're going to escape this. That I hunted down the woman who'd led you to your torment, and systematically ended the life of her and everyone at whose hands you suffered.'

'David!' I cry out, agonized at hearing these words from him.

'They'll believe it,' he answers, energy in his voice. His eyes are locked on mine. He intensely wants me to comprehend what he's saying. 'It's rational. And it's not like it isn't something I've craved doing my whole life. Of course I wanted to track down those men, so many times over these years. But I could never risk upsetting what we'd created here. Our life. Your recovery. Still, I thought about it more times than I can count. The only difference is that now I'll have actually gone through with it. "Enraged husband, grieving the memory of his sister, seeks retribution for the pain inflicted on his wife." You read the papers every day, even you have to acknowledge – it's a perfect headline.'

'They'll find the same records I did,' I protest. 'They'll find out we aren't married. They'll piece together that you've concocted a charade for my whole life.'

'Let them! It'll only help spell out my obsession with you, my desire to steal you away from your former life. Make you mine.'

There are tears in my eyes now, to match David's.

'You did make me yours, didn't you?' They roll down my cheeks.

'No one else needs to know the real reason why,'

430

David continues. 'To keep you from going down a path I'd seen before. To offer you hope. To the world I'll be an obsessed stalker who invaded your life and spilt the blood of everyone I felt had harmed my prized possession.' He takes a few deep, controlling breaths. 'I've also left a large bottle of the drug I've been using on you. You'll find it on the counter by the sink. That will clinch the story. I drugged you secretly, forcing you to be a part of my games. No one will doubt my guilt, Amber. No one.'

I can't bear to hear him say these things. 'I won't let you do this. I won't permit you to live with that . . . that shame. You've done things that are hard to forgive, but so have I. You're not going to take the blame for this alone.'

The tender resignation returns to his features.

'I'm afraid you still don't understand. And that's okay, it really is.' He takes another step closer. 'I won't be living with any shame at all.'

He lifts both hands to my face, cupping my cheeks in his warm palms. Our eyes lock – two lovebirds intertwined in the midst of the water – and he leans in to kiss me. My lips part into his, and we're connected. The warmth flows through me like a new surge of life.

His hands slide down my face, over my shoulders, rubbing human warmth into my arms.

As his left hand meets my right, with the knife still in my clutch and the blade still pointed at my skin, he gently unwraps my fingers from its handle. The man who loves me, drawing the instrument of suffering and death away from my side.

'But please,' he says, breaking our kiss and whispering so closely I feel his breath drift across my face, 'just once before this is all over, tell me it's okay. That you'll be okay. That for all I've done wrong, it hasn't been entirely in vain.'

I look into his eyes. God, I've always loved his eyes. But I don't know how to answer him, and he seems to accept this.

Then, without moving his face, he wrenches the rest of his body in a firm, singular contraction. His eyes stay fixed on mine, lingering in my gaze, but something changes in their presence.

I am drawn to look down, a sudden compulsion, and clarity instantly comes. With that one movement of my head, I finally understand the fulness of David's plan.

The knife I'd held in my grip is in his, and the blade is deep inside his flesh. His fingers are still clinging to the handle, even as blood pours out of the deep wound in his stomach.

'Oh God! David!' I cry. Comprehension of what he's done comes crushingly. 'No! Don't do this! Don't—'

But his other hand is firmly on my arm and he tilts me back to gaze into his eyes again. His face is whiter, but his features are warm and loving.

'Shh, Amber. It's already done.'

I can't speak. I can only sob.

He forces a smile, though the action pains him. 'The

killer, racked with guilt, takes his own life in the end, you see?' A little laugh – spots of red at the corners of his lips as it comes. 'The only ending to this story that works. The only one that sets you free.'

I realize that there is nothing I can do. His colour is draining, he's already starting to slouch. My rock and my stability is wilting, turning to sand.

I reach out to him, wrap him in both arms as he starts to crumble. With all my strength I embrace him, enclosing him in myself. I feel the life ebb from his body, his weight increasing in my arms. And before he's fully gone, I say the only phrase that comes into my heart.

'I love you, too, David.'

And then there's one phrase more, as his body becomes too much for me to hold and I lower it into the gentle flow of the water beneath us. A phrase I don't expect, and may never understand.

'Thank you.'

Epilogue

Months come and go in a steady rhythm. The tides ebb, the tides flow. The world spins.

I've read all the pages of the story that went before, most of them from a computer screen, secreted away in the solitude of home; but more recently, from the stacks of papers in my desk at the bookshop, where I've gradually returned. It was horrible, my story. Painful, but also filled with love. With sacrifice. And like all compelling stories, it's hard to admit when it's genuinely come to its end – when the last page has been read and the back cover closed, and there are no more revelations to be had. No more threads to follow or questions to be answered. When the book has to be put down, and the next step of life taken up.

It didn't end the way I would have hoped for. Then again, it didn't begin the way I would have liked, either.

But we're not always the authors of our own stories. We find ourselves characters in a saga penned by others – by their desires, by their faults, by their virtues. Shaped by actions heaped upon us, rather than those we've sought out or embraced. But they become our story, still.

As that one concluded, I had to deal with all the trauma of its closing pages. I had hated so many of the characters and so much of the plot; but others I had loved. Some had filled me, for a time, with a joy deeper than I'd ever known.

How can you not be grateful for a story that gives you that?

The investigations came, and the enquiries, and the interviews. David's note was the lynchpin he'd hoped it would be. He admitted to each murder, described it in detail, offered facts about the crime scenes no one else could know, including homes in Felton and Santa Cruz where three of the murders had taken place. The drugs mixed in the bottle on the counter had enough psycho-tropic power to them that the only emotion shown towards me in the whole process was pity. *You poor creature, look what that vile monster did to you! Thank God you made it through.*

I had no trouble bringing forth the tears that were expected of me throughout the process. My agony wasn't feigned, it was just of a different sort than any of them expected.

I remember the headline our local paper ran when all the details had finally come to light.

435

STALKER STEALS A LIFE, TAKES FOUR, THEN TAKES HIS OWN

Simple, unadorned. The stealing, the taking – just the right bit of wordplay to pass as journalistically witty while not crossing any lines.

I read the story. We all did. Chloe, Mitch, and everyone else in the shop. We read it, came to grips with its reality, and then realized we had to move on.

The final page of that book had been turned. The cover closed. But we would move on. And we decided we might as well do it together.

I find myself now at the first page of a new story. I'm meeting new characters – above all, a new protagonist, a woman and a self I'm only beginning to know. At this stage, at least, she's also going to work in the little bookshop in downtown Santa Rosa, with the staff who have been so supportive of her, so much like family. She's in therapy and counselling and on the right kinds of medication; and above all she has these friends, and she wants to learn to fall on them more. To let them be with her. She'll move house – she can't quite bear to stay in the same apartment where so much took place – but she'll stay in the area. At the edge of nature, with an orange-furred dog and a love for flowers.

She's broken, this new protagonist. She has a past. But she also has a strange optimism, that as awful as yesterday was, and as painful as today feels, tomorrow can be better. That life is not just the sum of past experience. That it can be held, driven, and propelled towards something new.

I don't know yet if it's to be a heroine's tale, if she's some great monument to fortitude and strength who will come blaring through the pages to a trophy finish; or if she's the gentle maiden, tossed about by the storms we get here in the springtime, who will be broken up as much as she strives to be made whole. There will be pits and there will be mesas, darkness and light. There are glimpses of her I can already see, and so much that still remains a mystery.

I only recognize a few similarities, in these opening pages, to the woman in that other story I so recently finished. Each morning, her blue eyes stare back from the mirror and tease her. The same straw-coloured hair falls to her shoulders.

But she's afloat in a new reality. There's a new breath in her lips, and her chest rises and falls with a different strength.

And she blinks. And life is starting again.

Acknowledgements

The Boy in the Park, the book I wrote immediately before this, proved to me that a novel could be both astonishingly engaging to write, but also surprisingly painful. That story dealt with some of the darker realities of human experience — hardly the happiest of realms in which to submerse oneself, but one that I was able to explore in a way that, I'm relieved and delighted to say, so many of you found a captivating, haunting read.

I could hardly have imagined that a follow-up could be even more painful to write, but entering into the world that has eventually become *The Girl in the Water* proved just such an experience. Behind what I hope is the tension of the psychological twists and thrills, is a world of suffering and pain beyond the comprehension of most people — but not all. As before, I am fortunate not to have experienced such suffering myself; but to all who have, and especially to those who have opened themselves up to me with their very real stories — far more terrible than anything I could fictionalise, and yet often far more inspiring, too — to you the better parts of this book are dedicated.

My setting for this book is the peaceful, in so many ways idyllic, world of the Russian River basin in northern California. There, in the hills of a wine country that is less well-known than Napa Valley, just to the east, winds this strangely beautiful river that meanders through the hills and countryside until it meets the pacific along a cliff-shorn coastline that is almost too spectacular to be real. I'm sorry that for the purposes of our story I've filled such a peaceful quarter of the world with evil and more than its reasonable share of corpses, but I hope in my own strange way this serves as a tribute to a section of North America of which I truly stand in awe, and which I visited several times while writing this novel. My thanks to the kind people of Santa Rosa, Windsor, Santa Cruz, Felton, and all the other locations I scouted out during writing, and who were hospitable and friendly one and all.

I continue to be represented by the industry's finest, my friend and literary mentor, Luigi Bonomi of LBA Books. We must have another lunch, Luigi, and soon. Every time we do, a new book seems to be the result — and because of you, each one is better than the last. I also owe a debt to Dani Gerard of LBA, who pushes me forward with drive.

This book is in your hands because of the tireless

devotion and advocacy of Kate Bradley, Senior Commissioning Editor at Harper Fiction and extraordinary advocate of my writing. Her enthusiasm for *The Boy in the Park* couldn't be matched — except perhaps by her dedication to this book. Not only is she an extraordinary publisher, but also a gifted editor whose creativity and conceptual know-how brought out the very best in this novel. I'd also like to thank Charlotte Ledger and Kimberley Young, who head up the list at HarperCollins and who continue to champion my books. My gratitude likewise to Nicki Kennedy, Sam Edinburgh and all their colleagues at ILA, who continue to do such wonders with international rights and translations.

I wish to thank Thomas Johnson for correcting my ornithology and ensuring that the impossible phrase, 'the cormorants were singing' didn't make its way into this book; and Martina Velasquez, who helped ensure that my men didn't sound too much like the women, and that all the women didn't sound like her (though the thought that I might speak in her cadence is an entirely happy one).

Finally, I want to thank the readers of *The Boy in the Park*, who took to my writing with such amazing enthusiasm — both in its English original, as well as in various translations: especially to my readers in Germany, who propelled the German edition up the lists with ferocious abandon. Your responses, reviews, social media posts and personal notes to me have been a source of real encouragement (I read every one), and I hope I've done you justice with this second offering.

441